No Weapon Formed

(Book II in the "Boaz Brown" Series)

Michelle Stimpson

Published by Michelle Stimpson
MichelleStimpson.com

Acknowledgments

Thank You, God, for a wonderful ten years as an author. Writing for Your glory is the best life—the life of Christ in me. Thank You for the gift and for guiding me as You promised through Your Holy Spirit.

Thank you to the dozens of people who have written to let me know how the first *Boaz Brown* touched lives. I'm amazed. People have actually gotten married to folks and accepted in-laws they would have otherwise overlooked and changed the floor plans for their homes based on LaShondra's prayer closet experience! One woman, in her 80s, said she didn't know you could pray anywhere until she read *Boaz Brown*. It changed her view of our God. I am humbled!

God uses that book in particular to break down barriers. The struggle continues, and the body of Christ continues to be victorious in Him. Thanks to those who did everything possible to put *Boaz Brown*, a debut novel, front and center: Denise Stinson (we miss Walk Worthy Press, by the way), Carol Mackey (made it a Main Selection for Black Expressions), Maxine Thompson, Miss Till at JoKae's Books, and so many more that loved and embraced me from that book forward. Thank you!

Thank you to my family and friends who are so supportive. Whether it's a prayer or a Facebook share, I appreciate you! And to my FB friends, my goodness – besides being wonderful people in the first place, you all ARE the grapevine when it comes to information about books. Thank you!

Thanks to all the individual readers whom I don't hear from but I know are on the lookout for books. I know there are plenty of folks supporting silently. I see you!

Thanks to the book clubs who continue to support the work and spread the word over nachos and potlucks!

Help for this sequel came in many forms through many people. Toyce – thanks for the *Bible for Hope* – it came in handy. Thanks to fellow authors April Barker, Lynne Gentry, and Rhonda McKnight for being sounding boards. Arquila Todd gave me info about aviation guidelines. Dormel Thompson and Dana Grieb filled me in on Nanny-world. Jayne Knight, Tia McCollors, Rochelle Moss, and Chrystal Hurst are or were awesome stay-at-home-moms with little ones. Thank you so much for your insight!

To the ladies at my Life On Life Table, thanks for your sisterhood and wisdom.

Johnetta J. Hochstetler advised me on current issues facing interracial marriages, and I'm go grateful!

Thanks to my editors, Karen McCollum Rodgers and Vicki Prather. You make my work shine!

Finally, to Serena Wells, thank you, thank you, thank you for sharing your experience and insight about chronic disease. I stand with you in claiming your complete, symptom-free healing in Jesus name!

Two are better than one, because they have a good return for their labor:
If either of them falls down, one can help the other up.
But pity anyone who falls and has no one to help them up.
Also, if two lie down together, they will keep warm.
But how can one keep warm alone?
Though one may be overpowered, two can defend themselves.
A cord of three strands is not quickly broken.
Ecclesiastes 4:9-12, NIV

❧Chapter 1

Hwuuuuu. Sheeeee. Hwuuuuu. Sheeee.

"Stelson. Turn over on your stomach." I shoved my husband's shoulder, attempting to wake him.

No response.

Hwuuuuu. Sheeeee. Hwuuuuu. Sheeee.

"Stelson. Roll over." A little louder, a little stronger push this time.

The television illuminated his glare at me, displaying the kind of anger that only a Church of God in Christ usher gives a member chewing gum in the sanctuary. "What?"

I demanded, "Roll over. You're snoring."

"No, I'm not."

"Yes, you are."

"I'm not even sleep," he protested.

"You think I woke you up so I could lie to you?"

He crumpled up his face, flipped onto his stomach with a grumble and turned his head away.

I didn't care about him getting upset. He wasn't the one who had to rise at 5:00 a.m. so he could work out, get himself dressed, and then get a 6 month old and a 4 year old up, fed, dressed and at the daycare before 7:15 a.m.—all the while hoping to make it to work by 7:45 a.m.

To be fair, Stelson would have helped with the kids if I'd asked him. But why should I have to ask? Shouldn't it be instinctive to think, "Wow, my wife is really busting her behind with the kids. Since I have a morning off, I should use it to help her."?

Apparently this is not common sense.

Within seconds, my husband was at it again. Only this time it wasn't so much the sound as the annoying vibration of the rattle in his throat and nose. *How have wives slept through snoring husbands for centuries?*

I sat up in bed, staring at the back of his clean-shaven head. In that instant I wanted to grab my goose-feather pillow, raise it high, and slam it down on his head like an amateur wrestler.

My hand clenched the pillow even as I reminded myself that it wouldn't be godly to attack my husband in the middle of the night.

Since the first time Stelson worked a 10-hour day after we married, I had become fully acquainted with his snoring ways.

I actually used to think his snoring was "cute". Endearing. Made me feel like a bona fide wife to complain about the sound of sawing logs in my bedroom.

But that mess wasn't cute at two in the morning after nine years of marriage.

I had a choice to make. Stay in the bed and get no rest, which would ruin my entire day and throw off my week because I wouldn't have a chance at making up the lost sleep-time until Saturday, or go to the guest room and savor the next few hours of peace.

With every intent to disturb my husband, I threw back the sheet and comforter, exposing my legs to the cold air circulating in our bedroom, thanks to *his* hot-natured body.

Though I knew exactly where I had placed my robe, I switched on the nightlight to create an extra disturbance. If I was going to have to leave my cozy bedroom, the least I could do was make sure Stelson knew how much I suffered so he could sleep well.

He stirred. "Shondra."

"What?" I shot back. I grabbed my pink satin robe from its place on top of the other clothes littered across the ottoman near the foot of our king-sized bed.

"Whereareyougoing?" his words slurred together.

"To the guest room. I can't get any sleep with you snoring like that."

He murmured, "No. Wait."

"Wait for what?"

He mumbled, "I'll go."

I cinched the belt around my waist and stood, waiting for his body to comply with his mouth and his heart, but before he could put action to his words, sleep overcame him again.

His gesture, albeit sweet, was empty.

Not that I was any better. Work, exhaustion and life often caused me to fall short of my word, too.

"God, help us."

I turned out the light and felt my way through to the door, pushing aside a pair of kitten-heeled shoes I'd worn to Sunday service earlier that day. My mother would have shaken her head at me if she'd seen the way I let my house go. I knew better. But when one child is hollering for milk and another one's footsteps can be heard in rapid succession running through the house like a madman, taking the time to properly store a pair of shoes—even those few seconds—takes low priority.

Once I'd cleared our bedroom, the smooth travertine floors in the kitchen and main hallway paved the way to the east wing. Since I did insist that those areas stay clear of debris, I walked swiftly, aided by the light of the moon. Too bad it wasn't a full moon, because I failed to take note of the baby's new high chair.

Wham!

My foot hit the side of that thing and I went down like Mike Tyson had just given me an uppercut. In an instant I was on the floor trying to catch my breath, holding my left foot.

The pain in my pinky toe was so swift and severe, words wouldn't do it justice. I slammed my hand against the cold floor, hoping to distract my nerve cells and possibly distribute the pain throughout my body. No help there.

"Jesus," I finally was able to whisper. "Jesus, Jesus, Jesus. Help me."

I dragged my body over to the couch, pulling myself onto the puffy leather couch with my elbows. On a scale of one to ten, the throbbing had to be an eleven. If I could have bent over and gnawed off my foot, I would have. Alas, the baby fat lingering around my waist had reduced me to a sideways method of putting on shoes, so I knew the gnaw-off wasn't gonna happen.

With one hand nursing my foot, I used the other to shed some light from the living room lamp. If I'd seen a trail of blood from the kitchen to the couch, it wouldn't have surprised me.

The light-click revealed something far more ridiculous. My baby toe was off on a path of its own, sticking out as though it didn't even belong to the rest of the foot. No doubt, it was broken. Or dislocated, if there was such a thing.

No! No! No! I didn't have time for a broken toe or a broken *anything* for that matter. The whole scenario flashed through my mind: I'd have to call the doctor, set up an appointment. I couldn't take the kids with me, so I'd still need to get them to daycare. Go to the appointment, wait around for the X-rays and diagnosis of what I already knew to be true. Sit there and have him tell me, "There's really nothing we can do except let it heal on its own." (This I knew because my younger brother, Jonathan, broke his toe once.) After that non-helpful diagnosis, I'd pay a $30 co-pay, get a lame prescription which was probably equivalent to taking four Aleve, then go to the pharmacy to have it filled. By the time all that was finished, it would be time to go pick up the kids again.

Forget that. Clearly, the toe was broken. It needed ice. I had Aleve already, and plenty of it. No need to involve Dr. Wheeler and mess up my routine with a whole bunch of extra running all over town.

With my left foot balanced on the heel, I hobbled over to the pantry and fished through the shelves for a plastic Ziploc bag. Careful not to swing the door near my foot, I slowly backed out of the area. The marble countertops sustained me as I maneuvered to the refrigerator, where I pushed the dispenser button with my hand instead of a glass and caught the falling ice with the baggie. I swiped a bottled water while I was standing there, then cautiously continued my trek to the guest bed, leaving the light on in the living room. I could not risk tapping that toe against anything on my way to bed.

The remaining few steps were taken with every precaution because my four-year-old, Seth, was notorious for leaving his kids' meal toys all over the house. "They're playing hide and seek," he would claim whenever I found one cleverly placed between the sofa cushions or standing next to a toilet seat.

His imagination amazed me sometimes.

After sliding into bed, I quickly realized that my foot would not tolerate even the weight of a sheet on top, let alone an ice pack. All I could do was rig up the ice beside my toe with a pillow and hope for the best while I tried to catch the remaining Z's available.

And then my ears caught the sound. The sound of discontent, angst and perhaps fear. Zoe was crying. She must have heard me rambling around in the kitchen. If she cried long enough, she'd wake Seth. And if *he* got up, that would squash all hopes of any rest because he only had two speeds: *On* and *Off.* Nothing in between.

I used the walls to help me get to Zoe in record time, for a person with a broken toe. I turned the light on just long enough to pull her from the crib and secure her in my arms. She stopped crying.

Despite what all the professionals recommend, this child was sleeping in the bed with me tonight.

She laid her head in the crook of my neck and threw one of her plump arms over my shoulder and began patting my back, a gesture of comfort she'd already learned from me.

I kissed her chunky cheek. "Momma sure needs that right now."

She wiped her eyes and yawned.

We made it to the guest room without incident. She squiggled up next to me and quickly fell asleep.

In the seconds before I followed Zoe to dreamland, it occurred to me that I hadn't grabbed my cell phone before I left the master bedroom, thus I had no alarm clock.

But at that point, I didn't even care anymore.

If somebody reported me for being late tomorrow, that would be too bad. They'd just have to write me up. *Shoot, my middle name is not Superwoman.*

Chapter 2 ❧

Good morning, God. Jesus. Holy Spirit. I prayed silently in the moments before getting out of bed. *I miss You. I miss how we used to spend time together in the mornings before I had to face the world.* That 10-second prayer was the only time available to commune with the Lover of my soul.

Of all the changes in my life since becoming a mother, the lack of quiet time with God was the one that discouraged me most. Going to church on Sunday and most Wednesdays was inspiring, yet I felt like I was running on spiritual fumes most of the week. My relationship with God seemed like a series of snippets whispered throughout the day. Text messages. No conversation. No intimacy.

When I was single, living in my own house, I had an entire bedroom to call my prayer closet. My journal, my Bible, my music—everything that ushered me into our sweet, daily communion—greeted me each morning. We curled up together in His Word, He taught me, loved on me, filled me with fresh grace and mercy each sunrise. Sometimes we disagreed. Sometimes I got mad or ignored Him because I didn't like what He'd showed me in His Word or in prayer. But I couldn't stay away from Him because everything fell apart when I tried to go my own way.

The fact that I was still functioning without a personal prayer life was a testament to His grace. *I'm tired, Father. So tired. I hope You understand. I still love You. I know You still love me. Thank You for being faithful even when I'm not.*

As much as I wanted—needed—to curl up in His presence, my life awaited me on the other side of the bedspread.

Painfully aware of each step, I showered, dressed, and groomed myself before waking the baby and Seth. Breakfast. Veggie Tales cartoons to hold one's attention while I took care of the other.

Stelson moseyed out of the bedroom only minutes before it was time for the kids and me to leave. "Babe, what happened to your foot?"

"I stubbed my toe." With both arms at a ninety-degree angle, shuffling around the house on one foot and a heel to get ready could have been counted as my workout. It would *have* to count, seeing as I'd missed my usual wake-up time.

"Come here. Let me look at it," he coaxed while sitting on the counter stool.

"I can't lift my leg up there."

"Well, let's go to the couch."

The thought of having my husband examine my foot and make a big fuss over my injury was quite romantic, actually, but I didn't have time. "I'm already running behind."

Stelson's blue eyes sank in defeat as he sat one elbow on the kitchen island and parked his chin in his palm. He raised both eyebrows, summoning the wrinkles in his slightly-tanned forehead, the result of his three-day-long business trip to LA.

Must be nice to attend conferences at beach-front hotels.

"So you're just going to hop around all day with a sock on your foot?" he pressed.

"No. I'll wear a slipper. It'll be fine."

"Shondra, why don't you take off today? Let me drop the kids off at daycare on my way to work, and you can go get an X-ray," he offered. Again, a decent gesture. But left up to my husband, the kids would arrive two hours late.

I packed the last bottle in Zoe's bag and zipped it closed. "Can't. We're interviewing new teachers today. And Seth has a field trip. He can't be late."

"How can anybody be late to daycare?" Stelson questioned, which only proved my point.

Seth came barreling into the kitchen from his bedroom and all I could think was: *Save my foot!* I snatched my leg and turned my entire body away from him. "Seth, it's time to go."

My husband swooped up our son and pulled him into a tickle-hug. Seth's brown locks swayed as he attempted to break free of Stelson's grasp. When all else failed, Seth struck back by tickling my husband, who burst out in contrived laughter. "Oh, you wanna tickle me back! You wanna tickle me back! Well, I'll tickle harder!"

Seth's laughter filled the room. Even baby girl found their game hilarious. She opened her mouth wide and let out a wail that Stelson couldn't ignore. With Seth still in his embrace, my husband walked toward the deadly high chair and used his other hand to gently tickle our daughter under her slobbery chin.

Of course, her full cheeks pushed her eyes closed as she laughed uncontrollably. Zoe's tighter curls didn't whip around like Seth's. Her features aligned more with her African-American heritage than our son's, who could have easily passed as Caucasian with his blue eyes and fair skin.

God knows I wanted to join in their game, but the clock was ticking. We were already seven minutes past leaving time. I placed a hand on Stelson's arm. "Alright, we gotta skedaddle, honey."

Stelson set our son on the floor. "Go get your shoes."

For some reason, Seth always obeyed my husband's orders the first time given. I wished I could record Stelson saying every command and just play it for Seth.

Still in his bathrobe, Stelson leaned against the stove. He crossed his arms and eyed me as I stuffed baby carrots into one of the compartments of my lunch container. Sometimes, he just watched me. Admired me, he'd say. I'd heard that men were visual, but I think my husband was even more visual than the average man because he could go from zero to "let's go to the bedroom" in ten seconds if I walked past him in a wraparound dress and a pair of heels.

Well, he used to be able to turn it on that fast. Lately, though, he wasn't as excitable. Maybe we were just getting older. Maybe I was having a hard time shedding the second-baby weight. Or maybe both.

I continued my routine, giving him an eyeful of me doing everything possible to keep myself looking good for him. But when I realized I'd forgotten to pick up another salad mix at the grocery store, I huffed, "Aww man!"

"What?"

"Forgot to get the salad mix." As soon as the words left my mouth, I remembered exactly how I forgot. I'd caught Seth popping a grape in his mouth and given him a two-minute lecture on how that was almost like stealing. In response, he started gagging and hocking, trying to bring the swallowed grape back up, which drove me to the point where I was almost ready to slap him on the behind and end the whole scene.

"No! You don't need to vomit."

"But Jesus doesn't want me to steal," Seth had whined sincerely.

"Jesus understands," I said. "Just don't do it again."

Yep. That's how I forgot the salad mix. "Never mind. I'll order delivery for lunch."

"You don't have to do this, you know," Stelson said in an I-told-you-so tone.

I shut the refrigerator door and faced him. "Do what?"

"Work outside the house."

I rolled my eyes and limped toward our bedroom. "Let's not go there this morning, okay?"

He followed, which annoyed me all the more. "Could you put her in the swing?" I pointed at Zoe to throw him off.

A minute later, he was beside me again, watching me dab on lipstick and brush my light brown skin with powder. Thankfully, my flawless complexion had returned after giving birth to Zoe. I unwrapped the scarf on my head and brushed my hair out of its sleeping position and into the chin-length bob style that required almost no maintenance. Though this style wasn't its best without bumping the ends with a flat iron, I had to give myself credit for wrapping it up the previous night so I wouldn't have to throw a donut back there.

Stelson started in again. "This is the kind of morning I want to avoid. You're rushed, the kids are rushed. We can't even enjoy a game of tickling—you won't even go get your foot X-rayed because it's go-go-go."

"No. It's go-go-go because I didn't have an alarm clock. And the reason I didn't have an alarm clock is because *you* were snoring so loud I had to leave the bedroom in a rush, which is also the reason why I hurt myself." I knew better than to tell him the whole truth—that my toe was a bit worse than "hurt".

"I'm sorry about last night," he apologized.

"I know you don't mean to keep me up. It's just...I can't get any sleep when you snore. That wouldn't change if I stopped working."

"I don't like sleeping with the TV on, either, but I've learned to work around it."

"TV is background noise. Snoring is...invasive."

My left foot grazed the bedroom covers, which alarmed me. Maybe Stelson was right. *Maybe I should stay home, prop my foot up, and protect it from the likes of 700 high school students who might be roughhousing in the hallways and accidentally step on my toe, which would cause temporary insanity, thereby making me knock the fire out of somebody.*

Note to self: Stay in the office today by any means necessary.

I balanced myself on one leg and bent over in the closet to retrieve the purple foldable slippers I usually reserved for clean-up after a long day of activities at church. The satin, barely-there shoes were the only option for my swollen foot. Hopefully. But seeing as I couldn't actually put them on in Stelson's presence without him inspecting the damage, I crammed them into my Louis Vuitton bag and slung it over my shoulder.

"My work is part of my ministry. We've already discussed this. "

"What about your ministry at home? To me and the kids? "

"Am I not a great wife and mother?" I challenged him. "I mean, I'm up sometimes all night with Zoe. If not with Zoe, with you snoring. And Seth...God knows he drains me to the very last milligram of my patience sometimes. "

Stelson eased toward me.

"Watch the foot," I warned.

He planted a kiss on my nose as he caged my waist in his arms. "Honey, you're a great wife. An exceptional mother. And I know the kids and teachers at Plainview High School are more than blessed because of your service as an assistant principal. You gotta look around, though." He threw his glance at our unmade bed, at the stack of clothes on the ottoman, and the shoes strewn across the scraped hardwood floor.

"Hey. You've got two hands, too," I reminded him.

"It's not just the mess. It's the fast food. It's you. You're always stressed. The kids get what's left of you after work," he listed.

"I know. I told you, I've got some people lined up to interview. A personal chef and a housekeeper. I just have to find someone I trust enough to leave alone in our home," I reminded him.

He squeezed my behind. "And I'm not getting enough of you."

I pulled back. "Is that what this is about? Sex?"

An exaggerated frown appeared. He nodded. "That's part of it. A BIG part of it."

"We just did it before you left. Thursday night," I refreshed his memory.

"Yeah, and now it's Monday," he said.

"And? Can I help it if you weren't actually here?"

"No, but when I come back from a trip, I would like some time alone with you," he said with a tad bit too much machismo for my taste. And yet, his puppy-dog eyes and the soft lines in his forehead gave him a distinctly desperate expression that outweighed my annoyance. Can't blame a man for wanting to have sex with his wife.

"Okay, okay. You win."

His eyes squinted. "I don't want to win, Shondra. I want us both to win—which, coincidentally, is not what happened Thursday night."

He had a point. Lord knows I was tired Thursday night. Just rolled over in bed like "go ahead." I'd thrown in a few sound effects, but my mind never veered into the passion lane.

"It's not that simple for me, Stelson."

"We've never had this problem before," he recalled.

"We've never had two kids—"

Zoe's cries from her swing signaled the end of our morning routine, finished or not. "We gotta go."

Seth was crouched on the floor in his socked feet with one shoe on his foot, the other on the couch where his behind should have been.

I checked my phone. We were now officially twelve minutes behind schedule.

Before he could protest, I hoisted Seth onto the couch and shoved the other shoe on his foot.

"No!"

"Seth, honey, we're late."

He covered his shoe laces with both hands. He begged, "Mommy, I can do it."

"I'm sorry. Maybe tomorrow," I said, grabbing one set of laces and quickly tying them.

"But Sister Heller said I can do all things through Christ which strengthens me, Fer-ip-i-gans four and fifteen," he cited.

"You're close. It's *Philippians* four and *thirteen*," I corrected him, "and Jesus will help you tie your shoes faster if you practice more, in the future."

Because he knew better than to resist me physically, he threw his head back against the couch and voiced his objection through cries.

Stelson came dashing into the living room. "What's wrong?"

Seth answered for us, "Mommy's tying my shoes, but I wanted to tie them."

I finished the second shoe and gave Seth directions to go get his backpack from his bedroom. He obeyed, albeit with tear-filled eyes.

Stelson parked his hands at his waist and whispered, "Why wouldn't you let him tie his shoes?"

Zoe's continued cries divided my attention. I answered Stelson as I pulled her from the swing. "Because it's taking him too long and we're in a hurry."

"It's important for him to be able to do things for himself," my husband lectured. "What's going to happen to him when you're not around, Shondra? You want him to be the type of kid who can't do anything without Momma?"

"He's *four!*"

Stelson slapped his hand into his palm. "He's a boy who will one day be a man. I don't expect you to understand this, but you have got to let him try to do things on his own. Maybe you could get him up a little earlier."

I motioned for Stelson to hand me the baby's diaper bag from the kitchen. "Um, no. If I wake him up earlier, that means *I* have to get up earlier. Not gonna happen."

"Then I'll take him to school," Stelson suggested.

"When? On the one or two variable days a week when you don't have to be across town by six o'clock? I don't think so. It's not worth confusing the routine. We gotta go."

I left Stelson standing in bewilderment, thinking to myself: *He just doesn't get it.*

Chapter 3 ❧

I dropped the kids off at daycare without incident, staggered back to the car and sped out of the parking lot with every intent to clip off as much lost time as possible. My Honda was getting to be as old as Methuselah, but she could get up and go when necessary.

I called my best friend, Peaches, on my way in to work. She lived in Philadelphia, which put her an hour ahead of me, so I knew her morning was well underway.

"Hey, girl."

"Hey. You're just now heading in to work?" she questioned.

"Don't start. I've had a crazy morning already. Stelson snoring, baby crying, and I stubbed the mess out of my toe. My foot is so jacked," I vented.

"And you're headed to the doctor's office, right?" she asked in her mothering tone. I suppose as the mom of four children, she had mastered the art of indirectly telling people what they ought to do.

"No. I'm going to work. If it gets worse, I'll go to a twenty-four-hour clinic when I get off so they can confirm that it's broken—after Stelson gets home from work."

"Girl, you crazy," she dismissed my perfectly sane plan. "A broken bone is good for at least two days off work in my book. And you know I was the H-R queen."

I could only agree as she recalled the person she used to be. The best friend I used to know. In the five years since she'd married Quinn, Peaches had turned into the most domesticated, all-natural guru in my phone contact list. She had jumped into wifehood and stay-at-home-mommy-world with both feet after vowing "I do". Took some convincing to get her down the aisle, mind you, but once she married Quinn, she never looked back. Just packed her stuff, scooped up her nine-year-old son and kissed Texas good-bye. Then she popped out two more stair-step kids—a girl and a boy—and put the brakes on her career in order to take care of house and home.

"Just ask the doctor to give orders to keep your foot elevated and iced for the next forty-eight hours. Maybe you can catch up on the sleep you lose to snoring. Did you try the lavender snoring remedy I emailed you?"

"No! You know I don't fool with all that natural stuff you send me. I'd be running all over town looking for frog sweat and ant spit, listening to you."

Peaches coughed and faded for a moment. "I almost choked on my smoothie. Shondra, you stupid."

Frog sweat and ant spit. I had to laugh at my own joke. "Girl, I'm tired. That's what I am. Deliriously tired."

"So what happened with the housekeeper?"

"I haven't found one yet."

"You know my mother is chomping at the bit to get her hands on Zoe. Since my kids and I are out of town and no one in my family has had any babies lately, she's always asking about yours," Peaches reminded me.

"Your mom is a grandma. They're supposed to step in every now and then, not every day," I said.

"Have it your way. But are you even looking for help yet?" she nosied.

Oh, the hazards of having a best friend who knows you too well. "You know, I can't open my house to just anybody. Don't you have to give the housekeeper a key? A pass code to the alarm system? I'm not comfortable with the idea."

"Well, I'll be praying for you to find the help you need. *If* it's God's will," she chastised.

"Have you been talking to Stelson?"

"Not exactly," she avoided my question. "But you know…he and Quinn are Facebook friends. Every once in a while, they might IM one another."

"Uh huh." *A conspiracy.* "Look, Peaches, you know I can't stay home with my kids. They would drive me crazy. I'd be depressed. I'd get fat. It would actually be counterproductive, I promise. But why am I explaining all this to you. You *know* me."

"Yes," she sided with me, "I know you. And I know you're always tired, which makes you extra cranky, irritable, and very hard to deal with, I might add."

"Look who's talking! You were the president of the bad attitude caucus for *several* consecutive terms," I reviewed the record for her. "And you were the card-carrying member of the independent woman club. Almost cost you a relationship with Quinn because you didn't want to lose your identity!"

"True that, but I resigned from both clubs when I learned to rest in Christ," she said. "His yoke is easy, His burdens are light."

I, too, had memorized Matthew 11:30 in Sunday school. Back then, the problem was: I thought a yoke had something to do with eggs, and I thought a burden was a wooden log, for some reason. Yet, I had to admit to myself that even with a developed vocabulary and forty-one years to my credit, the verse didn't mean much more to me now as an adult. My life wasn't a tragedy, but it was nowhere near easy and light.

I turned in to the school's parking lot. With only a few minutes before the first bell, the closest slots were already taken. My spot, however, was reserved clear as a bell: *Assistant Principal Only.*

However, somebody in a late model red Kia Optima couldn't read. "I know this person did *not* park in my spot," I shared my thoughts aloud.

"Don't get mad. They were probably in a hurry," Peaches attempted to calm me. "And you *are* late, sweetie pie."

"What time I get here is irrelevant. And there's not another empty parking place for, like, fifty yards! I can't wobble all the way across this lot!"

"Go in peace, Shondra."

She got on my nerves sometimes, riding around on her Jesus-bike. "Enough with the kum-ba-ya, Peaches. Talk to you later."

"Bye, girl."

I circled the lot a couple more times. Nothing. Except for one spot marked with bright blue and white. Handicapped Only. *I am disabled at the moment.* I eased into the spot, making a mental note to look out my window in half an hour to see if the non-reading culprit had backed out of my reserved space. If so, I'd ask one of my colleagues to move my car to its rightful position. If not, I'd ask our campus officer to write the offender a warning ticket.

I worked hard for this position! How somebody just gonna park in my spot? I felt my heart rate increase with every step from my car to the main entrance. Since every other step sent a painful jolt up my foot, I grew even angrier. *I wonder if they'd park in the nurse's spot! The counselor's spot! No! They would NOT!*

Granted, the handicapped spot had actually put me closer than my normal position, so I should have been happy to take a few less steps. But was I? No. I was mad. *Why is everyone against me? Why did Stelson get so upset about the shoe thing? When will Peaches get over her natural self and stop trying to make everyone live to be 150?*

I, for one, didn't want to be 150 so I could sit around and watch everybody I cared about die. No way. I'd had enough of death since my mother passed away three years earlier. I was still struggling through holidays and birthdays without her. Couldn't imagine going through a century and a half worth of the pain of losing my friends and family.

As I struggled with my purse and the laptop bag which I had taken home on Friday but didn't even get the chance to open over the weekend, out of the blue comes a crew of kids with a microphone, a camera, and a bright light.

"Mrs. Brown! We saw you park in the handicap spot. What do you have to say for yourself?" He thrust the microphone in my face.

I recognized the investigative reporter right away. Michael Higgins. Though a senior, he was barely five feet tall and had tried to add the illusion of an inch to his height with a spiked Mohawk. He was one of those bright kids whose clever ideas sometimes landed him in trouble. In fact, he was on my radar for the senior prank.

For effect, I limped a little deeper as I answered, "Well, Michael, as you can see, my parking spot was taken." I motioned toward my car. "Also, I'm wearing a sock instead of a shoe, which means I'm hurt.

Walking is very painful—"

"But rules are rules, Mrs. Brown. You don't have a handicap parking sticker, so it's illegal for you to park there. You wouldn't encourage *us* to break or bend the rules due to someone else's negligence, would you?" he pressed as the camera crew got a little too close to my foot.

"Can you step back, please?"

"Yes, ma'am," the girl holding the lighting respectfully answered as she yanked her head, signaling for the camera boy to follow my orders—as though her words carried more weight than mine.

I stopped and looked at the camera squarely. Gave my hair a confident flip. "I agree, Michael. It's wrong for me to break the rules, even under these circumstances. Anyone who breaks rules needs to be prepared to pay the consequences. If I get a ticket, I'll pay it. At this moment, every step I've saved in pain is worth whatever it might cost me financially."

Then I motioned for the videographer to aim low. "Can you zoom in on my foot? Clearly, it's swollen. Anyone who has ever stubbed a toe in the middle of the night can empathize with me."

"Cut!" Michael announced. The camera drooped. All eyes focused on him. "That's a wrap."

"Wait a minute! You can't tell *half* the story, Michael," I antagonized him a bit.

He sighed. "We're chucking this story. It's too goody two-shoes."

I joked, "What did you think I was going to do? Deny what I'd done? Make up some kind of a double standard?"

"Ummm…yeah!" he smirked. "The news is supposed to be sensational. Scandalous. Salacious. But you…you're like being honest about it. Taking responsibility. You'd come off looking like the victim. We'd never win the journalism competition with *this* story."

The collective moans let me know I was off the hook.

"Don't worry. We'll find something else," he instructed the team as they walked back to the arts wing. "We've got 'til February."

"Hey! Any of you private investigators see who parked in my spot?" I asked before they got too far.

"Oh. It's mine," camera girl admitted.

"So this was a set-up from the beginning, huh? And who are you, anyway, young lady?" I knew most of the juniors and seniors, but I couldn't say the same for the underclassmen.

"Janerica Woods." She batted her fake eyelashes at me timidly.

I liked to see kids with a healthy fear of adults, so I decided to go easy on her. Besides, I had to give them some credit for spending some of the last days of summer break up at the school. They were already working on the yearbook layout and planning for competition. "You guys need to make sure you have your next story approved by Mr. Conway. You baited me into a trap by parking in my spot. It's called entrapment. Not a good idea," I warned them.

The girl shot a dangerous glare at Michael, as if to say she'd told him so.

"Move your car, Janerica," I ordered.

"Okay, Mrs. Brown."

They scrambled on their way and I hobbled on up to the main entrance of our massive three-story red brick building. I waved the magnetic strip on the back of my ID in front of the school's security sensor. The door clicked and I entered, giving the front desk staff a quick greeting as I headed down the hall toward my office.

Millicent, my secretary, was the first to notice my limp. "You okay, Mrs. Brown?"

"Yes. Stubbed my toe," I replied with a yawn.

She trailed me into my office. Since Millicent was twenty years older, I always had a hard time seeing her as my professional subordinate. I couldn't have asked her to stop following me. Good Southern manners die hard.

"Let me take a look at it," she said.

Her long brown hair riddled with streaks of gray and the off-centered glasses reminded me so much of Momma. "Okay," I gave in. "But don't freak out."

I dropped my bags at my desk and ambled over to the small, circular meeting table. I sat in one of the cushioned chairs and plopped my injured foot up on another one while Millicent watched with worry written across her lined face.

When I bent over and removed the sock, her expression morphed from worried to repulsed. "Mrs. Brown! You have *got* to get to a doctor."

"It's only a broken toe," I mumbled, attempting to wriggle my other toes so she'd be satisfied. Unfortunately, the attempt ended with my face contorted in pain.

"Toes are close to vessels. Broken bones can damage veins within your toe. What if it needs a steel rod? I saw on the news one time where this lady lost her leg from the knee down because she didn't get help after stepping on a sea shell." Millicent painted the worst-case, most far-fetched scenario, same as Momma would have done.

I can't count the number of times Momma and I were simply sitting in the back room watching the news and I ended up getting a thirty-minute lecture about something that happened to some child way in North Carolina. "See, Shondra, this is why I don't let you run wild! If that girl would have been at home, she never would have..." fill in the blank with every calamity imaginable. Let Momma tell it, everyone would be alive today if they'd just stayed at the house.

"That's like a one in a million chance, Millicent," I reasoned.

"Well, somebody's got to be the one, right?" she said, wagging an authoritative finger.

"Well if you think I'm the one, you wanna go buy me some lottery tickets?" I teased.

"No, ma'am," she declined with a smile. "But I will go get you some ice at least."

"Thank you, Millicent."

The bag of ice sat against my foot all morning as I sat across from Jerry Ringhauser, a hulking, jowly man, who was the campus principal. He and I met alongside academic department heads to conduct teacher interviews for the few remaining unstaffed positions. Being so late in the summer, the pickings were slim. The top graduates had jobs lined up before they even walked across the stage. What we had left was a group of people who'd majored in something unmarketable, couldn't get a job right after graduating and were scrambling for a way to start making their first student loan payments. In other words, candidates for whom teaching was "plan C".

Nonetheless, we needed teachers as much as the applicants needed jobs. As we questioned each potential employee, I silently asked the Holy Spirit to help us ask the right questions and give discernment about which ones might actually be falling right into their destinies, despite the fact that teaching wasn't first on their agenda.

But what if I hadn't been there? What if I had been at home taking care of Zoe and Seth and missed the opportunity to hear from the Lord about something as serious as choosing a remedial reading teacher for my struggling students who would probably end up dropping out of school without the right help? *My work at Plainview is as important as Peaches' work at home, isn't it?*

"Mrs. Brown, do you have any more questions?" Jerry asked abruptly. That was our pre-arranged cue to end the interview.

"No. I think we've heard enough to make a decision," I said in a phone operator's tone, standing so that the applicant got the hint. "We'll be in touch with you in the next few weeks."

The interviewee, Lyndsie Adams, shook everyone's hand and promptly left the conference room. Jerry and I talked with Mrs. Sedian about the interview for a short while. None of us wanted Lyndsie on our staff. She was too sarcastic. Borderline obnoxious. We had enough of those on the roster already.

Mrs. Sedian, who had just used up one of her precious summer days to interview for her English department, grabbed her purse. "Call me when you get the next interview scheduled."

"We'll keep looking," I assured her as she left the room. "And thanks for coming in."

"No worries. If we don't hire the right person, it'll mean more work for me in the long run. I'm glad to help now."

Mrs. Sedian had barely shut the door good when Jerry sighed, "This is going to be one rough school year." He tilted back in his chair and covered his lips with a fist. I'd been working with Jerry for three years. He was a man of relatively few words. When he spoke, he meant business.

"Why do you say so?" I asked. Not because I didn't have an idea, but because I valued Jerry's perspective. He was the only person to whom I didn't mind losing my bid for the top position at the district's premier school.

"Six brand spankin' new teachers. Ranier *didn't* retire, which only means he'll cause more trouble than ever because he doesn't want to be here. Fielder's going to be out on maternity leave almost as soon as we start," he listed. I really had forgotten about Mickey Fielder, the head officer of security. She was a small woman with a giant attitude who kept kids twice her size in check.

On top of personnel issues was the fact that the state had changed the mandatory testing requirements. Again.

"Just be prepared," he warned, rising from the table. "We need you here. Every day. On time."

My mouth clamped shut as Jerry exited the room. He had been so gracious about my shoeless foot. But there was no mistaking the tone of his last words. He'd observed me coming in late that particular morning and, perhaps, many more, thanks to my unpredictable life with a baby and a four year old.

The respect I had for Jerry prevented me from snapping back with an excuse. Really, there was none. He wasn't threatening me or my job. He'd simply reminded me of where the bar stood. If I wanted to stay viable in the workforce, I couldn't play the Mommy card anymore.

❧Chapter 4

By Wednesday afternoon, my foot had darkened around the toe. Stelson snuck a peek at me while I was changing from the purple slipper to the pink, which matched my clothes. He almost hit the roof. "We are *not* going to church tonight. I'm taking you to see a doctor."

He called my father and asked him to watch Seth while the rest of the family forged onward to an urgent care clinic with my heroic husband at the helm. X-rays showed that my toe was broken. Worse, they had to tape it to my next available toe so that it could heal properly.

"Otherwise, it could cause you to end up needing surgery where they have to re-break the toe in order to set it straight again," the doctor informed us.

Stelson, who was sitting on the stool next to me, crossed his arms while Zoe slept in her portable car seat. I avoided his glare, though his eyeballs were burning a hole in my cheek.

I held my breath as the fairly young physician gently pushed a piece of cotton between the two toes, then taped them together for stability. The process was quick and relatively painless, though nerve-racking.

Moving forward, I asked the doctor, "How long will it take to heal?"

"Six weeks. Stay off your feet as much as possible. Elevate and ice if it starts to swell again. You should be back to yourself soon."

Now *that's* what I wanted to hear. With the good news, I was finally able to look at my husband. "See, babe? I'm fine."

But on the way to my father's house, we got into yet another tiff. "This is silly, Shondra. You were too preoccupied with work to take care of your own health."

"What? You want me to be a hypochondriac?" I knew I was taking my side to the extreme, but for real, *I'm a grown woman. Shouldn't I be able to make choices about when I want to see a doctor?*

"It's not just your foot. It's your *life*. You put your job before *everything*," he overgeneralized, "and we're only in summer school. What's going to happen when the regular session starts?"

Since giving birth to Zoe in January, I had been afforded some degree of luxury. I returned to work in May. By then, the extremely disruptive students had already been worked through the system and were matriculating at RightWay, or district's alternative school. Final exams were quiet time. And the last week, seniors were off campus, which took care of a third of the disciplinary battles. Kids were skipping or attending class out of dress code, but most of the teachers were too tired to care enough to go through the referral process. When our test scores came back with higher-than-expected results, the entire campus had gone on cruise control until the last day.

That said, Stelson had a point. I was about to hit the ground full-speed in the next few weeks. Still. "You act as though I'm the only working mother in the world. Wives balance home and work every day, honey. Single moms have it even worse, but they're doing it, too."

"True. Many women are doing it. The question is, are they doing it *well?*"

I refused to incriminate womankind. "I can't speak for every mom who works outside the home."

"Just speak for yourself, then." He parked in my father's driveway. Looked at me. "Do you believe you're going to be able to give the kids, our home, me, and even yourself your best while working? If you can honestly answer 'yes' I won't bring it up again."

Stelson had thrown the kids and our household into the equation, but in my heart, I knew he was pleading for himself more than all of the above.

"You're asking me to predict the future."

"No. I'm asking you if the past and the present are an indication of what we can expect in the future."

Sometimes, I thought it would have been easier if I'd married a man who didn't have any godly expectations. Then *I* could be the only "holy" one in the family, like my mother and my grandmother had been. No one would be able to question my motives.

But Stelson was no ordinary husband. He was my Boaz. The godly man I'd asked for. Waited for. The father of my children who worked hard to provide for us and lead us as the Holy Spirit led him. Even if I disagreed with him, I had to respect his position.

The loud exhale I gave him, however, wasn't quite as respectful as the Lord would have wanted. "Okay. I'll do better. I promise. I'm gonna get a housekeeper. I'm gonna get in touch with that personal chef lady who catered the women's conference at church. Her meal preparation service was reasonable, remember?"

I reached across the center console of our Chevy Tahoe and rubbed his shoulders. The rock-hard tension caught me by surprise. "Stelson, honey, this is just a different season in our marriage. We have little kids. We're busy. We'll make it through."

"You know..." He rolled his lips between his teeth. "We can hire someone to help with the house and the cooking. We can even hire someone to help with the kids. But we *can't* hire another wife."

My neck and my hand snapped back. "What is that supposed to mean? Is that a threat?"

Zoe stirred with the sharp tone in my voice. Sitting in the car seat without the vibration of a moving car was prime cause for a hissy fit in her world.

"No. That's not what I'm saying."

"Then what *are* you saying?"

"I'm saying that in this *season*," he slung my churchy term at me, "I'd like for you to slow down."

"What about you? Are you going to slow down, too? I don't like it when you travel and when you work late. Makes me feel like a single parent."

He nodded. "That's fair. I can slow down, too. I did most of the traveling when Cooper's kids were younger. I'm sure he'd be willing to return the favor if I asked."

Of course he could slow down. He was the "Brown" of Brown-

Cooper Engineering. He was one of the bosses, and his partner was a perfectly reasonable man who would do anything to help Stelson through a rough patch.

Zoe's whimpering permeated the car, causing me to tear away from the conversation with my husband. "It's okay, Zoe," I bubbled.

In baby language, she told me that she wanted out of those straps.

Stelson went to retrieve our son while I dug through Zoe's bag for a toy to keep her occupied. She smiled as I presented her a plastic key ring. "Here you go!"

With my baby temporarily distracted, I whispered to God, "You gave me this man. You gave me this family. You also gave me my degrees and my job. You know I just can't see myself as a stay-at-home mom. Am I wrong for—"

The screen door of my parents' house swung open violently as Stelson ordered Seth to get in the car.

Father God, what did my child do now?

Seth skipped to my side of the car and opened the door. "Hi, Mommy." He hopped in. He rubbed his forehead across Zoe's forehead, a roughhousing move that she adored. "Hi, Zoe, Zoe, Zoe!"

He didn't act or sound like a little boy in trouble.

Zoe giggled in complete awe of her big brother. He was the only one who could invade her space with such gruff treatment and get away with it.

Stelson went back into the house, but the main door was still open so I could hear him and my father having a simmering discussion. I pressed the button to lower my window and eavesdrop, but I couldn't make out their words.

"Seth, honey, what are Daddy and Grandpa talking about?"

"Oh, I told Daddy that Grandpa said I'm gonna be a negro when I go to pre-kindergarten," he informed in a most innocent tone.

"A *what?*"

"A negro. Black. And I gotta be real smart, Grandpa said. And he showed me a big, big chapter book with a lot of words. It had pictures with black people in them, and they were *really, really* black from a long time ago. But I told him I'm not gonna be black," Seth continued. "And

I'm already really smart."

Though there were still a thousand questions to be answered—like how he and my father had gotten into this conversation in the first place—I wanted to chase the color-rabbit in Seth's head. "What's wrong with being black?"

"I'm not black," he said.

"Well...you kind of are," I said. "I mean...I'm black. And I'm your Mommy..."

"You're not black, you're brown," Seth corrected me. "We're all Brown because of our last name, so we're not black."

"I see. Go ahead and get your seatbelt on."

This was not the kind of conversation I wanted to have with Seth without Stelson. And it certainly wasn't the conversation my father should have had with Seth, *ever*.

If it wasn't so hot outside, I would have pulled the brake, lowered the windows, taken the keys and gone inside for a minute to diffuse things. Leaving the kids alone in the car without air, however, wasn't an option. Dragging them inside wasn't an option, either.

I tapped the horn.

Stelson emerged from the house, stomping toward the car as my father yelled from the porch, "I only told the boy the truth!"

"Ooh," Seth gasped as his father descended the driveway. "We should change Daddy's last name to Red."

Chapter 5 ～

With Seth in the car, Stelson and I had to wait until we got home to discuss my father's unauthorized history lesson. Stelson put Seth in the tub. I took care of Zoe's last bottle and her kitchen-sink bath. My husband held it together long enough for me to read them a story. Then, he uttered a quick family prayer before we put the kids in bed.

And then I followed him to our bedroom to get the full story. "What happened?"

He helped me prop up my foot on two pillows before he answered. "Seth can't go over there anymore. Not until we come to an understanding."

"He has to go over there. Daddy picks him up on Tuesdays and takes him to piano lessons at Mrs. Gambrell's, remember?"

He probably didn't. I could barely keep up with the taxi schedule and I was the driver. "Besides, Daddy really could use the company."

"He may have to go to a senior center or something. Hang with people who want to hear his philosophy."

I ignored the not-gonna-happen suggestion. "What, exactly, was said?"

Stelson chewed on his bottom lip for a second. "Basically, he told Seth that because he's black, he'll have to work harder and be smarter than the white kids in his class in order to be successful."

Honestly, I thought Stelson would be more upset about the whole 'negro' thing. "Well...," I proceeded with caution, "I mean, my dad was out of place for having *the black talk* with him before we did. But it's not like he told Seth a lie."

"It *is* a lie," Stelson stressed. "And there's no such thing as having *the black talk.*"

"Yes. There. Is." I raised off the headboard. "Granted, you probably never heard it. But Seth is biracial, which makes him a minority. Historically and racially speaking, he *is* at a disadvantage. He *will* have to be at the top of his game in order to compete with his counterparts, assuming his skin will darken over time. I don't think he should hear this talk at four years old, but it is necessary."

Stelson hissed, "I can't believe you're saying this. On what grounds do you agree with your dad?"

His words stung me as his wife and as my father's daughter. "What planet are you on? Seth is black. And even if he never looks black, Zoe sure will. You've got to see things for what they are. America will label them black. And that label comes with *the black talk.* You have one in elementary school. Have another one when their hormones kick in, especially for boys. Another one when they go off to college, the military or wherever."

I contained my wincing as Stelson sat down near my foot, causing the bed to bounce slightly. This certainly wasn't our first disagreement about the kids. I believed in swatting Seth's bottom any time he disobeyed. Stelson was more on the "save spankings for major infractions" page, use "time out" for everything else.

He thought I bought the kids way too many clothes. I said our kids represented our family and should be well-dressed.

I believed in lavish Christmases with a ton of gifts under the tree. The joy of watching Seth open them filled my heart. Stelson believed kids should only get a few toys for Christmas because it's a celebration of Christ, not us.

Hands down, Stelson was better at listening to my arguments. Or at least he'd pretend to listen. In the end, if he didn't change his mind, we usually defaulted to his leading since he was the one who had to report to God on behalf of our family (I learned that in a Titus 2 class at church).

Anyway, that night was no different. He stopped churning through his anger and disbelief and genuinely asked me, "What *is* the black talk anyway?"

"It's where we sit them down and tell them about our history in Africa and America. Then we tell them there are still some people who will look down on them because they're black. We let them know that when people see black kids, they're prejudged. We teach about Emmett Till and Rodney King and Treyvon Martin. Teach them not to run from police officers or be disrespectful because cops will shoot first and ask questions later," I filled Stelson in.

"Being disrespectful and running from cops is a bad move for *anybody*, not just black people."

He wasn't getting it.

"Shondra, when and if Seth faces discrimination, after pointing to Christ, I'm going to refer to President Obama so my son will know that if a man with the same racial makeup can become the President of the United States of America, there's absolutely no reason why Seth can't achieve his goals as well."

Stelson's brow drew into a knot. "Is this what black people are telling their kids?"

"Society will tell them if we don't." I rubbed my husband's strong, muscular arm. My heart ached for him and I could only imagine how his heart must have been breaking with the news that he would have to prepare his children for a future he couldn't imagine.

But instead of agreeing with me, Stelson shook his head. "No. I'm not going to pour the fear of man into Seth and Zoe."

"We have to prepare them for *real life*," I said.

"Life in Christ *is* real life," he argued. "I don't want Seth and Zoe to think that the promises of God end where their skin color begins."

"But the *world* is not in Christ," I reasoned.

"Since when does the world determine anything? I mean, do you think when God declared 'I know the plans I have for you', He forgot to say that the plans are only valid if you're not black?"

My entire schema as an African American and as a believer clashed almost as much as when I'd found myself falling in love with Stelson. There I was again, deciding which side to lean on: my blackness or my faith.

"I can't do this tonight." I gave up as Stelson's new philosophy coursed through my head, all the way down to my throbbing foot.

"Let's pray," he offered.

He kneeled on my side of the bed, his bald crown reflecting the light from our ceiling fan. My poor husband had tried to hold on to the sides and front, but he finally had to let them go when someone told him he looked like George Costanza from Seinfeld.

He was still sensitive about his hair loss, so I refrained from stroking his head. Instead, I rested a hand on his shoulder, touching in agreement.

"Father, we come before You today thanking You for Your grace. Thanking You for the blessing of health in Christ. I speak healing into my wife's foot. I thank You for sustaining her, strengthening her to be a great wife and mother and assistant principal. I pray that we would both be obedient to the plans You have for us. Finally, God, as You have done so many times before, I pray that You will bring us to an understanding about how to raise the precious children You have given us, Zoe and Seth. Give us wisdom to know how much of the world's system to expose them to. Like Christ told the disciples, we want them to be wise as serpents, but innocent as doves. Teach us the balance. Teach us..."

That's about all I heard before I dozed off on my husband's prayer.

I figured I'd give my father a few days to calm down before I went over there after work to have a certain discussion. "Daddy, you cannot take it upon yourself to teach Seth how to be a black man."

"Stelson sure can't do it, and you can't either. So who does that leave?"

My father took another bite of his syrup sandwich and chewed it as though it were a T-bone steak. His face thin, eyes sunken, skin dry. It was hard to tell whether old age, poor eating habits, or sorrow was eating away at my father.

Sidetracked by his meal, I asked, "Why aren't you eating the frozen dinners I brought you last week?"

"I don't want no freezer food. Too many preservatives. This here," he held the slices of bread in the air, "is good, fresh eatin'. Back when I was growing up in Ellerson, Momma used to pack these for our lunches every day, and other kids was jealous because we actually had two slices, *and* something in between 'em.'"

To increase my aggravation, he stuffed a super-sized bite into his mouth, almost causing himself to gag.

Lord, how did my mother put up with this ornery man for almost fifty years? I loved my daddy, but he was a bonafide grouch who had gotten even worse since Momma passed away. Now there was no one to counter his negative spiels or tell him to turn off CNN because he was getting too riled up about all the bad news reports.

Get back to the business, LaShondra. "Like I was saying. Stelson and I would really appreciate it if you would let us decide when and how much to tell Seth about growing up African American. Can you respect that?"

He poked out his bottom lip. "Well tell me this, then. What exactly do you and Stelson plan on tellin' Seth about being a black man in America?"

I still wasn't completely sold on Stelson's plan enough to articulate it well. And I realized that I didn't owe my father an explanation. But the sincerity in his deeply set eyes reminded me that if my brother, Jonathan, didn't settle down soon, Seth might be the only grandson my father would ever meet. "We're going to raise Seth to have more faith in God than fear of man."

Daddy pushed his back against the chair. "So, y'all gonna let him live in fantasy-land, basically, where he won't know anything about his history, how white people destroyed his ancestors? You gonna make him think he's white?"

"Seth *is* half-white as much as he is half-black," I reminded my father. "Do you want him to hate half of himself?"

My father tapped his index finger on the kitchen table. "It's not *hate*. It's *education*. He needs to understand why every time he looks up, there's a black man being arrested on TV. Media manipulation." My father's voice rose. "He needs to know why there's hardly any black kids in the books he reads. Oppression and discrimination. If he knows what's really going on, he won't internalize all the hidden messages." By this point, spittle was collecting in the corners of my father's mouth as a product of his passionate plea.

I couldn't even argue with him because he had a point. Seth didn't know he was half-black or half-white. Seth really didn't care. Stelson and I hadn't planned on making a big deal out of race with our kids. And yet, children are observant. As sure as the little black girls preferred white dolls in the Drs. Kenneth and Mamie Clark black/white doll experiments in the 1940s, Seth and Zoe would leave their impressionable childhoods with concepts in place.

Pressing my fingertips over my eyelids, I gave my father his due. "I hear you, Daddy. I do. Stelson and I will figure this out. Just don't go black-history-month on him again without running it by us, okay?"

"What's wrong with you?" he asked.

I sat up straight, let my hands fall to the table. "What do you mean?"

Daddy raised his chin. He looked down his nose at me, examining my face. "You look tired."

"I *am* tired. I've got a six month old, a four year old, and a demanding job. What do you expect?"

"I expect Stelson ought not make my daughter work like a Hebrew slave," Daddy said as he lowered his glare.

"Stelson doesn't *make* me work," I clarified. "I work because I enjoy it."

"If you say so," my father gave his two cents. He backed away from the table and walked toward the trashcan to throw his napkin away.

The garbage was overflowing, as was the pile of plates in the sink. Momma never went to bed with a dirty dish in the sink. A part of me wanted to fuss at Daddy, but after reflecting on my own housekeeping flaws, I decided to keep my mouth shut. "I've gotta go pick up Zoe. Daycare closes at 6:30. Would you wake up Seth and send him to the car for me?"

"You know he's gonna want to spend the night," my father snickered. "He's crazy about you."

"I know," my father agreed proudly as he stood.

"Give Zoe a kiss for me," he requested.

"I will."

"You take care of yourself, Shondra. You can always move back here if you need to. All bills paid."

Are you kidding me?

He gave my arm a reassuring squeeze. In that moment, I decided not to take offense. Instead of asking him why on earth he would suggest that I leave my husband, I took Daddy's offer for how he meant it: a father reminding his daughter that she would always be his baby.

"Thank you, Daddy."

Of course, my father's gesture put me in a sentimental mood as I drove to pick up Zoe. He loved me. He wanted me taken care of. And the more I thought about my father's love for me, I couldn't help but think of my heavenly Father's abounding love. He wanted exactly what Daddy wanted for me: Peace. Well-being. All this exhaustion, this lack of focus, this scattered attention couldn't be His plan for me. And the bad thing was, I couldn't even take time that evening to pray about the situation because I had a portfolio full of teacher performance data to review before another staffing meeting in the morning.

Not to mention Seth's new weekly read-to-me requirement. His teacher had done a good job of putting the fear of God in them about getting an adult to sign off on the reading log. If anyone should have been "on it" about getting a child to read, it should have been me. An educator. A principal, no less. But I was so busy making sure other people's kids got an education, my own son went to pre-k not knowing how to read which, in Plainview, was not a good start.

Note to self: Get Daddy to do some time with Seth's reading log.

After securing Zoe in her car seat, I rattled my brain for a dinner plan. Didn't hear one. Besides, cooking and cleaning up would add another hour to my evening agenda. I was already in the red, time-wise. McDonald's to the rescue.

I limped through the house with sacks in one hand, Zoe on a hip, my purse and laptop bag handles in the other hand. Evidence of the morning's mayhem still sat where we'd left it: bowls in the sink, Seth's night clothes on the couch, Zoe's comb and brush on the coffee table. Conviction all over the place.

Nothing like coming home to a messy house.

Maybe He had graced some women to do many things well. Maybe some women *had* to be a jack-of-all-trades because they didn't have husbands, for whatever reason. But as for me, LaShondra Denise Smith Brown, I was clearly not capable nor was I anointed to run this many races at once.

Something had to give, but I wasn't ready to figure out who or what.

Chapter 6 ❧

I called Peaches first because she knew all the ins and outs of human resources. "What do I say?"

"You tell them you're taking the rest of your family medical leave. Don't say 'I'd *like* to' or 'I *need* to'. This isn't a request, it's a legal right. You can take up to a year off work to care for your baby."

"But I went back to work already," I said. "Doesn't that count against me?"

"Technically, yes, but you're in Texas, which is an employment-at-will state. No reputable employer wants to force anyone to work somewhere they don't actually want to work, especially not in your field," she explained.

"I so wish you were here, Peaches."

"Well if you get a phone upgrade, we can FaceTime," she badgered again.

"I don't have the mental capacity to learn another operating system right now," I pushed her suggestion aside. "Now, what if they don't want to let me go?"

"If your H-R person tries to act funny about it, you might have to wiggle through some of the loopholes in the law. I can send you some stuff if it comes to that."

I pushed the gear into park as I finished the free consultation with my resident expert. A quick survey of my surroundings put my mind at ease. There were no other co-workers present to overhear our conversation through the car's speakers. Stelson had rigged up the hands-free system to make the car safer for me and the kids.

"Anything else I need to know?" I probed. "It can't be this simple. How can I just walk in one day right before the start of school and say 'I don't want to work right now'?"

"What if you won the lottery and you resigned the next day?" she posed. "You think it would be any different?"

"I don't play the lottery."

"How about, God forbid, if you got hurt and you had to take off to care for yourself?"

"That would be different."

"No, it wouldn't," she explained. "Right now, your *family* is hurting and you have to go take care of the family unit."

Never thought of it that way.

"Why can't *dads* take care of the family?" I argued.

"You can ask Stelson to take a leave of absence. I mean, nobody's saying the person handling the house and kids has to be you," she replied.

I'd be a fool to ask my husband to give up his business. Stelson's income ran circles around mine. Non-profit sector salaries couldn't compete with the for-profit arena. "Never mind. I just can't believe I'm actually going to do this."

"What did Stelson say when you told him you were taking a leave?"

"He did the running man dance."

"Naaaaw."

"Yes. Elbows and everything."

Peaches cracked up. "Girl, he is going to love having you at home. So will the kids. Are you considering homeschooling?"

"Absolutely not! This is *temporary*. I do not plan to be at home long."

"What's your timeframe?"

"Long enough to get a handle on things. Get back in shape, get the housekeeper and chef on a schedule, get back into my regular prayer time, reconnect with Stelson," I ran through the agenda. "Six months ought to do it."

"And what if it doesn't? Or what if you actually *like* being home?"

"I won't," I relieved her of that worry. "Six months. I'm back to work in March. Finish out the school year, take another breather in the summer. I'll be good."

"Okay. Let's do this."

All day, I kept an eye out for an opportune time to speak with Jerry about my plans. Meeting after meeting, however, prevented us from grabbing a moment until almost three o'clock. We were both in wind-down mode by that point, but I had to break the news. The sooner the better, Peaches had said.

"Jerry," I said, knocking on his half-open office door. "Can I talk to you for a second?"

He looked up from the stack of work on his desk.

How can I leave him with all this work?

"Uuuh…is this a good time?"

"As good a time as any," he chuckled.

I shuffled toward the empty chair across from him.

"This doesn't feel like good news," he growled. "What's up?"

I took a deep breath. *Am I crazy? It took me years to get this high up in the district!* "I've been thinking about how to balance my life with this job—"

"I know. Me, too," he nodded. "Sarah's on me all the time about working too much."

Relief swept through me as I released the ball of pent-up air in my chest. "It's a lot to handle."

"I know," he agreed. "I've asked the superintendent for another vice principal to divide the work. If enrollment is as high as projected, we may have the budget for it."

Okay. Having another VP would relieve some of the workload. Less work, less stress. I could swing this.

My resolve to leave crumpled. "I sure hope so, Jerry. I think we could both use some help."

I didn't answer Peaches' call that night. Wasn't quite sure how to tell her I'd punked on the plan.

Stelson, however, could not be avoided. I told him the truth. The hopeful truth. "We're adding another vice principal," I offered as though Jerry's proposal was already set in stone.

God, please let it be, I prayed. I didn't like telling my husband half-truths.

With only two weeks before school started, my prayer was answered. Jerry got the green light to hire another vice principal. We looked in-district first for newly certified candidates. The only ones available had already been picked over and turned down by other campuses, which spoke volumes.

Our search led us back to the district's open pool of applicants. Jerry and I combed through dozens of resumes. We narrowed them down to four. We interviewed all four, selected two contenders. Interviewed again, and finally decided on one: Natalie Lockhart-Gomez.

Natalie's background working with diverse populations clinched the position for her. She was bilingual (English/Spanish), which was a plus given our campus's ever-changing population. Jerry and I both looked forward to sharing best practices with her.

We submitted her name to H-R for a final review.

Meanwhile, Jerry and I got busy preparing for back-to-school inservice and countless meetings with counselors and the dean of education, Marty Williams. Marty was a genius when it came to matching teachers' strengths with student weaknesses based on the data analysis Jerry and I provided. It felt good to be part of such an awesome team. Double-good as a black female. Right or wrong, my work was fulfilling—even if it was a never-ending job.

"This year is going to be wonderful," I told myself over and over again, even as Stelson made little comments here and there about how they could have just as easily hired two last-minute vice principals as one.

I stopped talking to him about anything involving work because the conversation would morph into a low-level disagreement. Stelson wasn't really one to raise his voice. Sometimes, his ability to make a point and then shut up immediately afterward left me almost wishing he'd soften his words with a bunch of other irrelevant gibberish. Other times, I just wondered if it was a "white" thing because every black couple I knew could go tit-for-tat until the cows came home.

When we argued by not arguing, I thought about my father's philosophy; the idea that black men were fundamentally different due to historical influences. Maybe white men didn't argue because they didn't have to. Why argue when you already have the power? And maybe black men argued because if they didn't advocate for themselves, they'd never be heard.

Where does that leave Seth?

I couldn't worry about the future. Not when two of my strongest math teachers were being heavily recruited by the district office for coaching positions.

Jerry and I threw ourselves into last-minute mode, which included registration, staff development, and meetings with the technology team regarding the digital book adoption for several core classes. We needed to help develop our policy regarding use and abuse of the new e-readers we'd be distributing to students. The whole transition was a booger-bear we'd been putting off for years. But since technology waits for no one, we had to hammer that whole plan out in a matter of days.

Stelson pretty much took over Seth's enrollment in pre-K. I met his teacher, Miss Osiegbu, and let her know in so many words that Seth was the son of a long-time district administrator. If she knew anything about Plainview school district, she would know that we all looked out for each other's kids especially. An unspoken perk which, incidentally, was the very reason I'd "requested" Miss Osiegbu for Seth. She had a reputation for challenging kids beyond the state curriculum, per the school's counselor, who used to be on my staff at the middle school.

The Friday before school started, I finally stole away from the campus for a lunch break at Wal-Mart so I could buy Seth's school uniforms. The trip to the store alone saddened me because I knew if Momma had been alive, it would have been her joy to take Seth back-to-school shopping.

Come to think of it, if Momma had been alive, she would have helped me with the kids a lot more, and Stelson wouldn't have been on my back so much about quitting.

Momma. I wish you were here. Being a mother without a mother was extra hard.

We were all set to go—or so I thought—until the actual morning of the first day, when we got up and I slid those navy blue uniform pants up

Seth's legs.

Seth leaned over and examined the inch of empty space between the top of his foot and the hem of those pants. "Mommy, I'm too big for these."

"Turn around."

Seth twirled. I flipped up the back tag. They were a size four, just like I thought. But the last time I'd bought him a pair of pants was before the summer. He'd worn nothing but shorts pants, even to church, for the past few months, which explained the problem.

How can I not know what size my child wears?

I turned the hem of his pants inside out to see how much extra material we had to work with. "Take your pants off. Wait right here."

Taking out the hem robbed me of six precious minutes, but I couldn't send my child to school looking neglected on the very first day. And I sure as heck didn't want Stelson to get wind of the crisis at hand.

After I freed the hem with a steak knife, I told Seth to get the glue out of his new backpack while I went into the laundry room to iron his pants.

"Okay." He seemed glad to be helping.

So long as Zoe remained silent in her crib, we would be fine.

Standing at the ironing board, I eyeballed a straight line. I folded the fabric, then starched and pressed a new seam into the bottom of his pants. Seth brought me the glue, which would have to do until I saw him again after school. I tacked the new hem in place. "We'll give it a few minutes to dry and you can put them on again."

"Yes!" He raised his hand for a hi-five.

"Teamwork, baby!" I congratulated him, slapping his palm. "But don't tell Daddy, okay?"

"Don't tell Daddy what?" my husband's voice poured over my shoulder.

Dang it!

Seth slapped both hands over his mouth.

I played it off like no big deal. Motioning for my son to come near, I placed myself behind Seth's body as I helped him step into the newly-crafted slacks. "Well your son, here, must have hit a growth spurt. We had to let out the hem in his pants."

"You're getting pretty tall there!" Stelson gave our son his second high-five of the morning. "Why would this be a secret to keep from Daddy?"

Though his eyes were fixed on our son, I knew Stelson's question was aimed at me.

I truly did not want to mislead my husband again, but I didn't want to give him another log to throw on his you-don't-have-to-work fire. "We had a wardrobe malfunction. No worries. We fixed it."

Quickly, I sent Seth back to the kitchen while I got Zoe up and dressed. Stelson spent a few minutes talking to Seth in the kitchen reiterating our expectations and God's expectations of him in pre-school.

My ears remained on high alert to see if their conversation diverted to the subject of Seth's pants. Thankfully, Stelson let the topic fall.

I'm sorry, Lord. I don't like tricking my husband or recruiting my child for deception. But how else was I supposed to avoid conflict while getting what I wanted out of life at the same time? After all, it was *my* God-given life. I wasn't the first working mother, and I wouldn't be the last. There had to be a million moms worse than me, too. At least my kids were clean, fed, well-dressed (with the exception of Seth's slacks) and loved. Seth was smart, Zoe was hitting all her developmental milestones. So what if they ate fast food a little more than the surgeon general recommended. *Who died and made him boss of the food pyramid anyway?*

Forget Peaches. Forget Stelson. I was not Martha Stewart or June Cleaver. I was *LaShondra Smith Brown.* LaShondra was a good wife and good mother, and I wasn't going to let anybody make me feel bad about wanting it all.

I closed my fist tight around the dream of having it all and refused to let it go.

❧Chapter 7

"Hey."

"Yes. Who is this?" I asked.

"This is Taylor Austin. I'm from the Mommy-coo service."

"You mean Mother's Chief of Operations service?" I corrected this girl.

She smacked, "Same thing. I'm calling for my...um...'nitial nanny phone interview."

"This interview is over." Call me picky, but I would have liked for my children's nanny to at least sound like she'd graduated from high school.

The previous potential nanny had sounded intelligent enough, but when she'd asked me to hold on, she'd failed to properly mute her phone. I heard her cuss somebody out with expert diction and a fine choice of escalating insults.

Hung up before she knew I was gone.

Obviously, I was using the wrong service. Or perhaps God was allowing me to see people's true colors ahead of time. I couldn't decide if it would be better to hire someone with a small, apparent flaw or choose the "perfect" one and find out later that she'd been a rat all along.

If we were talking about a personal trainer or even a teacher, I could live with being fooled for a month or a year. My babies were a different story. Finding out I'd been snowed after-the-fact wasn't an option.

Back to the drawing board and on to Seth's school.

After the first few days of pre-k, I was able to drop him off without a blur of tears—my tears. By Thursday, he had the drop-off routine under control. He'd unhook his car seat, hop out of the car, strap on his little backpack, and run inside without even looking back.

Every effort was made to preserve my mascara as I drove to the school on autopilot. *It's almost like he doesn't need me anymore.* I merged into traffic on the farm to market road as my brain shifted from Mommy-mode to VP-mode.

Thankfully, I was needed at Plainview High School. The counselors were busy leveling classes while sifting through a ton of schedule change requests, while the administrators did what we could to keep it all running smoothly. *Ask Marty if it would help to put one of the aides in Mayfield's classroom.*

New students were still enrolling, and the troublemakers who had been released back into the general population were already working on their return trips to RightWay. *See if the Watson girl has ever been tested for an emotional disorder.*

Jerry and I were compassionate to an extent. Kids are kids. Yet, those who disrespected teachers and disrupted the learning atmosphere met with serious consequences. After two or three parent conferences and a few suspensions, we turned them over to the disciplinary experts at RightWay. Some kids actually fared better in a structured environment with very little peer interaction. Whatever. I just knew they couldn't stay on *my* campus and keep up all that foolywang. *Find out who the new secretary is at RightWay.*

Fast forward to thoughts of what we would eat for dinner. I'd forgotten to take out the chicken. *Boston Market.*

The morning hadn't even started, and already I was yawning as I took my rightful parking spot. I grabbed the computer bag from the passenger's floorboard.

"Hhhhh. Hhhhh. Hhhhhwaaa."

My God!

I quickly turned toward the sound in my back seat. *Zoe!* In my haste, my rush to leave the house, the new routine, my tiredness, I had failed to take her to daycare. Worse, I was about to leave her locked in my car on a hot August day.

My God! What would have happened if…

Suddenly, visions of news stories where babies had died in hot cars—

forgotten in back seats or unaccounted for on field trips—flashed through my mind. This row of cars was already filled. There would have been no one casually walking by to see or hear my baby inside crying, suffocating in the stifling Texas heat. *Jesus! Thank you!*

Tears streamed down my face as I fumbled out my door and to the back seat of the car to retrieve my baby. I pulled her from the carrier straps and held her in my arms, rocking back and forth in the back seat kissing her pudgy round cheeks relentlessly.

What if Zoe hadn't made a sound?

I stared into her gray eyes. She stared back at me, puzzled. Another round of tears sprang forth as I imagined what could have happened. Her life cut short. My beautiful baby gone forever. All because I was too distracted, too busy to focus from point A to point B?

Thank you, Lord.

I didn't even go inside the building. From the car, I called Jerry. Told him—not asked—*told* him that I was taking a leave of absence.

"LaShondra, I don't understand," he puttered.

"The other week, when we talked about how hard it is to balance work and this job. I should have told you then. I'm sorry. But I can't do it anymore. Not for a while, anyway. Maybe you can still get the candidate we declined."

Jerry stuttered, "B-b-but, we've got Natalie. We've got help. Your responsibilities—"

"I almost left my baby in the *car*," I blurted out, my voice filled with emotion as my composure crumpled. I was breaking all kinds of professional rules, but I needed Jerry to feel me on this. "If Zoe hadn't started crying, I would have left her inside. And then…then…I'd be…planning a funeral, losing my mind."

"You left her in the *car*?" he asked, ridicule lacing his tone. "I mean…I'm sorry, LaShondra. I didn't know you were so stressed."

I sniffed. "Well, I am."

"Maybe we could work something out. Four-day weeks," Jerry practically begged.

Zoe flapped my nose with her hand. Her smile, a reward in itself, propelled my response. "No. I'm heading over to H-R. Please ask

Millicent to pack up my office."

"I have to warn you, LaShondra. This will *not* look good in your file."

"How would it look if I were in jail and you were accused of failure to recognize that one of your employees was cracking up?" I flipped the table.

Jerry exhaled. "Fine. I'll let Dr. Hunt know you're on your way."

Of course, I knew Dr. Hunt from my previous involuntary leave of absence, when I was investigated for showing disciplinary leniency in favor of African-American students in my Junior High assistant principal days. The whole thing was a setup, really, but in accordance with policy, I'd been placed on administrative leave during the investigation.

This time, we'd be meeting on different grounds.

I dropped Zoe off at preschool. While there, I picked up the center's brochure to acquaint myself with part-time and drop-in rates. Thankfully, no one asked me why Zoe was late or I would have gone into another crying spell.

Dr. Hunt was expecting me. Her secretary sent me toward a larger office.

"LaShondra. Good to see you again." She remembered me.

"Same here, Dr. Hunt. How have you been?"

"Counting down the days to retirement," she gave an I'm-dead-serious laugh.

"Oh? When?" Her stay in Plainview schools had become a running joke. Every year she said she was retiring. Never happened.

"At the end of this school year, definitely," she informed me. I got the feeling she'd shout it from the rooftops if given the opportunity.

Retirement. What would happen to my retirement? If I stayed off work until Zoe started pre-k, would I have to work until I was darn near seventy? Stelson and I hadn't made it that far in our discussion.

"Congratulations. We'll have a hard time filling your shoes," I complimented her, taking the guest's chair. Her office décor hadn't changed at all in ten years except to add more plaques, certificates, and family pictures.

Dr. Hunt won't be here when I come back! The next H-R director might not remember me so fondly.

I swallowed. Replayed the video of Zoe's life-saving cry on the big screen in my head. *I'm okay. I'm okay.*

"Jerry Ringhauser called ahead. I'd like to hear straight from the horse's mouth, though. What brings you here?" She laced her fingers and leaned forward.

"I'm going to take some time off to be with my baby," I said.

She nodded. "Good idea. I had three of my own. I hope to be able to do with my grandkids what I couldn't do with mine."

The sadness in her eyes dissipated the lump in my throat. I didn't want to wait until the next generation to enjoy my offspring.

"I'm sure your grandchildren will love having you around."

"Yes, yes. And when do you plan to return?"

"Um…I guess late spring, maybe? Or next fall?"

Dr. Hunt laughed. She cut her eyes at me and shook her head. "I'll make note of it, but I wouldn't be surprised if you changed your mind and stayed home longer. Babies have a way of rearranging plans. You thinking about having another one?"

"Oh, noooooo," I quickly denied.

Dr. Hunt laughed. "That's what we said after the second one. Things happen."

No, ma'am.

I completed the necessary forms and signed my name on the dotted line, so to speak. Dr. Hunt assured me that I wasn't the first person to leave with no notice. "It may be better for them to start the year off without you. The new person won't have to compete with your legacy. Start off fresh, you know?"

"Got it."

Dr. Hunt pushed off the table as she stood. "Well, Mrs. Brown, if I don't see you anymore before I get out of here, it's been a pleasure."

"Same here."

I walked back to my car thinking, *That wasn't nearly as bad as I thought it would be.* I guess I thought they were going to bring me before a judge or something. Rake me over the coals. Maybe Peaches was right—nobody wanted me there if I didn't want to be there.

My current predicament would make me think twice about holding on to teachers who were ready to resign.

I was planning to make the news of my leave a surprise for Stelson, so I hadn't texted him. Instead, I cut a path across town to meet him for lunch. There was always the possibility that he wouldn't be available or even present in the office, but I took my chances.

Brown-Cooper Engineering occupied a good portion of the third floor of the Chase bank building. Stelson's office, of course, boasted breathtaking views of the surrounding hills. Too bad I rarely got to see them, with my head buried in my own world.

Not today.

"Hi, LaShondra! How are you?" Stelson's administrative assistant, Helen, asked.

"I'm great. You?"

"Great."

Sometimes, I felt like I talked to Helen more than Stelson. We fell into an easy hug. Her shampoo had to be straight up Prell. Old school all the way, with her polyester flower-print dress. I'm not trying to be funny, but she was precisely the kind of drama-free, wholesome, great-aunt-lookin' secretary I wanted around my sexy husband.

She flounced down in her chair again. "Stelson didn't tell me you were coming by today."

"Oh, he didn't know. I won't be long. Just wanted to chat with him for a second. Is he available?"

"I believe so." She pressed the red conference button on the phone. "Stelson, your wife is here to see you."

Seconds later, Stelson rushed out of his office. "Is everything okay?"

I scrunched my face. "Yes. Everything's fine."

His shoulders fell an inch. "Okay. Come on in."

"I'm going to lunch," Helen told him. "Take care, LaShondra."

"You, too."

She grabbed her fanny pack and left.

Stelson led me into his office. The green trees and clear sky peeking through the vertical blinds gave me an appreciation for God's handiwork.

If only I'd had this landscape to gaze upon every now and then, my job would have been easier to bear.

The spacious room housed his desk, a full couch, a conference table for eight, and a wall full of plaques and certificates attesting to the company's excellence.

Stelson shut the door behind us. "What's up?"

I twirled to face him. "I did it."

"Did what?"

"Took a leave of absence."

The residue of anxiety drained from his countenance, replaced by a full grin as the corners of his eyes softened and lifted. He snatched me into an embrace and kissed my forehead. My cheeks. Finally, my lips. "Thank you."

I couldn't bring myself to tell him about the Zoe incident. Frankly, I was too embarrassed. I wished I hadn't told Jerry, either.

"You're welcome, baby."

He tilted my chin up with an index finger, kissing me more deeply than before. A surge of fire ran from my head to my feet and back up again. I couldn't remember the last time we'd kissed. *Really* kissed.

"I've got a present for you." His warm breath swept my nose.

"A present? How'd you know I was going to quit my job today?"

He walked to the office door and pressed a gold button to lock it. "I didn't. I just knew that whenever, wherever my prayer was answered, I'd have a special thank you ready."

I squinted. "A thank-you gift?"

He twisted the plastic rod that closed the blinds. "Yep."

I whispered, "Stelson, what are you doing?" though I already knew the answer. Somewhere in the hustle and bustle of becoming a new mom, I'd forgotten how marvelously spontaneous my husband could be.

"I'm preparing to give you a *big* thank you." He loosened his tie. Threw it on his laptop.

My eyes popped open wide, looking around the office. "*Here?*"

"Yep. Wouldn't be the first time. Remember?" Stelson said as he started on my neck.

"But we haven't done it here in a very long time," I croaked.

"Unfortunately."

I dropped my purse. Hopped up and wrapped my thighs around his waist as he lifted me. I could only hope that the conference table would hold as sturdy as it had before I'd gained twenty pounds carrying two kids.

He set me on the surface, teased my lips with his tongue as we both scrambled to remove only the necessary clothing.

He stopped. Put a finger on my mouth. "No screaming."

I giggled. "Same goes for you."

ﾍﾞChapter 8

Benefit #1: mo' sex. Benefit #2: *better* sex. Benefit #3: #1 and #2. We hadn't quite figured out exactly how we were going to reorganize the family budget, but intimate time with Stelson definitely added to the bottom line that first week I was home from work.

Once we'd finished with the kids' baths in the evenings, you would have thought we were newlyweds who had just recently discovered God's bonus perk to being married.

We finally came up for air on the weekend. Stelson served me breakfast in bed that Saturday morning.

"Where's Mommy?" I overheard Seth asking my husband in the kitchen.

"She's resting."

"*Resting*?" Seth asked as though it weren't humanly possible.

"Yes. She's resting in bed."

"Can I see her?"

"Yes, when she's ready."

Since Zoe was only good for about twenty minutes in her swing and Seth wasn't the type to sit in front of a television without finding some other way to entertain himself, I scarfed down the toaster waffles, turkey sausage and orange juice.

Plus, I wanted to see my babies. I couldn't have Seth feeling I'd all but abandoned him.

As I showered, washed my hair, and blow-dried my straight, brown mane, I wondered how my appearance would change with thick, curly coils like Peaches' hair. I pulled my bangs back and took inventory of my forehead. Head-on, it was fine. But the profile. *Nuh-uh. Too big.* Besides, people said natural hair was way more work than permed hair. The whole point of me leaving my job was to *gain* more time, not reallocate it to caring for my hair.

My little ones both squealed when I joined the family in the living area. "Hi, Mommy!" Seth threw his arms around my neck.

"Hey, Seth!"

Still a bit protective of my toe, I tucked it safely underneath the rim of the couch.

"Daddy said you were resting. Are you sick?"

"No. I'm feeling great."

"Then why were you resting?" His long eyelashes fluttered as he questioned me.

"Can't mommies rest?"

"No," he insisted.

"Well, *this* mommy does." I tickled his stomach.

He backed away, laughing.

I hoisted Zoe from her swing and smooched on her neck until she burst into gurgling giggles. I cradled her in my arms as I joined Stelson and Seth on the couch again.

And there we were: the picture-perfect all-American family. Dad, mom, and son, and a baby daughter. All we needed was a dog, which Stelson and I had both agreed wasn't going to happen until Seth was old enough to assume the responsibility.

"Who wants to go to a movie?" Stelson asked, though he must have already known the suggestion alone would drive our son bonkers.

"Me! Me! Me!" Seth jumped, raising his hand in the air.

"Okay. Let's make it happen."

The theater hadn't been on my agenda, but how could I resist all this delicious family time? This was my new identity, right? No longer super-*every-woman*. I could whittle it down to super-*wife* and super-*mom*.

With the promise of movie plans, Seth hopped on his Saturday chores—straightening up his bedroom and picking up trash in the back yard—while Stelson and I had our monthly budget meeting at the kitchen table while keeping an eye on our son.

My husband presented a Dave Ramsey disciple, a spreadsheet with color-coded categories and clearly labeled dollar amounts. Most of the time, I came to the budget meetings and simply listened. Really, I didn't care what Stelson did with the money in our joint account so long as the bills got paid and money was both given and saved.

The only account I watched like a hawk was my personal account, which was separate from what I put in the family pot. Stelson didn't mess with my personal account. I didn't mess with his, either. We could both view each other's account activity online, but I had learned early on not to even click on his links if I didn't want to get upset about how much he'd spent on a pair of cufflinks.

"So," he started, "in order to stay on track with the kids' college funds and our retirement accounts, looks like we're going to need to renegotiate some of our existing contracts and cut back on several non-essentials."

"Like what?" His definition of non-essential was usually different from mine.

"First, the cell phones. With you working at home, your data plan can be reduced because you'll have your phone tapped into the house's Wi-fi."

Made sense. "Okay."

"I estimate lower gas expenses as well."

"True," I said as I continued perusing the charts. "Wait. Zoe's daycare."

"What about it?"

"I wanted to keep her in two days a week."

He shrugged. "Why would we pay for daycare when you'll be home?"

"So I can get stuff done around here," I said.

He sat back in his chair. "Ummm…I'm not following you."

"I need some transition time."

"For what?"

"So I can get the hang of being a stay-at-homer. I want to practice doing it the easy way first."

"Why would you practice the easy way when you'll be doing it the hard way in the future?"

I couldn't think of a good comeback.

"I'm not saying no," he clarified, "I'm saying it doesn't make sense to me."

Now that he'd destroyed my whole practice-easy theory, it didn't make sense to me, either. If this was the way he dealt with contractors, I felt sorry for them. My husband didn't play when it came to numbers.

He shrugged, "If you want to pay out of your personal account, knock yourself out."

Not gonna happen. "You're right."

The clothing budget had shrunk along with the car insurance. Both were highlighted in green. "What's the deal with these?"

"Seth wears uniforms and you're working from home now. Clothing expenses, dry cleaning should go down, right?"

I breathed out. "I suppose." Now, my eyes were scanning for a decrease in any category related to him. *Nothing.*

"What about this digital TV bill? Must we have so many channels?"

"No. If you can get us a better deal, let's do it."

"What about my mad money?" I asked.

"Mad money?"

"Yeah. Money that I can just blow on whatever."

"Don't you have some money in your personal account?"

"Yeah," I concurred peacefully, "but it's not going to last forever."

Stelson laid his paper flat on the table. He took my paper and repeated the action. "What's on your mind, Shondra?"

I sighed and told my husband the truth. "I feel like I'm losing my independence."

"Welcome to the club."

"What club? You're not in the club. You're still working, still bringing in a paycheck."

"Babe, Cooper and I realized a long time ago that every penny that comes into our business came from the hand of God Himself. We all depend on Him."

"Well, I mean, yeah," I agreed, "I know He takes care of us. But I don't like the idea of me having to justify everything, explain every single purchase. It would make me feel like a child. Not a child of God, a child of *you.*"

My husband poked out his lips and, immediately, I realized I'd hurt his feelings. "I'm sorry. That came out the wrong way."

"Do you trust me?"

"Of course I do," I replied. "Stelson, this is not about you. It's about *me*."

"No. It's about *us*. We're a team. We need you on board."

Staring into his blue, sincere eyes, I surrendered. "You know I can't resist you, right?"

He stole a kiss. "Big Daddy's still got it."

I smacked his arm. "No you didn't!"

We tweaked the grocery budget and added a few back-to-school expenses to the bottom line. Stelson adjourned the meeting in prayer and we were off to the movies.

My husband let Zoe and me out at the ticket booth while he and Seth found a parking spot. After the restroom and diaper-change run, we got our popcorn and drinks. Seth begged to visit the arcade. When he whined at my 'no', Stelson told him if he didn't stop crying, we'd give his ticket to a grateful child.

Seth straightened up.

We found three seats in a row smack dab in the middle of the theater. I hoped Zoe would sit still through the entire show, but she ran out of patience about a third of the way through.

I took her out and gave her a bottle, which ended her fussing and sent her off to dreamland.

By that point, I'd missed the most important part of the movie, apparently, because two cats who couldn't stand each other had become best friends.

I squirmed back to my seat. Stelson held out his arms for Zoe, so I passed her off and straightened out my shirt again.

I scrunched down and asked Seth, "What did I miss?"

"They had a fight and Pumpkin won but he didn't really want to hurt Stripes real bad so then they liked each other," he gave me the run down.

"Okay. Thanks."

Ten minutes later, Seth's foot began bouncing on the edge of his seat. I already knew what was coming next.

"Mommy, I gotta go use it."

Since Zoe was snuggled up with Stelson, I grabbed Seth's hand and apologized profusely for making a third trip past fellow movie-watchers.

We made a trip to the women's restroom, where the atmosphere alone caused me to have to go, too.

"Wait for me when you get finished, Seth," I instructed him since his stall was two doors down from mine.

I heard him flush and listened to his feet pounce away. I assumed he had taken it upon himself to wash his hands, which would be a sloppy wet mess probably, but I was learning from Peaches: Making messes is what boys do best.

I finished my business and stepped outside of my stall, expecting to see my son.

But he was nowhere in sight.

"Seth?"

No answer.

I asked the lady at the hand dryer if she'd seen a little boy leave.

"I'm sorry. I wasn't paying attention."

A quick inspection of the feet under the stalls yielded no sign of his green Toms boat shoes.

"Seth?"

I doused my hands in water and left the restroom, my heartbeat quickened at thoughts I didn't want to consider.

Outside the restroom, I visually searched the main lobby, sidestepping through the popcorn lines. No sign of my child. I could feel the blood rushing through my veins. *God, where is my baby?*

Quickly, I ticked off the other options: Maybe he went back into the theater. Or outside. But why would he go outside unless somebody...

A loud ringing sound caught my attention. *The arcade.*

I ran to the carpeted area and pushed past a horde of teenagers. Sure enough, there was Seth sitting in a racecar pretending to drive.

I snatched him up out of that racecar, swatted his behind three good times, and growled, "I told you not to leave the restroom!"

Those licks probably didn't hurt, but the sheer astonishment at having his whole world change in an instant brought a wail from Seth's throat.

"You stop crying. Stop it now, Seth."

As my own fear-fueled adrenaline subsided, I gave Seth a moment to collect himself.

My voice in control now, I ordered, "Dry your tears. Now."

He huffed a few more times, using the back of his hands to complete the job.

"I told you to wait for me, didn't I?"

"Yes," he agreed.

"Then why did you leave?"

"Because I wanted to play the game," he murmured between sniffles.

"You cannot disobey me. We'll talk about this after the movie." I grasped his hand firmly and led him back to our show. I slid my hand into the oversized door handles, and just before I yanked them open, I felt a tap on my shoulder.

"Ma'am?"

I turned to find the cinema security guard staring me down.

"Yes?"

The young man, dressed in blue with a yellow brooch too large to actually be taken seriously, said, "Someone noticed you striking this child."

"And?"

"Yeah, that's her," a woman, slightly older than me, with thin lips stepped from behind him. "She's the one who was hitting this little boy."

"This little boy—"

"Don't deny it!" she fussed. "I saw you. And I'll bet if his mother knew you were—"

"I *am* his mother," I set the record straight.

Seth tugged my arm. "Mommy, can we go inside?"

Shock splashed across their faces as my son confirmed our relationship. Suddenly, it occurred to me that I was the only dot in the picture.

"I'm sorry, ma'am." Security gave a sheepish grin and pointed at the woman. "She just said there was a black lady beating somebody's kid and…we have to protect the public."

I wanted to send Seth in to sit by his father so I could confront both the guard and the woman and ask if they would have been as concerned if the child were black. Or even if we'd both been white. But I didn't want to go there in front of my son.

"Your concern is misplaced," I seethed.

"Well, you two don't look like..." her voice trailed off as I shot her the duck lips, daring her to say another word in front of my baby.

She threw her hands up and walked away. Didn't even apologize.

For the second time, however, the guard reiterated his regrets, probably hoping I wouldn't report him to his manager so he'd be relieved of that fake Underoos-lookin' plastic badge.

I was beyond hot with both of them. "I'll accept your apology, but I hope you learned a lesson."

"Mo-meee!" Seth jerked my sleeve. "We're missing it."

Without another word, I followed my son into the darkness of the theater. We sidestepped down our row again and joined the rest of our otherwise normal family.

Sometimes, I could *almost* forget we were a cross-cultural family. That Stelson was white and I was black, and that our kids were halfway in between.

Almost.

I told Stelson about the incident later that day, after we'd finished with all our family fun. I guess I didn't want to spoil our good time, though I had been suddenly thrust into the world of black-and-white and noticed all the people of various races who took special notice of us. Observing us like we were a spectacle. Visually examining my children's hair texture. Matching up Seth's eyes with Stelson's, Zoe's darker skin color with mine.

They made me want to put my fingers in my ears and stick out my tongue. Then at least they'd have something worth gawking at.

Stelson, of course, picked up on my change in mood and that's when I let him in on the spanking followed by the interrogation.

He wanted to know why I didn't text him so he could come out and handle it.

"Honey, you can't *handle* prejudice," I said. "It's in people's hearts."

"Some people are ignorant," he said. He rubbed my neck as I secured my wrapped hair with a scarf.

Really, his hands were in the way, but I didn't want to shoo him away at the moment. "Out of the overflow of the heart, the mouth speaks," I quoted the Word.

"Mmm," he grunted. "Can't argue."

My husband tried. He really did. But in light of what happened at the movies and what my father and I had discussed, I wasn't sure if Stelson knew exactly what he was up against, what we'd both signed up for as an interracial couple raising biracial children.

Lord, help us.

Chapter 9 ❧

For some reason, every single Sunday morning was a struggle, no matter how early or how late I set the alarm clock. Even before I got married, this was a problem, but without someone waiting on me to leave, I didn't notice it.

Having kids didn't help. Sometimes we each took one child to get dressed. And yet, I could never hold up my end of the bargain.

If there was one thing my husband hated, it was being late. Drove him nuts.

I, on the other hand, wasn't nearly as perturbed by lateness to church, work, or anywhere else. What I *really* didn't like was being rushed by someone who only took ten minutes to get dressed.

Stelson honked the horn again. He and Seth were already in the car, and he had managed to give Seth the extra time it took for him to tie his own shoes.

I was still stuffing Zoe's feet into her white patent leather shoes, hoping they would make it through a few more weeks on her growing feet.

"Zoe, Zoe, your Daddy is ready to go-eey!"

I must have swung her from the crib too quickly because a stream of puke came flowing out of her mouth and onto her green cotton dress.

"No, Zoe. Nooooo." I flubbered my lips in exasperation, which caused Zoe to smile. And, of course, my baby's smile was contagious.

"Shondra. What's taking so long?" Stelson barged into the baby's room. "What are you doing?"

"I'm—"

"Looks like you're in here making goo-goo eyes with Zoe."

"If you'd let me finish a sentence, you'd know that she just spit up on her clothes. Now I have to change her."

He threw a hand in the air. "What happened to her bib?"

"I hadn't put it on her yet," I defended myself against what I perceived to be unspoken allegations of inadequate motherhood. *Look, man, I done already quit my job. What else do you want from me?*

Stelson shook his head and stormed out again.

How we managed to get so off track right before Sunday service always confused me. The corporate worship experience was supposed to be the most sacred event of the week. The time when I felt most holy, an opportunity to be inspired and refocus. And all I could think about on the way to church was how I wished the Lord would slap my husband upside the head.

Seth sat in his seat staring at us through the rear view and visor mirrors as I put the finishing touches on my makeup. My son was probably wondering why Stelson and I weren't talking. Zoe must have felt the tension, too, because she got fussy on the way. Seth tried to entertain her as much as possible, though his seatbelt wouldn't allow much more than holding her hand.

Stelson dropped the kids and me off at the side entrance, then drove off to find a parking spot. From the looks of things, he'd have a long walk back to the sanctuary, which wouldn't help his attitude.

Parents, mostly moms, stood in the check-in line. If they were anything like me, they were counting down the seconds until they could be child-free.

Of course, the scripture painted on the wall would have to convict me. "Children are a heritage of the Lord, offspring a reward from Him." Psalm 127:3 NIV. How could I have so quickly forgotten all the infertility hoops Stelson and I had jumped through to have children? *Forgive me, Lord.*

After waiting in a short line, I checked both kids into children's church at one of the kiosks, grabbed their printed stickers, and pressed them onto each child's back.

"Hi, Sister Brown!" Ebby, one of the faithful children's church leaders, greeted me. "How are you?"

Despite the anger simmering in my heart at the moment, I replied with churchy flavor, "Good! How are you?"

Ebby hugged me, which gave Zoe ample opportunity to grab hold of a fistful of Ebby's dreadlocks.

"Zoe, no," I said, prying her fingers from Ebby's hair.

Ebby laughed heartily, "Happens all the time. Kids are fascinated by my hair."

I had to admit that the mysterious twists on her head were interesting to me, too. In fact, I'd taken the liberty to register the texture with my finger as I loosened Zoe's grasp. The light brown locks were softer than I'd imagined.

"This one certainly loves your style," I complimented Ebby.

Her soft, shiny cheeks rose to a full crest. "I'll see you later." She rushed off to wherever she'd been headed before she took a moment to speak to me.

Ebby's patient, pleasant demeanor with Seth as a baby set me at ease with leaving Zoe in the care of the nursery volunteers at Living Word Church. And Seth was learning so much in his Sunday school and children's Bible study classes that I knew his teachers took this special ministry seriously.

During the hair-pulling distraction, Seth had managed to crawl behind the kiosks and was, apparently, busy trying to discover where the sticker paper came from.

"Seth! Get out from around there!"

He obeyed quickly, with a mischievous smile. I pinched his arm with enough force to let him know I meant business without leaving a mark.

I dropped the kids off in their respective classes, then left that building trailing the covered walkway to the main sanctuary. Waiting for Stelson, I sat on one of the benches in the foyer. He finally arrived, and we proceeded—without discussion—to our regular section of the church. Right side, second section of pews. The ushers knew our preference. We were regulars, and Stelson was one of the long-time members. Not that we had special privileges. I suppose it was like how Mother Bohannan had her spot at Gethsemane COGIC. People expected her to sit there as much as they respected her routine.

Living Word Church had grown into an adult-heavy congregation. There was a good chunk of teenagers, but there weren't as many kids around as I remembered when Stelson and I first married and I joined the church. The rainbow of colors present had always made for a pleasant, gawk-free experience. When all our hands were raised toward heaven, the spectrum of color was beautiful to behold. People from every nation praising Him in our mid-sized sanctuary.

Almost half of each service was spent in praise and worship, which instantly lowered the temperature of the anger brewing in my chest. "Here I am to worship..." *I know it upsets my husband when we're late, Lord. I need to do better.* "Altogether wonderful to me."

As I blessed the Lord with the fruit of my lips, gratefulness coursed through my soul.

Without notice, the pain of losing my mother sprang up fresh. Threatened to overtake me. But in truth, recollections of Momma added to my praise. I could only thank God for the years she *was* alive, pouring into my life. Not everyone had a mother when they were growing up. Some people's mothers didn't get to see them finish high school, college, earn a master's degree, become a professional success, and walk down the aisle to say "I do". Some never got to see any of their grandchildren.

Other people didn't have good mothers, and instead of suffering the pain of loss, they suffered the inexplicable pain of neglect, abuse, or indifference.

My mother was good. And she was in the presence of a good God. "I'll never know how much it cost..."

Counting my blessings brought thoughts of the wonderful man He had brought into my life ten years earlier, who was standing at my side. Stelson was an amazing husband. He loved the Lord, he loved me, and he was proving himself a great father to our children, despite the fact that Stelson lost his own father to cancer when he was only nine. It was hard to believe now that I'd almost missed out on the blessing of being married to a man of God because Stelson was white. The way God changed my heart through Stelson's love and companionship was nothing short of an earth-moving miracle testimony. I didn't know many women—black *or* white—with a husband like mine.

The final stanza of the song was a reflection of how much it cost Jesus to pay for our sin, which sent tears trickling down my face as my hands flew toward heaven. I didn't deserve God's goodness, but He loved me. *He loves me.*

Skylar Woodland, the worship leader, led us in a moment of prayer, thanking God for His Son, Jesus. And then she asked us to pray with someone near us.

Of course, this brought Stelson and me face-to-face. Immediately, I folded my arms around his neck and whispered in his ear, "I'm sorry."

He locked onto my waist and prayed as we swayed to the slow beat of worship, "Father, I thank You for this beautiful woman. Thank You for our family. Thank You for teaching us both to be obedient to You and submissive to one another, as Your Word directs. We stand against division in our home. Help us to put aside hard feelings this morning so we can hear Your voice. And please God, *please* help us to get to church on time in the future. Amen."

Now, that last request wasn't quite the prayer I think Skylar had in mind when she'd instructed us to go before the throne. But I let it slide because Stelson sealed the prayer with a peck on my cheek.

"Amen," I agreed.

The announcements, which followed worship, found Stelson and I scrunched close together. *Thank you, Lord, for giving us both hearts to forgive easily.*

Assistant Pastor Gales reiterated the upcoming church Labor Day picnic to be held at Ronnie Reed Lake. The fellowship team was planning a day of kayaking, a trail hike, and barbecue.

Stelson nudged me. "You wanna go?"

"Uh, that would be a no."

"Why not?"

"You know I don't do outside."

"Oh, come on. Didn't you ever go camping when you were a kid?"

I snarled my face. "No."

"Camping's great. Lakes are fun. You'll see."

I exhaled, knowing once my husband got it in his mind he was going to expose our kids to an adventure, he would make it happen.

I'm not trying to be funny, but this was definitely not something from the COGIC list of things to do. Barbecue, yes. But hiking trails and kayaking? Absolutely not. Anything that might mess up a black woman's hair couldn't be placed on an official church agenda.

The multi-cultural mix of people at Living Word had introduced me to a world of cuisines, traditions, and customs through various celebrations and missions' updates. So far, except for a few bites of food discreetly spat into a napkin, there had been no serious setbacks.

After Pastor Toole's timely message on asking the Holy Spirit for help when we've reached the end of our ropes—or better yet, *before* we come to the end of ourselves—new members received the right hand of fellowship and church was dismissed.

Stelson, the kids, and I trekked to my parents' house after service. According to Stelson, he and my father had conversed by phone and had respectfully agreed to disagree about Seth's future as a black man. For now, Daddy would hold off on the hard-core facts.

"I didn't know you two talked," I mumbled as I read through the Sunday program again. "Why didn't you tell me?"

"Some things are man-to-man."

Hmph.

We stopped and picked up a meal of rotisserie chicken with French fries and green beans. "Baby, get an extra chicken. I want Daddy to have some extra for the next couple of days," I said to Stelson at the drive-thru order screen.

The smell from the plastic bags sent Zoe into a tizzy until we reached Daddy's house and I gave her a pinch from a French fry to swish around her gums. This child was not supposed to be eating table food, according to all the doctor charts.

I remembered when I'd gotten angry with my mother for putting cereal in Seth's milk when he was only five months old. "Momma! He's not supposed to have cereal until next month!"

"Says who?" she'd fussed.

"Says all the books! It leads to food allergies and teaches them to overeat!" I informed her.

Momma rinsed Seth's empty bottles and packed them into his diaper bag. I cringed, thinking of all the germs still inside since she hadn't used the special anti-bacterial bottle-cleansing soap I packed. Those bottles would have to be washed again when I got home.

"Shondra, you gon' get enough of readin' books to try and figure out how to raise your baby. What color is the person who wrote that book, anyway?" she asked.

"What difference does it make?" I asked, crossing my arms and leaning against the counter.

"Makes a world of difference. Black babies are different. We got a different makeup. Different genes. Everything that works for white babies don't work for black. Now, I'm not sure what's going on with my grandbaby since he's half-and-half, but I know one thing—he was hungry, so I fed him. And he wouldn't sleep, so I had Jonathan pick up a little thing of cereal. I put a few pinches in that bottle, widened the nipple a little with a fork. Next thing I knew, Seth was out for the night. He woke up this morning with the biggest grin on his face, like he was glad *somebody* finally filled his little tummy."

I clawed my forehead. *Why, Jesus? Why couldn't she just stick to the schedule and follow the plan?*

"Look." She snapped her dish rag at me. "I done took care of plenty kids, including you and your brother. Y'all weren't obese. Now, if you go and get fat now, that's on you. But so long as you pay attention to your baby, figure out what he needs, listen to your mother's intuition, and listen to your *mother*"—she tilted her chin down—"this baby will be just fine."

Oh, how I wished Momma could see Seth now. She'd been right. Seth was a perfectly well-adapted four year old. My biggest battle with him wasn't *over*eating, it was *picky* eating.

Daddy welcomed us into the house, giving Stelson a manly hug and kissing Zoe. He boxed with Seth for a moment. "Y'all come on in."

We gathered around the table, using Daddy's Styrofoam plates and plastic utensils (Jonathan's brilliant idea to help keep the kitchen decent after I told him about the crazy stack of dishes). Stelson prayed a blessing over the food, and we all dug into a meal that Momma never would have deemed an appropriate after-church meal. I could almost hear her fussing: *store-cooked for Sunday dinner? Blasphemy! You ought to have more respect for the Lord's day!*

I would have given anything to hear her quote the strict laws she had raised us to follow, even though I wasn't condemned by them anymore, thanks to the revelation of grace.

Stelson was unusually quiet. His way of feeling my father out since their talk. Daddy was tiptoeing around Stelson, too, talking mostly to the kids and me.

"Is Jonathan coming over?" I asked.

"Said he might," Dad answered. "You ought to know, though. Don't you talk to him more than me?"

"No. Not since he took that second job at the gym. Seems like he never figured out how to sit down and relax when he left the navy. Is that some kind of disorder?"

"Might be," Daddy said, chewing at the same time.

I hoped Seth wasn't taking notes.

"You know what they say on those commercials," Stelson finally added, "they do more by sunrise than most people do all day. Oh, wait, is that the army?"

"Yeah, that's the army," my father seconded.

"I wanna go to the army," Seth announced. This had to be his fifth career choice in a month.

"Really?" Stelson encouraged with a smile. "Why?"

"'Cause they get to fight!"

"Nuh-uh," Daddy quickly let the air out of Seth's chest. "Whole world is against us since we elected a nig—"

I shot Daddy a look that stopped him mid-sentence, thankfully.

"Since we elected President Obama. We be the first ones on the firing line. Well, we already were, but they pushed us up even more so now."

Stelson swallowed his food quickly. "Don't you think things have changed some? I mean, it's not perfect, but it's not 1960 anymore, either."

Lord Jesus, why did he have to go there? I knew my husband. He had every intention of enlightening my father. But I also knew my daddy. He was like a tree planted by the water; he would *not* be moved in his opinions. Those two never needed to discuss religion or politics with each other. Ever.

My father closed his eyes and spoke with as much passion as people usually reserve for when they've closed their eyes to sing. "Just because it's a new century, just because we've had a black president, and just 'cause we got Oprah don't mean the world ain't full of Paula Deens."

The debate commenced over food. Thankfully, Stelson and Daddy were both so hungry that consuming the chicken tied them to a reasonable volume.

Seth pulled my sleeve and cupped his mouth. I leaned down to hear his secret.

"Momma, I thought President Obama was brown."

"He is, honey," I whispered behind a palm.

"Then how come PawPaw keeps saying he's black?"

"Some people say brown is black when we're talking about people's skin." I knew that was confusing.

"Are there people who really *are* black?"

"Yes. There are. Beautiful people. And some of them were your great-great-great grandparents from a long time ago."

"Oh. Do you think I will look like them? Like PawPaw said?"

"Listen to me. You just be *Seth*. Don't worry about your color. Go ahead and finish up your green beans."

Stelson and my father's discourse ran another circle. Next thing I knew, my son let out a wail that could have called the cows in.

"Waaaaaah! Waaaaah!" he screamed, wiping real live tears from his eyes.

All conversation ceased as I searched his mouth to see if something had cut him or if he was hurt.

Stelson flew to Seth's side of the table and knelt. "Son, what's wrong?"

"I don't *wanna* be black!" he exploded.

Daddy jumped right on it. "See! Now that there is a shame!"

I gave Daddy the hand. "Shhh."

"I don't wanna be black!" Seth repeated.

"I'm not gonna shush when it comes to my grandson," Daddy raised up from his seat. He leaned over Stelson, as though he might need to intervene somehow.

"What's the deal with being black?" Stelson gently probed.

"'Cause my last name is Brown. If I'm black, then people can't see me," Seth tried to make us understand. "Like when you use the black con-struct-no paper in class, nobody can see when you write on it."

Stelson smothered his chuckle. "No, son. Being black isn't like being a piece of black paper. It's totally different. Everyone can see black people."

"Depends on who you ask," Daddy mumbled under his breath.

Stelson redirected Seth's anxiety. "Here. Wipe off your face and let's go outside for a minute."

My husband and son walked outside to the swing set that was working on its second generation in my parents' back yard.

Daddy and I stayed behind with Zoe as I cleared the table.

"Now, Shondra, I know you think your husband's doing the best he can with Seth. And maybe he is. But he's going about this thing the wrong way."

I stuffed the empty plates into the trashcan. "Well, how do you think Stelson should have handled it, Daddy?"

"He should have told him that black was beautiful. Not no 'what's the deal?'" he mimicked my husband. "Even if Seth don't never turn brown, he can't walk around with a hatred for his own people. What you want him to do—grow up and marry a white woman?"

Daddy's words stung my heart. Startled me, really. "Is that what you still think of me? That I grew up to marry a white man?"

He pinched the fullest part of his nose. "Naw, Shondra. I didn't mean it like *that*."

I blinked back tears to keep from turning this into a fiasco.

"I'm just saying—I don't want our bloodline to turn *completely* white."

"That's enough. We're gonna go now."

I heaved Zoe up from the high chair.

"Wait a minute, Shondra," Daddy tried to talk me down from the emotional cliff.

"You know what, Daddy, you have a right to feel what you feel and believe whatever you wish. But I will not sit here and let you insult my husband, me, and my family."

"It wasn't an insult. I'm only trying to give you advice. What are grandparents for? I know I'm not your Momma, and I don't have all that churchy stuff to tell you, but I got some years behind me. Been through some things. You gotta give me credit for knowing something about how to survive in America."

More than anything, I wanted to process my father's words through logic over my feelings. The most hurtful part was the genuine nature of his comments. These words had come straight from the abundance of his heart.

"Good-bye, Daddy. I know you mean well. You really do. And I love you." I smacked his cheek with my lips. "But really, *really*, I need you to trust this to me and Stelson, just like we discussed the last time. All right?"

My father agreed, though I knew he wasn't convinced we were doing the right thing.

And Daddy wasn't the only one with doubts.

❧Chapter 10

The second honeymoon was over. Stelson had a busy work week ahead of him, full of meetings and presentations. He told me not to expect him home before seven any night.

Honestly, I didn't mind. I was looking forward to the extra hours. I figured they would give me plenty of time to make sure the kids were taken care of, dinner was prepared, the house was tidy, and also to make myself especially presentable before Stelson walked through the door—like all those "be a good wife" articles suggest women do.

Didn't quite work out that way.

I promise, I got up and took Zoe and Seth to school at 8:00 a.m. Then I worked out. I went to the grocery store, stopped to eat a bite, and finally handled some business at the post office. I might have watched an episode of Judge Mathis while checking a few emails. And then, lo and behold, it was 2:20 in the afternoon. Only forty minutes left before I had to go pick up Seth from school, since he was no longer enrolled in after-school care. If the morning drop-off bottleneck was any indication of the logjam I could expect at 3:00 p.m., I really needed to be there no later than a quarter 'til.

How can it be time for him to come home already?

Nonetheless, I savored the last few moments of silence, seasoning the red potatoes I'd put in the oven once I returned with Seth.

Wait. Only Seth?

If I picked him up at three, that would put me back home at 3:30 after fighting the school zone traffic; I'd have to go right back out for Zoe. Hardly worth another pilgrimage.

I gotta do better tomorrow.

The potatoes would have to wait until I returned home with both of my kids. Meanwhile, I folded a basket of clothes in five minutes flat so I could get a head start on the other stay-at-home moms by leaving my home at 2:30 p.m.

. Imagine my surprise to find myself still three cars away from the turn-in curb.

Do these other moms ever leave the school?

In exasperation, I called Peaches. "Girl, this is some foolishness. I'm here to pick up my baby from school, twenty minutes early, and we're already bumper-to-bumper."

"Hey, people do it every day."

"People without lives!"

"What's your real problem?" Peaches went straight in.

I made use of the headrest. "I didn't get anything done today."

"What did you do?"

The short list of accomplishments took every bit of ten seconds to relay.

"Okay," she said. "What's wrong with that?"

"I feel like I didn't do anything *important* today."

"Important like what?"

"Important like...I don't know...save the world."

"How is making sure your household runs smoothly *not* important?"

Since I wasn't moving anywhere any time soon, I put the car in park and poured my heart out to my best friend who *had* to be somewhere under all that B. Smith. "Peaches, this is ridiculous. Our parents did not pinch pennies and work extra hours to put us through college so we could grow up to be housewives. I mean, not unless we get a reality television show or something."

Her voice dipped low. "Now, you know you ain't gotta be a real housewife to be on a housewife show. You might stand a better chance as a live-in girlfriend these days."

"Right," I chimed in. "But I'm saying. I feel like I'm not using my *brain*. My *skills*. My *education*. This is boring and pointless and it's sucking the life out of me."

"You haven't even been home a whole week yet!" Peaches yelled.

"I know! Can you imagine what I'll be like in a month?" I whined.

"You want me to go call the *wam*-bulance? Please, do you know how many women would love to be in your shoes right now?"

"I don't care about those other women. This is *me*. *My* life!"

"Okay," she sighed. "I'm not going to tell you how to live your life. But let me ask you this—have you prayed about this whole situation?"

"No."

"Start there," Peaches ordered. "Just get up tomorrow before everyone else, like you used to when you were working, and pray. Get your mind right. Ask God to show you what to do in the next 24 hours, and see what happens. Got it?"

"Mmm hmmm." When did *she* become the big sister?

"I gotta go. Silent reading time is almost over," she said.

"What's that?"

"It's when the kids have to do something silent after playtime. It helps them get calm before homework," she spelled out.

"You can *play* before homework?"

"You can do whatever works for your household," she said. "Get some kind of schedule going—you know, so much time for this, so much time for that after school. And then for the house, decide what you're gonna do on certain days. Rotate mopping, dusting, a little bit every day. And plan a week-long menu. Girl, you'll have the Browns runnin' like a well-oiled machine. And then if you go back to work, it'll be easier to plug your assistants back into the equation."

The school bell rang and the first children, whose teachers must have had their noses pressed against the glass, zipped out of the doors. The children's backpacks bounced heartily as they found their rides waiting in the circular drive-up.

Once Seth came bounding out of the building, the rest of the evening flashed before my eyes.

Stelson texted me once to say he'd be even later than he thought, but I didn't care. I got Zoe and Seth in bed as soon as possible, and I was right behind them. When I worked, there was only a two-hour span between the time I scooped them up from daycare until I turned out the lights. Now, with *five* hours...

Lord, You changed my mind and caused me to make this decision. Now I need you to change my heart to match.

Beep. Beep. Beep. Beep.

My alarm clock showed six o'clock. Not too much later than the time I used to rise when I actually had a job.

But this is a job, I reminded myself. Actually, the thought was so contrary to my feelings, the words probably hadn't come from me. They were from my heavenly Father, the very reason I'd chosen to set the buzzer in the first place.

The aroma of Stelson's coffee was still fresh in the kitchen, though I'd heard him leave about ten minutes earlier. My husband was serious about getting in his exercise at least three times a week. After his gym workout, he'd shower and go straight to the office if his schedule allowed for khakis and a rugby shirt.

Hopefully, in weeks to come, we'd be able to see each other before he left for work.

But that particular morning, I was glad for the silence. Glad to return to a routine that had completely escaped me since Seth came into the picture four years earlier. Were it not for Stelson praying for our family and calling me into prayer with him sometimes, I would have been a guest in the upper room.

Quietly, I moved through the kitchen and made myself a quick cup of tea. That Zoe had super-sensitive ears, and I had come to believe that she could decipher my footsteps from her father's because she never woke up when he was walking through the house. Only me.

And then came the biggest wake-up call of all: I had no idea where my personal Bible case was. I'd carried my smaller, travel Bible to church Sunday, but the sacred one I'd owned since the previous century, with all the highlighting, my personal notes, along with my journal, was nowhere in plain sight.

That's just sad.

After searching through my nightstand, under my bed, and in Stelson's office, I decided that it must have been in my car's trunk. Going out to the garage was not gonna happen if I wanted the morning's peace to remain intact for another hour, so I grabbed Stelson's Bible from his desk along with a blank yellow notepad from one of his drawers.

I tiptoed to the guest bedroom, slowly closing and releasing the door behind me. I felt like screaming, "I made it!" but instead, tears overtook me as I fell to my knees at the foot of the full-sized bed.

This was the barest room in the house, consisting of only my old queen-sized bed and dresser. The closet was filled with clothes I hoped to wear again, at least in my dreams.

A reflection of myself in the closet mirror nearly startled me. There, with my head wrapped in a scarf, wearing an outdated robe, was a vision of my mother in me. I remember when I used to walk into her room to request money or ask her if she knew where something was, and I'd find her in this same position. On the floor praying. Rocking back and forth. With tears in her eyes.

Just like me.

Sometimes, I would slip back out of the room. Other times, she would look up and ask me if I wanted to join her. The older I got, the more I said yes, if only for a few minutes.

And now there I was, a grown woman doing what my mother had modeled for me all those years ago.

"Thank you, God, for her example."

I just knelt there and cried. Cried and cried and cried. Partly because I missed Momma—and anyone who has lost a mother will agree that it is possible to cry almost endlessly.

But I also released tears of joy because I'd missed *Him* and, finally, we were reunited. Just the two of us. And I sensed that He'd missed me, too.

Perhaps the reunion with Momma would feel the same.

Once I finished slobbing all over the bed's comforter, I propped myself up on the pillows and began writing on the makeshift journal. If memory served correctly, I hadn't written anything in my journal for months. And even then, my entries were short, sweet, and guilty: *God, I'm sorry I haven't talked to you much. I'm hoping this is only a season. - Shondra.*

With nearly a full hour to do whatever came spiritually, I popped in a praise CD and wrote to my heart's content, telling God how I had quit my job, telling Him about how Stelson and Daddy didn't see eye-to-eye about Seth, asking Him why Peaches seemed so foreign to me now. She was still my girl and all, but the more I wrote, the more I discovered resentment toward her, which surprised me.

I went on to discover resentment toward a lot of things: Stelson steering me to be more domestic, society saying I needed to lose twenty pounds, my dad acting like I owed him a dark child.

God, what is all this in my heart? Felt as though I was undergoing a divine intervention.

Daddy led me to the topic index in Stelson's NIV Bible, where I searched for the words "bitterness" and "resentment" and found references to plenty of scriptures that sanded down my recently-formed heart callouses. The third citation led me to James 3:13-18.

Who is wise and understanding among you? Let them show it by their good life, by deeds done in the humility that comes from wisdom. But if you harbor bitter envy and selfish ambition in your hearts, do not boast about it or deny the truth. Such "wisdom" does not come down from heaven but is earthly, unspiritual, demonic. For where you have envy and selfish ambition, there you find disorder and every evil practice. But the wisdom that comes from heaven is first of all pure; then peace-loving, considerate, submissive, full of mercy and good fruit, impartial and sincere. Peacemakers who sow in peace reap a harvest of righteousness.

I closed my eyes, rested my head on a pillow and let the truth of His words burrow deep into my soul. And then a verse I'd memorized in Sunday school, circa 1980, flashed on my mind's screen: If any of you lack wisdom, let him ask of God. I couldn't remember the scripture reference, but I knew it was in there. The Lord Himself must have written those words on my heart because they popped up like they'd been waiting for such a time as this.

With the simplicity of a child, I prayed aloud, "God, I don't want the world's wisdom. I want *Your* wisdom. Please give it to me."

I received it in faith.

Verse after verse confirmed His desire to pick up right where we'd left off. *For real, God?*

Proverbs 1 said: YES.

No probationary period. Just a willing heart and a desire to meet Him every day.

And an alarm clock to get me up in plenty of time to meet with the Lover of my soul. *Thank You, Jesus.*

That morning, I thought God was reviving our spiritual intimacy because I had been working too much, because I was tired all the time, or maybe even because He was tired of seeing those unfolded clothes on the couch.

But, really, there was much more at stake than I could have imagined.

Chapter 11 ∂

The next morning, I could hardly wait to get into the prayer closet and be alone with God. I had located my own Bible under the driver's seat of my car, told God I was sorry for losing track of it in the first place, and received His grace to pick up where we'd left off.

Being reminded of His love, His mercy, His teachings gave me a sharper spirit throughout the day. Aside from an ear to hear, my heart yielded easier to His nudges.

By Wednesday, I set the alarm fifteen minutes earlier, and I even wound down in the prayer closet after we got home from mid-week service. I'd listened to Pastor Toole's sermon and amen'd right along with the rest of the congregation, but I wanted to get back home and discuss the meaning of absolute surrender with the Author of the concept, personally. His text, 1 Kings 20, was Ahab's declaration, "My lord, O king, according to thy saying, I am thine and all that I have."

Yes, I had quit my job. Yes, I had (begrudgingly) been submissive to my husband and even my best friend's words confirmed what I had already been feeling. I had all the outward signs of obedience to the Lord, but deep down inside, my heart still hadn't come along for the ride. And when I admitted that to myself, I heard Him whisper in me: *I want all of you.*

All of me? I thought I'd already given Him all of me. I mean, I did believe on Christ as my Savior. I did know Him and seek to walk in His ways. What else did He want from me?

All of you repeated in my spirit.

I knew there was no sense in arguing with God. Not likely He was going to change His mind. He wanted all of me—even that little rebellious part that wanted its own way, couldn't stand to be taken advantage of, and always tried to make things easy for myself.

But what was He going to do with it? Kill it? What would I be without my defenses? I didn't want to be one of those weak people who let people run over her. Always praying, always hoping. Helping everybody else and then one day I'd wake up and realize I'd spent my whole life doing what other people wanted me to do.

I wanted to do me. LaShondra.

Not other people. Me. rose inside my mind.

His thoughts baffled me. Sent me back to the drawing board. "You, God?" I had to ask myself if it would be any easier to follow God's will than my husband's. Really, would my feelings change if I knew the plan was coming directly from God? Would that have made me receive this change with joy?

Probably not.

With that revelation, my eyes rendered tears of grief and repentance. "I'm sorry, Lord." *Lord.* Why was I calling Him that name if He really didn't have that place in my life?

"Jesus, I crown You Lord. Even if it means my worst fears come true, *be* the Lord of my life."

My back bolted straight up. Those sentences didn't even sound right. What would make me think that receiving Jesus as Savior *and* Lord would make my life worse off?

I flopped onto the bed and grabbed my journal. I made a list of all the bad things that I thought could happen to me if I actually surrendered all to Jesus, like Pastor Toole had preached.

Surrender Cons
1. I might have to go to some faraway place to be a missionary.
2. I would be poor and suffering.
3. I would lose all common sense.
4. I would be weak and whiney (God, you know I can't stand weak, whiney people).
5. I would be all "holier-than-thou", so heavenly minded I was no

earthly good. Can't relate to real life.

6. I wouldn't get to have at least one guilty pleasure in life.

7. I wouldn't get to do what I wanted to do in my life.

As I glanced back over the list of objections, my English degree kicked in. The subject of every sentence was "I". Everything was about me.

"But isn't this my life, Lo—" I couldn't even finish His name before Paul's words, something about 'not I, but Christ' slammed me with the truth. I flipped to Galatians because I knew the book, just not the exact verse.

The search results landed me at Galatians 2:20. *I am crucified with Christ: nevertheless I live; yet not I, but Christ liveth in me: and the life which I now live in the flesh I live by the faith of the Son of God, who loved me, and gave himself for me.*

The only question on the table: Whose life was this, anyway? Was I dead to sin and alive in Christ or not? Was I living for my glory or His?

Sure, I knew what the "correct" answer was. I suppose if I'd been in Christian autopilot mode, I would have gulped down this hard truth and promised God I would "do better".

But I didn't want to promise God something I didn't have a burning desire to do because that would only lead to an empty vow. That would only get us right back to square one; me going through the motions, just riding out this season until I got to a section of life I really liked, which may or may not have anything to do with Christ.

The war inside my body, between the flesh and the Spirit, was almost tangible. *Why is what I want and what God wants so different?* I was tired of doing the right thing but resenting it the whole time. But I didn't want to live my life without Jesus. I mean, I wanted Him *in* my life; I just didn't want Him to *be* my life.

Even after all the years I'd spent in church, all the time I'd spent getting to know Him. And despite the fact that I truly loved Jesus and I knew He loved me, I wasn't willing to die. Not all the way, all the time.

And yet, this was His request. This was why He had pulled me in so close to His very heartbeat. He wanted to be my Lord. My King. To rule every aspect of *my* life.

I had to shut my Bible and my journal on that somber note. I closed my eyes and prayed again. "God, you gotta change me 'cause I can't do it."

I left our set-apart space with more questions than I'd ever had about my walk with Him. Confusion wasn't quite the word for my state of mind; it was more an expectancy than anything. What would my life look like after He changed it? Would I recognize myself? Would I turn into one of those COGIC congregation mothers with the fierce scowls who testified that I had been "saved all day, no evil have I done"?

Stelson was already asleep in bed. The television was still blaring, which meant he must have been trying to wait up for me because he wasn't one to fall asleep with the tube going.

I, on the other hand, planned to take full advantage of the fact that he was already in dreamland. I switched the channel to TBN, hoping to find one of my favorite ministers preaching.

Instead, I got someone I'd never heard of on the screen, but a quick check of the guide showed a familiar Bible-teacher coming on in seven minutes, so I kept it there.

I must have underestimated what the prayer closet had taken out of me because I didn't make it past those seven minutes before drifting off myself.

All I know is, sometime in the middle of the night, my ears received supernatural hearing ability and I heard a minister—to this day, I cannot tell you who it was—saying, "If you're afraid of giving your all to the Lord, You obviously don't know Him. Everything He does works out for good to those who love Him. Take your eyes off of yourself. Reject the lies of the enemy. Behold the Lover of your soul, for He *is* good and merciful and kind."

Still halfway sleep, I could taste the sweetness of those words in my inmost parts. *God is not a bully. He's not out to hurt me. His plan for me is good.*

Somehow, in all my fears, I had forgotten Who I was dealing with. Underestimated His good thoughts toward me.

But not anymore.

"Thank you, Jesus."

Stelson stirred. "Huh?"

"Go back to sleep, baby. I love you."

"Yeah. Love you, too."

I still hadn't learned to beat the laundry game that week because I hadn't taken Peaches' advice about getting a formal schedule together. But the schedule was the last thing on my mind. My convictions weighed in every moment of the day, and the love of God so completely enveloped me that I had no choice except to agree with Him. Christ revealed Himself to me countless times throughout the day, sending me back to the Word for confirmation of the nuggets dropped into my understanding.

Am I really dead in Christ? Colossians 3:3.

Is my new life gonna be terrible? John 10:10.

What if I want my old life back? Matthew 16:25.

With cheeks covered in tears, I succumbed to a new, deeper understanding of the marvelous truth. I could no longer fight for a dead woman.

Okay, God. I surrender all. Take all of me.

Spending so many hours dedicated to His presence, between feeding, changing, and taking care of Zoe, put me in a bad position by the time Seth got home. I had to put him to work.

Little did I know, Seth was the absolute best towel-folder in the universe. I mean, he lined up those corners with a surgeon's precision and straightened the linens flat! Obviously, he'd inherited his father's ability to pay attention to details. The best part was that it took him forever to fold perfectly. I could get some serious work done while the boy was folding, and he was gaining the opportunity to lengthen his attention span.

He also came in handy for bending down to hand me the clothes so I could load them in the washer.

He intently watched me operate the shiny red machines. "Can I turn it on?"

"Maybe when you're older."

"But I'm in pre-k now."

"Yes, but you have to be tall enough, too. But don't worry, I'll make sure you start washing clothes the moment your arms can reach these knobs." I pointed at the silver disks, promising my child something I knew he would later regret.

When he asked, I explained the functions of laundry cleaners, because I fully believed in training up young men to do household chores. "Detergent is like soap. Bleach spray gets the clothes nice and bright, and fabric softener makes them feel soft and smell good."

"Like perfume for girls?" He recoiled.

"No, no. More like sunshine. Fresh."

"Okay." He seemed pleased to know I wasn't trying to turn him into a girl.

It seemed as though my afternoons were consumed by one question: What do we do *now*? I really didn't want to become the kind of parent who parked her kids in front of a screen and gave them half a Benadryl to make them drowsy (this I learned from watching way too much television myself).

Try as I might, the living room still looked as messy as ever by the time Stelson arrived. "Hey, babe."

"Hey." He looked over me at the kitchen table cluttered with paper and crayons. "Um...okay...I thought the house would be...you know...better."

Now that he'd mentioned it, I also looked half-thrown-together in my yoga pants, oversized t-shirt and dry ponytail. And yet, it wasn't as though I'd been sitting on the couch eating ice cream all day. "Busy day."

His mouth remained open as he nodded. "Yeah. Okay."

"What's that supposed to mean?"

"Nothing, Shondra. I'm sure it is tough getting used to a new schedule. And I love you for making this sacrifice for our family," he backpedaled.

"Thank you. That's more like it."

Chapter 12 ❧

Instead of focusing on the brainlessness of folding clothes, I sang songs of praise, knowing my children and my husband were gifts from God. Aside from that, there were countless women who would give up everything to be in a wonderful marriage with great kids. Gratefulness became the order of the week as, moment after moment, the Holy Spirit reminded me of who I was and Whose I was. I could have kicked myself for not accepting the fullness of Christ sooner.

But God knows when we're ready.

Stelson and I stayed up late one of those nights watching television. After putting the kids to bed, we snuggled up on the couch and indulged in messy, completely un-nutritious pour-over cheese popcorn.

"This stuff is so good," he smacked, wiping his fingers on his T-shirt.

"Ewww! Why are you doing that?"

"Because I've had it on all day and I'm gonna throw it in the hamper when I leave this couch." He smiled down at me.

Sometimes I thought Stelson did things to flirt his way under my skin. *Men.* I rested my head on the clean side of his shirt again. "Spray some spot-cleaner on it first, please."

He kissed my forehead with his greasy lips.

I slapped his chest. "Stop! That's gross!"

He laughed as I wiped the combination of saliva and processed goo off my skin. I rubbed the residue into his shirt.

"Ewww! Stop! You're getting my dirty clothes all dirty," he mocked me.

Laughter snuck past my lips. "You wrong for that, baby."

Stelson chuckled, too. "I know." The rumble of his deep voice vibrated against my face.

God, I love this man.

The day of the picnic, Stelson left before me so that he could help the brethren with preparations to host the twenty-five or so families registered for the event.

Of course, I started my morning with quiet time, conversing with my Father, thanking Him for new life in Christ and for His love. Really, I wished I could have spent all day with Him. Just go get a hotel room somewhere and have a spiritual honeymoon.

Zoe's whimpers wouldn't allow it, however. With Stelson gone, I'd have to get the kids up and dressed by myself. Thankfully, we had all gotten more than enough rest in anticipation of a busy, active day. I put a full breakfast on Seth's and Zoe's stomachs and was even able to throw in a power nap myself before we left at noon to join the festivities.

It was Labor Day weekend, so the park was packed. The line to turn in to the Marina stretched a quarter of a mile long as families with boats and jet skis waited to enter the camp and lake grounds. The temperature had reached 88 degrees and was expected to climb another 5 degrees. In Texas, 93 degrees in September is actually a fortunate break, but it still was enough to make a woman throw the hair back into a ponytail, slap on a visor and sunscreen, and call the beauty regimen "done".

Stelson had texted me pretty good directions to help locate the Living Word pavilion. I spotted his truck and found the next closest empty spot for my Honda.

I was trying to keep an eye on Seth while I held Zoe on one hip and retrieved our chairs from the trunk. Pastor Toole's twin pre-teen daughters, who were also getting out of their parents' car, rushed to me. "Hi, Sister Brown."

Their names were Brittney and Ashley, but I couldn't tell them apart. "Hi, girls!"

"Can we help with Zoe and Seth?" one of them asked.

"Sure."

My baby was already reaching out for the closest twin and Seth, who never met a stranger, eagerly took the other one's hand. With both limbs free now, I maneuvered the chairs and Zoe's bag from the trunk.

The five of us walked toward reserved grounds. My motherly instinct measured and determined we weren't too close to the water's edge.

Our church's pavilion covered ten long, rectangular tables with attached benches. Already, seven tables were taken with many of the church's lively, rambunctious families. As usual, most of the older crowd—with grown children—and the younger, single sector of the congregation had opted to leave all this outdoor fun to those of us with kiddos. I couldn't blame either group for bowing out because this was definitely not my cup of tea.

Alas, I was determined to make the best of it, as were my fellow moms and dads. The smell of barbecue, the joyous sounds of laughter, the beautiful view of the surrounding trees and the soft murmur of the lake was something I had missed when I was growing up. Exposing Seth and Zoe to God's creation would, hopefully, make them well-rounded people.

At least that's what I told myself when a mosquito bite brought me back to reality. *This early in the day?* I quickly set our belongings at an empty space and retrieved the bug spray from our tiger-striped bag. I sprayed my arms and legs between "Hellos" and hugs, trying not to appear paranoid.

Brittney and Ashley had taken my kids to the table with the rest of the pre-teens, where they were all ooohing and aaaahing over Zoe's tight, round cheeks.

I made a mental note to find some baby-friendly bug lotion in the future, but in the meanwhile, I sprayed some on my hand, then rubbed it on my baby.

Seth acted as though I was stabbing him, hollering loudly when the cold spray hit his arms. "That's cold!"

His antics sent the older kids into hysterics, which was exactly what he'd wanted.

Stelson tilted his chin up, acknowledging me from the grill. I winked, knowing this might be all I got from him until after all the food was finished.

Some of the other moms and I kept a watchful eye on our kids as we conversed about a variety of topics: good books, the new Aldi store, and the chicken pox vaccine, which I had recently learned was a requirement of the state. Back in my day, chicken pox was a rite of passage. You were "one of us" once you'd endured a week of those terribly itchy bumps and a little fever.

Somehow, the conversation drifted to losing weight, which made for a fifteen-minute-long lament. From my perspective, no one in our circle was really overweight, even for Texas. Shoot, some of them needed to *gain* a few pounds, if you'd asked me.

In times like those, I had to make a conscious effort not to go into a "they're not black" moment. Our circumstantial clique, formed because we all needed to make sure our kids and their on-the-spot babysitters didn't venture too close to the lake, consisted of four white women, one Hispanic, and two black, including myself. If I wasn't careful, I could almost draw a line between them and me (the other black woman on my side, of course) and start to interpret the conversation through a lifetime of Daddy's bitter commentary.

Why are white women so whiney? If an alleged extra fifteen pounds is your biggest problem, you need to go sit down somewhere.

Even after knowing Stelson for ten years, serving alongside diverse groups of people in the church—well, at least I did before I had Seth— and coming to the understanding that the first man in my life had been dead wrong for teaching me that all white people were undercover racists, still…the memories lingered. They had to be consciously challenged.

Don't go there, LaShondra. Stay who you are now.

I wondered if people who had experienced neglect at an early age had to remind themselves that not everyone would leave them. And did people who grew up without knowing when they'd get their next meal always feel the need to pack every leftover scrap of food into a doggie bag? Furthermore, were the white women at the table fighting to overcome their own prejudices as I sat in the circle? *Are we all fighting secret battles?*

Once I reeled myself back from black-isolation-island, I was more than ready to join the congregation in blessing the food. Pastor Toole and his wife stood at the head table, where aluminum pans overflowing with meat, potato salad, beans, and pre-sliced pound cake were already teasing my stomach.

"Let us pray."

After the 'amen' members from the hospitality team manned the serving line. In no time, we were all enjoying good food and time with family. Stelson had retrieved the kids and brought them to our table so we could make sure they ate.

After half an hour or so, Jim Moore, one of the men who worked alongside Stelson in the finance ministry, announced that it was time for the trail walk. "In light of the temperature, we're doing the shortest trail. Half a mile. You need good shoes and a water bottle. And you'll definitely want your cameras. It's a beautiful route."

Stelson raised his eyebrows. "You wanna go?"

Me? In a forest? I squinted. "What you talkin' 'bout, Willis?"

"Oh, come on, Arnold," he said. "Live a little."

"My foot's still not one hundred percent," I tried.

"It's only half a mile," my husband convinced me. "I'll carry you if I have to."

"Yeah, right." We both laughed.

Stelson went back to my car and got the baby harness from the back seat. I strapped Zoe to my chest because I wanted to be on the lookout for bugs trying to get past my bug spray. Seth nearly hopped out of his skin at the prospect of a jungle adventure. Stelson had a way of making our son think everything was a major excursion.

We started out at the foot of a massive thicket of trees. Once we got ten feet into the walk, the canopy of trees shaded us perfectly and a coolness I hadn't expected made it bearable to link pinkies with Stelson while he held Seth's hand.

My husband took a deep breath. "Reminds me of old times. Divine."

I couldn't quite wrap my mind around the smell—wild grass mixed with tree bark and a hint of flowers? Whatever the combination, the scent was not something I'd want in my clothes or my hair. Though the foot trail was fairly defined, the further along we went, the more pathways veered to the left and the right. One wrong move and a person like me with no sense of direction could be walking in circles for hours.

Overgrown brush poked into our walkway. Birds with unfamiliar calls screeched as we invaded their territory.

This whole setup was too naturely for me.

Seth tucked his water bottle in his waist. "Dad, did you used to come here when you were little?"

"Not this park, but we did camp."

"Ooh! Look!" Seth shouted, pointing into a thicket. "A bunny for Easter!" A white rabbit stood watching us watch him. The animal had unusually long ears. Reminded me of Bugs, actually, but he didn't seem like one of those friendly, carrot-eatin' rabbits.

The group slowed as Jim explained that as nice and cuddly as rabbit and deer were depicted in Disney movies, wildlife lives up to its name—*wild*. We shouldn't try to touch any animals we might find along the trail. "And watch out for snakes."

He shouldn't have told me that. "Snakes?" I whispered to Stelson.

"We'll be fine."

Selfishly, I tore away from my husband and eased toward the center of our pack. If a snake was gonna attack, it would have to get through five other people before it got to Zoe and me.

We did stop again as Jim told us about the various species of birds in the area. Eagles could be seen and heard if we came later in the day.

Our group couldn't have gone more than fifty feet before I looked back to double-check for Stelson's head. Not hard to spot, since my poor husband didn't have any hair.

We had made it to a point where we could see the next hundred yards or so pretty clearly. There would be no snakes nipping at our feet without warning, so I slowed down to join the other half of my family.

But when Stelson's full figure came into view, he wasn't attached our son.

"Where's Seth?"

"I thought he was with you."

Simultaneously, we turned toward the empty path we'd just traipsed. "Seth!" I yelled.

No answer.

"Seth!" Stelson's voice, much louder, called.

Still no answer.

"Jim, hold up a minute. Is Seth in the bunch?"

Everyone stopped. Their heads made three hundred and sixty degree circles, then shook ominously.

My stomach hardened.

"Seth! Seth!" my fellow church members began calling his name. Stelson took off down the original path. Jim followed him. I was about to be the third person in line when Nora, one of the ladies I'd been talking to earlier, put a hand on my arm and said, "No, LaShondra, stay with us. You've got the baby."

The baby. Yes, Zoe. Thank God she was strapped to me. I wrapped my fingers around her toes and squeezed gently as we waited. One minute. Two. I don't know—seemed like an eternity.

In the distance, we could all hear Jim and Stelson calling Seth's name.

"Let's pray," Nora said.

Those of us who'd stayed put formed a circle and locked hands. "Father, Your Word says there is nothing hidden from You. We pray that You would reveal Seth's location in Jesus' name."

Jim's and Stelson's voices were softer now. They were further away. "Seth! Where are you?"

I knew then that my baby was good and lost.

⁓Chapter 13

Seven whole minutes later, Jim and Stelson returned. Without Seth.

Stelson hugged me and stole a second to whisper, "Psalm ninety-one."

"We've called the rangers," Jim said to the group. "They'll help us find him. You all go ahead and follow this path. In another quarter of a mile, it'll lead you to a clearing and our pavilion will be on the left. You can't miss it."

I heard people's movements before I saw their feet actually moving away from the direction where we had last seen Seth.

"No! I'm not leaving him out here!" I locked glances with Stelson.

"Babe, we are going to find him. But we need the rangers to help us now because he's…off the path."

Confused, I shook my head, still tied to Stelson's eyes. "Off the path?"

Jim's fingers gripped my husband's shoulder. "It hasn't been long. And believe it or not, he's not the first person to get lost, LaShondra. We'll find him. He can't be too far."

I begged to differ. Seth could get pretty far pretty quickly.

"He can't be too far," Jim repeated himself.

"Shondra, go back. We'll wait for the rangers. Jim has given them our exact location. I'll text you the moment we find him. And remember Psalm ninety-one."

I couldn't remember my name just then, let alone a whole chapter of the Bible. *How did Seth get away so quickly?*

With each step toward the pavilion and away from my baby, my heart shattered again and again. I pictured my baby, probably following that rabbit, crawling into the bushes. Maybe the rabbit bit him. Maybe the rabbit ran away, and Seth chased him further into the woods, where a coyote was waiting. And Seth would mistake it for a dog. Try to pet it. And then...

No! No! No!

Nora linked elbows with me as tears escaped my control. Our feet crunched the gravel as we walked back to the pavilion. With every agonizing step, I imagined Seth's voice getting softer and softer. If he was calling for Mommy, I wouldn't have been able to hear him once we cleared the trail area.

He was so little. Frail. Anything in that giant forest could gobble him up.

"Jesus, Jesus, Jesus," I whispered repeatedly because I couldn't think of anything else except The Name.

My fellow church members ushered me to one of the picnic benches, where I rocked back and forth, holding on to Zoe, chanting His name. The congregation joined me, speaking requests for Seth's safe return aloud, encircling me in prayer.

Still, I only had one word: Jesus.

Somebody brought me a bottled water. I gulped it down, which must have triggered Zoe's thirst. Nora retrieved the baby's bag and offered to relieve me of the task of feeding, but I was too paranoid to let go of my baby girl. My shaking hands struggled to hold the baby's bottle steady.

I wished I could have called my mother. She was no park ranger, but having her there would have made me feel like someone else more responsible than me was present.

A camper from one of the adjacent pavilions came over and asked if everything was okay. "No," Nora shared. "One of our kids got lost on the trail. They're looking for him now."

"My goodness," the guest exclaimed with sincerity. "Well, we saw you guys gathered around praying. We've got about fifty people here with our family picnic. Let us know what we can do." He sauntered back to his group.

My personal, in-brain video recorder tried to pin-point the exact time

Seth must have gotten lost. *How did we lose track of him? I thought he was with Stelson.*

Fifteen minutes passed before I got the first text from Stelson. *Coming back to pavilion. Need to organize search party.*

Pastor Toole must have gotten the text in the same moment. "Okay, everyone, we haven't had any success in finding Seth yet," he announced with raised arms. "Everyone who's willing and able—we're gonna form search parties to look for him."

After another fifteen minutes, our pavilion was packed with people all up and down the lake shore who were willing to ditch their plans for fun in the sun to help find my baby. People I'd never even met were stuffed under the canopy, awaiting directions from the ranger.

Stelson held Zoe and cradled my shoulder while the rangers, along with a few police officers, explained how to use the buddy system. They laid out a map on one of the tables and gave directions to "squad leaders" as they called them—about seven men who'd volunteered to lead groups of people. Walkie-talkies were dispensed to optimize communications. "Set it to channel four."

Surely, with so many people looking for Seth, and such knowledgeable rangers, they *had* to find him.

"We've got about four hours before sundown. We need to make the best use of the sunlight," the main organizer announced.

I'm sure his words were simply a matter of fact, but terror eased up my back at the thought of Seth being lost after dark. Or overnight. I buried my face in Stelson's chest.

Two hours later, we still hadn't found Seth, but news reporters had found out about the story. The last thing I wanted was the media trampling on my nerves, but we couldn't stop them. It's a free, drama-starved country. One of my church members remarked that since it was a holiday weekend, news was slow. They were looking for any crisis to make the evening news sensational.

All the local networks were there—NBC, ABC, CBS, FOX, KTVT. The church women who'd stayed behind with me kept me fairly insulated. The media spoke to the police, mostly, and took footage of kids who'd stayed behind playing in the shallow end of the lake.

Daddy really wasn't the one I wanted to have present with me in a time of crisis, but I didn't want him to find out on television that his grandson was missing. "Daddy, umm..." I steadied my voice, "We're having some trouble finding Seth. We were at a picnic today at the lake, and—"

"What lake?"

"Ronnie Reed."

"He got lost?"

"Yes."

"Well, who was watching him?" Daddy asked.

"He was with me and Stelson and some other church members." *Why does this feel like a lecture?* "Anyway, we were on one of the walking trails and he got lost. They've got news reporters and everything out here. Won't be long before they put it on television."

"Ronnie Reed Lake, you say?"

"Yes, sir."

"I'm on my way."

After ending the call with Daddy, I called Jonathan and filled him in. He fussed for a second, asking why I hadn't called him earlier.

"I really thought we would have found him by now," I cried.

Jonathan relented. "Don't worry, Shondra. The woods don't go on forever. He's in there, and he will be found. It'll take me about an hour to get there, but I'm coming to help."

I was hoping to have good news by the time Jonathan arrived, but there was none. And as the search crews began rolling back in without Seth, my stomach churned. No sign of my baby, and sunlight wouldn't be on our side much longer.

The news crews were still hanging in their heavily wired vans. "As the search continues for a missing four-year-old boy at Ronnie Reed Lake, family and friends are gathered here under the shelter of the pavilion. People have been praying, waiting for good news or any news. At this point, police are not sure if the child met with some kind of danger or if he's simply lost. But one thing's for sure. His family, his friends, and a multitude of strangers are not giving up on finding him. We'll continue to follow this story into the evening. I'm Pauline Frazier. ABC news."

Daddy arrived wearing overalls, a white t-shirt and a straw hat, looking as though he might take off on his own private search for Seth. He pushed past the media and, with my word, through the church-member barricade. He hugged me briefly. "Where's Stelson?"

"He's out looking along with dozens more people," I said.

Daddy glanced at the acres of trees all around us. "What is Seth wearing?"

"A green shirt with blue jean shorts."

Daddy shook his head. "Wish he was wearing something brighter, like yellow or orange."

"You and everybody else," I voiced.

"I'm sorry. Where's Zoe?"

"Some of the teen girls are trying to keep her happy."

Zoe was beyond fussy by then. She'd tried to take a nap, but it was too hot outside for her to get comfortable.

"Can we get a press conference?" One of the media members yelled toward us. "We might be able to get more help."

Suddenly, all eyes were on me. The mother of the lost child.

Nora asked, "Do you want to?"

"No. I mean…yes, if it will *do* something."

"I'll see what they have in mind," Nora said.

That Pauline lady was allowed to enter our confines. "Hi. I'm terribly sorry about this whole situation. This must be awful for you," she sympathized.

For someone who made a living telling bad news, her vibrancy and girl-next-door beauty fell in second place to her sincerity.

"Thank you," I replied.

"Maybe if you and your husband could…give permission to use a picture…and make a plea to the public, someone might come forth with helpful information."

"Information like what?"

Pauline shrugged. "Well, I'm sure Seth isn't the first person to get lost on the trail. Maybe there's a cut-off or a hiding place someone knows about. Or maybe…if someone took him…"

I nearly vomited. "*Took* him? Is that what the officers are telling you?"

She shook her head vigorously. "No, no, no. I'm saying…if anyone knows anything, or if anyone can assist, conveying the situation on television will only help. It may bring more volunteers and maybe even raise awareness so the next family to go on the trail won't have to suffer." She threw a glance toward the lowering sun. "And the sooner the better."

I don't know what all went through my brain, but the words assist, information, and suffer struck a chord. "Okay." I texted her a picture of Seth for the story.

Pauline hopped up and hollered toward her van. "Okay, people, let's set the stage."

I texted Stelson: *Press conference.*

He replied: *Why?*

His question made me wonder if I'd made the right decision. *To get help.*

A few minutes later, Pauline approached me again. "Mrs. Brown, are you ready?"

"Ready for what?"

"To go on camera. Make a plea to the public."

Somehow, I had missed the part about me being on TV. I must have been thinking the press conference would be with the police department and the rangers. Honestly, I don't really know what I was thinking at that point. I was tired. Nerves fried. Emotionally drained. And I was hungry but I couldn't force myself to eat, not when Seth was probably starving by then.

Overwhelmed by Pauline's request, I sighed. "What…what do I have to do?"

"Just need you to say a few words about your son and ask for help," she prodded.

My phone buzzed with a message from Stelson. *Crews coming back in soon. Too dark. Don't worry.*

How could I *not* worry with a message like that?

Daddy must have read the expression on my face when I read Stelson's words. "What's wrong?"

"They're coming back."

"Who's coming back?" Pauline said.

"The rangers. It's getting too dark," I cried.

"That's it, Mrs. Brown. *That's* the emotion we need on camera. Share your experience. We're on in three minutes."

Pauline was trying to win her first Emmy, I gathered, as she walked back to her lighting crew to finish preparations.

Daddy, who'd been sitting by my side since he arrived, leaned over and whispered in my ear, "Is Stelson coming back now?"

"Yeah."

"You might ought to wait until he gets here. Let him do the conference."

Puzzled, I asked, "Why wait? We've only got a half hour until sunset."

Daddy poked out his lips for a second. "You gonna think I'm tryin' to be funny, but I'm dead serious. Stelson's white. The news gets one look at him, they'll probably send out the National Guard. But for a black kid...not gonna happen."

I felt like Daddy had bashed my face with a brick. *Not gonna happen.* My lips trembled. "B-but—"

"Shondra, you know I love Seth. I want him back as much as you do. That's why I'm telling you. Let *Stelson* do the press conference."

"What about both of us—" the words got scrambled in my throat as I witnessed Daddy closing his eyes, wincing with emotional pain.

"No. Just Stelson. You remember how people showed their true colors over that little biracial girl on the Cheerios commercial?"

My lungs deflated as I contemplated his argument. People weren't simply angry—they were irate that General Mills had portrayed an interracial family as "normal" and loving. Americans wrote so many terrible things on the YouTube page that a decision was made to disable comments.

I had no doubt that Seth and Stelson would pass for a white father and a white son. With me in the picture; however, our chances of getting Seth back might be lowered.

Stelson's hand on my shoulder interrupted my train of thought.

Immediately, I sprang to my feet and fell into his embrace. When I finally stepped back to look into his eyes, my blood froze. For the first time since this whole ordeal began, I could see that my husband was worried.

"Honey, we're going to do a press conference," I said.

"Yeah," he barely answered.

"Will you do it?" I blurted out.

He squinted. "Of course. Let's—"

"No. Just *you*," I stressed.

Stelson's countenance questioned further.

"Two minutes," Pauline declared.

I clutched Stelson's arms. "Listen. We stand a better chance of finding him if…if I'm not on the screen with you."

"Wh-what?"

I hated to have to spell it out for him, but he obviously wasn't getting the picture. I leaned in closer. "The general public doesn't respond to missing African-American children with as much…*interest* as missing white children."

Stelson looked past me, where Daddy was sitting. Stelson's face flattened as the entire picture must have formed in his head.

He focused on me again. "We're going on. *Together*."

"I'm not trying to be politically correct, Stelson. This is our *son*. Right now, we gotta do what we gotta do to get him back. We can change the world later."

In the ten years I had known Stelson, he had never given me the look I saw come across his face at that moment. Nostrils flaring, mouth pinched, eyes drawn together. If he had been anybody else, I would have ducked because usually, in a movie, that was the look the sane person gave before they slapped some sense into the hysterical person.

"We are doing this together. In faith. Period."

He took my hand and led me to the makeshift press room, which was nothing more than a wooden bench with microphones pointing toward the center.

Cameras flashed, lights beamed, and microphones poked at Stelson and me as we stood with an officer I had seen on television a few times already. Apparently, he was with public relations, from the sheriff's office.

He spoke first, "The missing child is four-year-old Seth Brown. He disappeared while hiking through the forest with his church group today. We've been looking for several hours now, but have yet to find him. We're asking for the public's help. It's possible that he may have wandered to the outskirts of the trail and beyond."

When he took a breath, the reporters inched their questions in, all at once. One stood out above the others, "Sheriff, does Seth have any food or water with him?"

"Yes. We believe he has a bottle of water," he answered.

The press clamored for attention again, settling on the question, "How many adults were with Seth?"

"Numerous."

"Then how did he get lost?" one of them yelled.

"It only takes a second for a child to wander away," he defended us.

I guess the media didn't like the sheriff's response. They fired questions at Stelson and me. We heard, "Exactly *how* did he get lost?" over all else.

My husband responded, "We need all the help we can get to find our son now." Stelson squeezed my hand. "He's fun. He's smart. And he's got a baby sister who adores him. If anyone has any information, if you saw him wandering near your campsite earlier today, *please* call 9-1-1. We thank you in advance for your prayers. And we praise God in advance for Seth's safe return."

"Mrs. Brown! Does your son have any experience with camping? Scouting?"

Stelson answered on my behalf, and it was a good thing because the only thing coming out of me was tears. "Seth is quite adventurous. Fearless. I'm sure he's making an adventure out of this whole event."

Thankfully, they didn't pressure us much more. The sheriff took it from there, answering questions about how long Seth had been gone, questions about the terrain and wildlife, to which he replied that the area was not inhabited by many harmful animals.

Someone asked about searching through the night. Helicopters. Planes. Heat-sensitive goggles. The sheriff seemed reluctant to make any promises which, quite frankly, rubbed me the wrong way. "We're following the protocol for missing children," was all he mentioned.

"Have you issued an Amber Alert?"

"No. This case does not fit the criteria for an Amber Alert."

I didn't even look at Daddy because I already knew what he would say. Words like "protocol" and "criteria" were the polite way of saying "red tape delay"; the kind of delay that doesn't happen when you know the right people, have enough money, or fall into a certain group.

We, obviously, weren't "in" enough. And maybe it was all my fault because I hadn't listened to my father.

⮞Chapter 14

Jonathan arrived just as darkness settled on the park. He joined hands with Stelson and me, praying for Seth's discovery. He and Stelson talked with the sheriff and the rangers, trying to think through how we could continue into the night. Evidently, military people have some secret camaraderie that immediately makes them trust one another. Jonathan's background put him in the thick of the conversation, giving Stelson a bit of a break.

The swarm of media had grown, but the number of searchers had dwindled down as people realized there was nothing more they could do that evening. Ebby volunteered to take Zoe home with her family while those who were able to stay waited for further direction. Thankfully, I had packed more than enough formula and diapers.

Jonathan was intercepting my cell phone calls so I wouldn't have to replay bad news over and over again.

Family by family, my church and the unselfish people who didn't even know our names six hours earlier checked out, promising to pray for us. Some of them even said they'd come back if we hadn't located Seth by morning. The rangers said, "We'll be here." as though they had no plans to try finding him at night.

I turned to Stelson. "We're not going to leave him out there until tomorrow, are we?"

"Honey, it's ten times darker in the woods than it is out here," he said. "They're working on a plan B."

"That's not good enough," I said. "We should *all* be out there now. Let's get some flashlights. Some orange vests. We can't let a four year old fend for himself overnight in the woods. That's ridiculous."

"Equipment is on the way," Stelson tried to calm me, but he was making me crazy.

I wanted him to *go off* on these people. They weren't doing enough to find my baby. Everybody sitting around like we're waiting on a shift change at a hospital. "Stelson, I need you to—"

"Hey! We've got a plane coming!" one of the reporters yelled. "A lady called in to the station. Said she empathized with the mom. Donated the use of her private plane to find Seth."

"Bless her," Stelson sighed.

This news breathed a second wind into those of us waiting for the next step.

"Hello?" The ranger answered his cell phone. "Yeah. We've got the manpower. Yeah. We're on it." He pressed a button on his phone to end the call. "Folks, we've got a plane. We've got everything we need to launch a night search. In some ways, this is better. We can use a night vision apparatus to help us spot him. If Seth is anywhere in these woods, we *will* find him tonight."

Just like that, protocol was overturned. God had given us favor with yet another stranger.

They called in some kind of special operations team, notified air traffic authorities, and it wasn't long before we heard the plane flying overhead.

"Jesus, please," I whispered.

Stelson took my hands into his and prayed, "Lord, thank You for sending us help. Thank You, God. Your timing is perfect, Your ways are good. Thank You for hiding him from all evil, according to Your Word. Father, enable those who have been trained for this experience to find our son. Father, position Seth so that he can be found. In Jesus' name we pray, Amen."

"Amen" echoed from everyone at our fly-by-night headquarters, including my father, who hadn't said much to me since I plastered my brown face on the screen.

For some idiotic reason, I sat down next to Daddy while Stelson and Jonathan manned the walkie-talkies, which were tied to a middle man who could communicate with the men in the planes.

"How you holdin' up, Shondra?"

"Pretty good."

"Yeah. You're a strong one. Always have been."

I wasn't sure what Daddy was trying to say, but I didn't have the energy to investigate what might have been an insult.

"They've got a visual!" Jonathan darn near screamed.

Instantly, we all hovered around the sheriff as he jotted down the coordinates relayed on the walkie-talkie.

I held my breath, waiting for more news through the static-y contraption. "He's mobile. Moving in a northeast direction…"

Mobile! He's moving! Alive and standing on two feet! I don't think I have ever been happier in my whole life. "Thank you, Jesus!"

Just then, an SUV from the Texas Parks and Wildlife Department pulled up. Boxes full of helmets with flashlights and what might as well have been canes, as far as I was concerned, were distributed. A group of men, including Stelson and Jonathan, set out to the designated area to retrieve my baby.

In the meanwhile, I got down on my knees and knelt over the park bench, praying non-stop until the moment I heard my husband yelling from the top of the trail, "We got him! We got him!"

I ran full force along the water's edge to meet my husband holding our child. The reporters ran alongside me, with their equipment bouncing along the whole way.

Even with limited light, I could see Seth's little legs, covered in red splotches, dangling under Stelson's elbows.

"Oh, baby!" I snatched Seth from Stelson and squeezed him. "Baby! We looked everywhere for you! Are you okay?" I brushed his hair back to get a good look at him. His skin was littered with insect bites, but he wasn't swollen or feverish.

Seth scolded weakly, "Mommy, I stopped to tie my shoe. And then you got lost."

I kissed him profusely as Stelson folded us both into his arms. Everyone clapped and cheered, slapped high-fives and congratulated one another on a mission accomplished. Stelson thanked them all.

Someone from the press asked the lead ranger for the name of the person who had donated the plane. My ears perked up for the answer.

"She wants to remain anonymous."

Stelson leaned over me and Seth and prayed, asking God to bless her for her generosity.

Paramedics gave Seth a once-over. We stripped my baby, thoroughly checking him for suspicious insect bites or evidence of anything that may have burrowed into his skin. Seth was given a clean bill of health and a sucker, which ripped off the paper stem.

He drank a bottle of water, tore into a chicken leg and ate like…well, like a boy who'd been lost in the woods for hours.

By the time we got home, people were blowing up our cell phones even more than after the press conference. Seth's misplaced accusation about *me* getting lost made the local hourly news and even a few of the national spots. Ours was the feel-good story leading almost every broadcast. Seth's blue eyes shined brightly despite the evidence of his very rough day dotting his skin.

Stelson, Seth and I stopped to collect Zoe from Ebby's.

When we crossed the threshold of our home, a flood of emotion rippled through me as Stelson and I held on to each other and our sleeping children.

We both smelled like pure funk, but I couldn't let go. Couldn't stop crying. Stelson released his bottled pressures, too, by way of sighing heavily and simply groaning. Speechless. That day could have turned out so much worse. But God.

Once my throat got unclogged, I offered a prayer from both of us. "God, thank You. Thank You, Lord, for returning our son. Thank You for all the people who came to help. And for the woman who donated the aircraft. You are amazing. You amaze me, God. Thank You for a husband who listens to You, without fear. And thank you for proving Yourself to me, God, even though You shouldn't have to. Amen."

"Amen."

We switched bathing duties; Stelson washed Zoe in the sink and I took the liberty of giving Seth a soapy, hot bath. He fussed, of course, because he was so tired he could hardly sit up.

"Seth, did you see any rabbits?" I tried to amuse him.

"No," he whined.

"Were you scared?"

"No."

"Seth, honey, where *were* you? Didn't you hear Mommy and Daddy calling your name?"

"Nooooo," he cried, wiping his eyes with closed fists. "Mommy, I want to go to sleep now. Plee-hee-heease."

I laughed because I don't think Seth had ever begged for sleep before. "Mommy has to give you a bath." I re-checked his ears, behind his neck, *every* crevice. I washed his hair three times and raked through with a fine-toothed comb which, of course, brought a low cry with a stream of tears from Seth's eyes.

My baby was pooped, but I wasn't going to let him hit the sheets just yet. I rubbed ointment on his arms and legs and doused him with Zoe's powder.

"I don't wanna smell like a baby. I'm a big boy," he protested.

"You sure are. And I'm proud of you, surviving out there all by yourself for all that time," I said as I helped him step into his pajamas.

"I wasn't alone."

Terror shot through me. I grabbed his arms. "Who was with you, honey? Did somebody—"

"God was with me," he stated with a face full of sincerity. "He told me not to be scared. And to drink my water. But there's something else, Mommy."

"What is it?"

"Ummm..." he sighed. His eyes closed involuntarily. "I had to do number two outside and I couldn't wipe. Is that okay?"

"Yes, baby. *This* time."

I made it as far as the kitchen before I broke out in a praise dance with no music except the fruit of my lips. "God, I thank You! God, I bless You!"

When Stelson got out of the shower, I told him about Seth's literal wilderness experience with the Lord. He joined me, kneeled beside me at the bed in thanksgiving.

"We bless You, God," my husband chanted, "bless Your name."

"Yes, Lord," I backed him up.

With Stelson having grown up in the Assemblies of God and my roots in the COGIC, our posture was nothing more than a picture of one of the good old-fashioned prayer meetings the older saints used to have. No agenda. Just petitions, praise, and thanksgiving because He *is* both able and worthy.

Though we were both pooped beyond words, I snuggled up to Stelson and apologized for letting fear cause me to doubt his leadership.

He kissed me. "We're not perfect."

"Yeah. I know. But sometimes I feel like you're pretty close, Babe." I thumped his chest.

"On that note, let me drift off to dreamland because that's about the only place I'll ever be perfect."

"I'm right behind you."

☙Chapter 15

Our church family celebrated God's answer to prayer during service the next day. Pastor Toole asked Stelson and me to share the testimony for the sake of those who weren't at the picnic, though I couldn't imagine most of the congregation didn't already know. No matter what color or doctrine, church folk have cornered the market on how to spread a word quickly.

My head was pounding after service. Just tired and emotionally spent. Nothing a good serving of comfort food wouldn't fix. Stelson, the kids, and I had lunch at Chili's. "Might be our last time doing this for a while," he said when the bill came.

"I know, right?" I agreed. "We're gonna have to find some places where kids eat free."

Our conversation was interrupted by two women who'd seen Seth on television the night before. "He is so cute! Thank God you two found him before I did. I would have taken him home with me!"

"Praise God." I smiled up at them.

After obtaining a full belly and some good rest, I was ready to tackle the week ahead. Starting each day with a quiet hour kept my mind "stayed on Jesus", as the older saints used to sing. Reading the scriptures, journaling the conversations between God and me, physically kneeling down in His presence…priceless. I wondered how I had ever managed to think I was fine without His peaceful good morning. I wouldn't have been able to have a quiet hour when Zoe was first born, of course. God knows our schedules. But now that I was back in the groove, I was determined to do everything possible to *stay* stayed, even after I returned to work.

I was hoping to connect with the women's Tuesday morning fellowship meeting at church, but my schedule got rearranged when the nurse called from Seth's school to say that he was running a fever. The worst-case scenario presented itself in my head on my way to pick him up from school: *He has malaria!*

Oh. Wait. We don't have malaria in Texas. Do we?

We went straight to the doctor's office after I retrieved Seth. I gave Dr. Bullock the run-down on Seth's adventurous weekend. After checking his lymph nodes and hearing the slight congestion in his chest, malaria was ruled out. "Looks like he's got a common cold. Now that school's started, kids are swapping germs every minute of the day."

"Yes, he started pre-k in public school a few weeks ago," I concurred.

"A bigger school brings more kids, more surfaces to touch, more opportunities to catch a virus. Just keep an eye on him. Keep his fever down. Look out for any rashes, given what happened this weekend." She pointed at Zoe, "And keep him away from this one if you can."

Keeping Seth out of Zoe's face was nearly impossible. With both of them at home with me throughout the day, it was only a matter of time before she started coughing and sneezing, too. We had to pass on one of the church kids' birthday parties that weekend. Sunday, the fevers were gone, but we stayed home as a precaution.

Stelson led "home church", which absolutely fascinated Seth. "We can have church at home?"

"Yes. Jesus said we *are* the church. And if two or three of His people get together for Him, He will be here with us."

"Wow! Jesus is *everywhere!*" Seth exclaimed.

Stelson charged our son with the duty of leading worship, which was a joy to watch. Seth insisted that we all participate in his extended remix version of "Father Abraham"—including wiggling our right and left knees *and* elbows.

I gave the announcements. "Zoe has a check-up appointment this week. We're praying for another awesome report. Seth knows all of his letters and their sounds. And Daddy has a birthday coming up soon."

We all clapped for Stelson. He laughed, "I *like* these

announcements."

Stelson opened His Bible. "I'm going to share something the Lord has been teaching me lately. It's in Ecclesiastes, chapter four."

I helped Seth find the book of Ecclesiastes in his children's illustrated Bible. Though he couldn't read yet, I talked him through the navigation. "Ecclesiastes…chapter four…oh, wait. Go back…yes…chapter four."

I pointed at the words as Stelson read from His Bible "Ecclesiastes chapter four, verses nine through ten. Two are better than one, because they have a good return for their labor: If either of them falls down, one can help the other up."

Seth had to demonstrate. He flattened his back against the floor. "You mean like this, Daddy?" he asked while reaching for Zoe's hand. Baby girl struggled with all her might to leave my lap as she responded to his gesture, trying to grasp his hand. Seth raised up to meet her hand, then hopped to his feet. "Thank you, Zoe! You helped me get up!"

"Yaaay!" we all clapped. Zoe was ecstatic.

"That's exactly right," Stelson agreed.

I made chicken noodle soup, thanks to a recipe I found on the internet. With Seth's stomach still a bit queasy, the soup was a perfect, light meal.

After we put the kids down for a nap, Stelson helped me clear the dishes. His "help" was really a cause for flirting, I quickly ascertained from his swats to my behind. I pretended to be annoyed, but we both knew I liked it. Who *wouldn't* want to flirt with a man who led "home church" when his family wasn't able to attend services at the sanctuary? And one who practiced what he'd just preached—lifting me up when I had lost track of the promises of God while Seth was missing.

Aside from his toned body, my husband's *character* was so juicy-sexy, it didn't take much to get me in the mood.

Stelson joked that I must have worked him too hard the night before because he woke up with a headache. I sent him off to work with a kiss, a few Tylenol, and the rest of the soup. Stelson didn't like taking drugs, but when I called him at lunch to check on him, he said he had swallowed the pills before a meeting because he couldn't concentrate otherwise.

"You think you need to see a doctor?" I asked.

"No. It's probably the virus the kids had last week."

"Probably so. I'll assess you when you get home," I promised with a hint of teasing.

"Man, I'm going to take a shower and get right in the bed."

I heard him sniff and surmised that he had indeed caught the bug Seth brought home from school. "Okay, baby. I'll have everything ready. What time do you think you'll be here?"

"Leaving here by five thirty. So, six at the latest."

"I gotcha. Bye."

"Bye."

I set an alarm on my phone for 5:40: *Run bath water for Stelson.*

I chocked up the fact that I didn't get sick to what my mother used to refer to as "Mommy Immunity." She said that, while we weren't invincible, God gave mothers an extra level of resistance to sickness because He knows families act like they can't hardly function without a Momma.

And, speaking of "functioning", I was quite proud of myself for getting the hang of running a household. My biggest help had been creating a family menu, rotating ten meals I could cook that everyone, except Zoe of course, would actually eat. When I emailed my spreadsheet to Peaches, she replied:

That's good, girl, but what about the snacks? Drinks? Desserts? Consider EVERYTHING before you go to the grocery store. And sign up for coupons online.

"Coupons?" I questioned my laptop screen. My time was worth more than the 25 cents a coupon would save me. If my best friend was combing through newspapers and email messages hunting down coupons, she was *out there*. Past Suzie Homemaker. Past B. Smith and Martha Stewart. It was time for Peaches to have her own reality show 'cause I had to see it live and in action to believe it.

Nonetheless, I went back to the drawing board. *Snacks and drinks.* In the past, I would just walk into the grocery store and pick up some things that looked fun—the brightest-looking fruit chews, cutest cheese puffs.

But now I had the time to sit there and think through what would be best for us all to eat at snack time. I added apples on Monday and Thursday, granola bars on Tuesday and Friday. Popcorn on Wednesday and Saturday. Ice cream had to go somewhere. *Sunday.*

The more I thought about it, I realized my father could use some meal-planning, too. Not that he would follow through.

You follow through bubbled out of my spirit.

My fingers were perched, still, on the keyboard. Waiting for more direction. And then the idea to include my father in our meal plans became clearer. I would make enough for him, too, and take it over to the house.

Yes. No. "How am I going to do this?" I asked. Since I couldn't exactly recall any scriptures on how to preserve food for the week, I went online and discovered a novel idea: freezing!

I was sold. I could cook on one day and freeze everything we would need for a whole week! They shouldn't have told me that. I was about to make myself the freezing queen.

Matter of fact, I figured if I got the cooking and freezing thing down, I might be able to go back to work sooner.

Zoe and I tackled the grocery store like two old pros. With the menu in hand, we were out of there in no time. I even got to come home and put the food away before we went to pick up Seth.

I was so excited, he was barely in the car before I informed him, "Your snack today is an apple."

He got a funny look on his face, I supposed wondering why I was so excited about apples.

I had to laugh at myself. "In case you were wondering, I mean."

It was a beautiful day. Cool enough for us to hang outdoors for a half hour or so. Zoe jumped in her bounce-walker and Seth sparred with an imaginary opponent once I got tired of getting poked by his plastic sword. I snagged a spot under the patio umbrella and just sat there watching. Listening. Thanking God for such a wonderful family to occupy this picturesque, lush green back yard with its 6-foot privacy fence.

Zoe's late afternoon nap was soon in order, so we brought the party inside. Seth wouldn't fall asleep this early. I gathered his coloring books, crayons and Legos and sat him at the table while I prepared our evening meal of chicken tetrazzini with light garlic bread. I'd save the cooking bonanza for a weekend day, when Stelson could busy himself with the kids.

The smell of melted cheese and chicken permeated the house. When I was a little girl, Momma made our house smell like heaven almost every day. Casseroles, chopped onions, breads, cookies. Enough to make me want to hop off the school bus and come running inside to see what she had in store for us.

But that was in the 1970s. Back when women—let alone *black* women—weren't considered for high-powered jobs. Most didn't have the education anyway, thanks to low expectations. My degrees hadn't come easy. I was proud of my accomplishments. And yet, standing there in the kitchen with my house smelling like Momma's, I had to admit to myself: *This is an accomplishment, too.* I wanted Seth and Zoe to have the best things in life, including feeling that someone who loved them had been thinking about them, preparing for their arrival while they were away.

My phone's alarm beeped, reminding me to run Stelson's bath water. My poor husband was pretty manly, but he could get downright baby-ish when ill. Worse than the kids, which was why I thanked God Stelson rarely got sick.

I knew I was in for some serious nurse duty when he walked through the door looking like death warmed over. He dropped his briefcase and let his jacket slide from his shoulders straight to the floor. "I'll pick it up later." His pale cheeks, red nose, watery eyes and disheveled hair told the story of a miserable day.

I rushed to him and checked his forehead with the back of my hand. "You're burning up. Sweating. Go get in the tub." I scooped his jacket off the floor and hung it in the coat closet.

"Hey, Daddy!" Seth lunged at Stelson's legs.

"Daddy's not feeling good," I pried him off. "He needs to get some rest."

"Yeah, buddy. I'll talk to you later."

Seth slinked away, disappointed.

Between my three babies, I had my hands full. Stelson missed work the next day. And the next. By the third day, the fever had gone and the congestion was clearing, but the headache didn't go away.

In fact, it got worse.

Chapter 16 ❧

"Daddy, what is the problem?" I pushed my chin forward, waiting for some ridiculous response.

"I don't like to fool with the microwave every day like you young people. Ya'll gon' wake up one day and figure out all that radiation is the reason for all this cancer y'all got," he fussed. One by one, he took my expertly prepared, carefully packaged meals out of the spectacular brown paper sack I had lovingly arranged them in for his benefit. He slung them on the counter.

"So what are you going to do with this food, then?" I asked.

He snapped the top off the turkey with garlic and parmesan red potatoes. "Well, I'll eat this one tonight since it's still warm." He sniffed my cooking. "I'll put the rest in the refrigerator. Guess I can transfer 'em to a tin pan and then put it in the oven, for the most part."

"If you can put stuff in an oven, you can make your own meals," I argued.

"I didn't ask you to bring this food over here," he bucked up.

The front screen door slammed. *Thank God. Jonathan's here.*

"Hey," he breezed into the kitchen, hugging my father and me. "I see you've got these nice home-cooked meals, huh, Dad? We ought to make a service out of it. Shondra's mobile kitchen."

"He doesn't want them," I interrupted Jonathan's sales pitch.

My brother crossed his arms, looking down at my father. I was so glad Jonathan was taller than Daddy. Jonathan Sr. needed someone to put him in check. "What's the problem now?"

"I don't want to eat a bunch of microwave re-heated food," he stubbornly replied, mimicking Jonathan's stance. "I already done told y'all that when you brought all those other freezer meals."

Jonathan sighed with enough contempt to get kicked out of a courtroom.

"But the food I've prepared isn't drenched in chemicals or preservatives. You know whose kitchen they came from. What's the problem now?"

Daddy raised up his nose. "If it ain't fresh from the oven or the stove, it don't taste the same."

Jonathan blinked. "Wait a minute. Are you the same Jonathan Smith who claims his family was so poor, Grandmomma Smith fried pancakes with Vaseline and you all *ate* it, happily?"

Oooooh! The Vaseline story. *Good one, Jonathan.*

I took a swing, "And didn't you always tell us that if we were picky about what we ate, we weren't really hungry?"

Daddy waved both of us off. He pushed up his glasses. "That was before I had a good job at the post office. Before I met your Momma and…well…you know how she was about cookin'. She spoiled me."

My father's lower lip began to tremble, which nearly threw me off the boat.

Jonathan slapped my father on the back. "We feel you, man. We feel you. We all miss Momma."

They got no further than a side-hug before Daddy pulled away. "But if y'all insist on me eating frozen food—"

"We do," Jonathan cosigned.

"I guess." Daddy piled three of the containers in the freezer.

"It's better than eating sandwiches every day," I assured him. "And you can recycle the containers if you absolutely don't feel like washing them."

He grumbled and walked to the den, leaving Jonathan and me to make sense of his foolishness.

"What's my half?" Jonathan asked.

"Don't worry about it," I said.

"No, I want to contribute. I mean, seeing as you ain't got no job and all," he teased.

I punched my little brother in the stomach. "I got a full-time job with your niece and nephew."

Jonathan's lean body hadn't changed much since he was in high school. Always a trainer, he regularly participated in marathons and triathlons for the so-called "fun" of it. I, for one, would never put torturing my body in the "fun" category.

"You can put, say, thirty-five on it every week, assuming that he actually eats the food. If he doesn't, I guess we'll have to see if meals-on-wheels can deliver something. I don't know."

Jonathan nodded in rapid succession as he pulled money from his pocket. "Oh, he's gonna eat this food. If I have to come over here every night, he *will* eat it."

I thanked him as I stuffed the cash in my back pocket.

"Oh, please." Now it was my turn to harass him. "I saw your little status change on Facebook the other day. Mister *in a relationship*. How are you *in a relationship* with someone we've never met?"

"I brought her over here."

"When?"

"Not long ago," he skirted around my question.

"Daddy!" I called to the back room.

"Aaay, aaay, *aaay*," Jonathan shushed me. "I said I brought her over here. I didn't say I brought her inside."

"What's wrong with her?"

He smacked his lips a little too hard. "Nothing."

"Why haven't *I* met her, at least?"

"Look, we don't need McGruff the crime dog here, all right? She's somebody I met running a marathon. Nice. Smart. Cool. Has a three-year-old son. What else do you want to know?"

"Is she black?"

He poked out his lips. "How you gon' ask me that and my brother-in-law is white?"

"I'm just asking. I mean, the last time I watched a marathon on television, I didn't see a whole lot of *us* pounding the pavement."

"*Y'all* do need to be pounding it, trust me," he remarked. "Sisters are tipping the scales these days. For some reason, y'all expect us to *embrace* the extra weight, like there's something wrong with *us* for wanting a fit woman."

"Whatever! *We* have a lot of stress. Single moms, working moms. Shoot, I'm blessed to be able to take a break until I get a handle on this."

"All I know is, I'm not trying to marry somebody I can't carry over the threshold," he reiterated.

"Whatever. Now, back to the original question. Is she black?"

"Yes. She's black," he stated.

"Okay."

"Why? Is that a relief to you?"

I should have known I couldn't corner my brother without enduring a psychoanalytical session. I sat down at the table. He eyed me, standing in front of the refrigerator.

"Yeah, for Daddy's sake. It is a relief. I think he'd be completely disappointed if both of his kids grew up and married people who weren't black."

"You've already put us at the white quota?" he laughed.

"Yeah," I joined his joke, "I don't think Daddy could take any more."

Jonathan sat next to me. "Dang. I gotta stay with the black, huh?"

I popped his arm. "You act like you've got a problem with black women."

"Not all of y'all. Not the northern sisters."

I couldn't believe these words were coming from my brother's mouth. Jonathan Smith, Jr., raised by my father, the black Archie Bunker.

"Go on."

"See. It's like this." Jonathan's hands stiffened like boards as he lined them up on the table for this grand, animated explanation. "Black girls, from the south especially, got raised by people like…" he pointed toward the den. "They taught them that it was black people against the world. And then people like Momma, rest her soul, taught black women that men were liars. Not to be trusted, only after one thing, heartbreakers. So then they've got this women versus men schema, too. I ain't got all my life to be trying to undo that mentality. I just want to be in love and get married to somebody who wasn't programmed to be suspicious and defensive all the time. That's tiring."

"And white girls aren't defensive?"

"Some of them are. Depends on how they were brought up. But for the most part, white girls are optimistic. They see the glass half full. And they don't have this...*bite* in 'em."

"I thought men *liked* bite. I mean, when you have a good, feisty, passionate, strong woman, you've got a good ride or die chick."

"I have no problems with a good, strong woman with bite. I just don't want her to bite *me*, especially when I haven't done anything to deserve it," he clarified.

My handsome brother. Strong. Black. Intelligent. Gainfully employed. Loved God. Family man before he was even married. If this kind of man was prone to prejudge black women, where did my daughter stand? "What about Zoe? She's going to be a black woman raised in the south. Would you overlook her?"

Jonathan pushed his lips over to one side. "Pssssh. Please. Zoe's gonna be fine 'cause, first of all, she has *me* for an uncle."

I rolled my eyes. "Second of all?"

"Second of all, she's got you and Stelson. Working together." He locked the knuckles from both hands together. "Y'all are a team. You keep it practical, and Stelson keeps it optimistic. Faithful.

"By the way, Daddy told me about the thing at the picnic. About how he didn't want you to get involved with the press."

"What did he say?" I asked.

"Said you got lucky. That wasn't luck, though. That was God."

"Truly," I agreed.

"So when do I get to meet this marathon-runnin' girl?"

"Soon enough." He smiled.

"What's her name?"

"See, you're already going too far too fast."

I whipped my cell phone from my purse. "I'm gonna look on Facebook."

"Give me that!" he jerked the phone from my hand.

"Dad-aaaaay!" I hollered.

Jonathan yelled over me, "Never mind! Everything's okay."

Some things never changed between us.

I came home ready to debrief Stelson about the progress with Daddy and even discuss or debate Jonathan's philosophy. My husband was absolutely brilliant and one of the things I enjoyed most about our relationship was the fact that he and I could engage in intellectual conversations through our varied viewpoints.

But when I returned to our abode, I found the kids unattended—Zoe in her play pen, Seth in his room with the door shut, watching television and playing with his gazillion happy meal toys strewn all over the floor.

"Seth, where's Daddy?"

"In the bed."

I found my husband just where my son told me he would be. He was a stiff lump with the comforter draped over his head. I lifted the hood. "Stelson?"

"Don't!" he snapped, yanking the covers back in position.

"What's…did y'all eat dinner?"

"Yes. The kids ate."

"What about you?"

"I can't," he said through gritted teeth. "My head is killing me."

"Honey, if it's that bad we need to go to the doctor. Did you take some Tylenol?"

"It's all gone."

"What do you mean it's all gone?" I railed. "I just bought it earlier this week."

"Like I said. It's all gone."

One glance in the trash can confirmed his statement. The empty 24-count bottle stared back at me. I rubbed my forehead. A sudden knowing happened in me. I can't explain how I knew. I simply *knew* this wasn't right. "Stelson, get up. Let's go to the emergency room. They need to do X-rays, an MRI, or something."

"It's…I'll go tomorrow."

"We really," I tried to speak without giving the enemy ammunition, "need to go."

"Tomorrow. Could you go get me some more pain reliever, though? Something stronger? For migraines?"

Speaking to him through the covers, I couldn't gauge his condition well. "If it hurts this bad—"

"Can't you simply do what I ask? Sheez."

I stood there for a moment, staring at the damask print black and white fabric as though a foreigner had addressed me from the other side of the blanket. *Had* to be somebody else because my husband didn't speak to me that way.

"I beg your pardon?"

"Just go. And get it. Please."

It was my pleasure to leave the house because the man lying in my bed was about to make me bite him for real.

❧*Chapter 17*
Stelson

Mornings were the worst. Seemed as though his body had spent the night in a brawl and he had to recover when the alarm clock buzzed. He'd caught the flu before and experienced the achy exhaustion, fever, and congestion that accompanied the virus. He'd never forget how it felt.

However, this was different. Not only was he in pain and tired, he'd begun to notice things no flu virus would produce.

As he parked in his reserved slot, he closed his eyes again, hoping the white spots in his vision would disappear.

He opened his eyes. White spots gone. For now.

Stelson took the keys from the ignition and got out of the car. He dropped his keys into his pocket—or so he thought until her heard them hit the ground. He'd miscalculated the position of his hand. Again.

"Hey, Brown," Orson Maxwell, the owner of an insurance agency in the building greeted as he waltzed to the garage's elevator.

"Morning, Maxwell."

Stelson bent over to retrieve his keys. He quickly grabbed his laptop bag from the back seat of the truck and hoisted it on his left shoulder, which wasn't his usual carrying spot. His right side had weakened so much that he was even afraid to hold Zoe on that side.

He locked the vehicle doors from the panel switch, then jogged to catch up with Maxwell, who was apparently holding the elevator for him. Suddenly, his right leg forgot how to step. Stelson stumbled but his left foot remembered the routine and put him back on track.

"Whoa! You alright there?" Maxwell asked.

"Yeah. I'm good."

"Looked like you were about to take a dive," Maxwell chuckled nervously.

"Naaaa. I was just making sure gravity still worked," Stelson joked, though his mind reeled from this bizarre loss of function. His muscles sometimes didn't follow the direction his brain gave them. Not that his brain was his friend, either, since it rarely ceased to pound inside his skull.

He boarded the elevator with Maxwell and they engaged in small-talk, which was something he hadn't forgotten how to do, thankfully. He could carry on a whole conversation and not pay attention to one word, which was exactly how he made it to his floor.

"See you later," Maxwell said as Stelson exited.

Stelson wondered if this was how it had been for his father. Did his father know that he was dying ahead of time?

Stelson gave Helen a slight 'good morning', grabbed the coffee she'd prepared for him, walked into his office and shut the door behind him.

He dropped his baggage behind his desk and fell to his knees in prayer at the desk. He didn't want to leave his wife and children the same way his father had left his mother.

"Please, God. If not for me, for LaShondra, Zoe and Seth."

Unbeknownst to his wife, Stelson had been reaching out to doctors on his own, ruling out the major culprit: cancer.

Still, there was no explanation for these peculiar symptoms. Just a bunch of guesses and hardly any relief from the throbbing in his head. He had even missed the last finance meeting at church because it was all he could do to go to work and back.

If LaShondra were still working, he would have taken off a week's worth of days by now so he could stay home in peace and quiet. But with everybody home most of the day, he would be less likely to find silence there than at the office.

"Brown," Cooper called out, knocking on the door.

Stelson quickly—too quickly—rose to his chair, which made his head spin. He massaged his forehead. "Yeah. Come in."

Cooper's head appeared. "You all right?"

"Yeah." Stelson let his hand fall to the desk. "What's up?"

"Got Dick Churchill coming in at ten. You ready?"

"Almost. Let me show you the numbers."

Cooper entered the office and the two men sat at the conference table reviewing the proposal for Churchill Fabricating. Stelson pushed past the agonizing headache, listening to Cooper's last-minute tweaks and making adjustments to his computer's files.

They were a good team. Always had been. But today, Stelson wished he'd never met Cooper. He wished he didn't even have a job because he'd rather be somewhere flopped on a bed with a towel covering his eyes indefinitely.

With the help of God and Excedrin, Stelson made it through the Churchill meeting with a slight decrease in pain and only a few spots here and there blinding his sight.

But he had to turn down lunch with the men because the meeting had drained his energy. "Maybe next time."

Cooper had flashed a disapproving glance, which prompted Stelson to offer a false explanation for why he couldn't attend a lunch with one of their newest, most wealthy clients. "Got an event at my son's school today."

Churchill smiled. "Family first. I've got three boys of my own."

Cooper winked, obviously satisfied that Stelson had cleared up the tension.

Of course, telling a lie only caused more tension for Stelson. In fact, this was his second lie today. When Jim Moore had called earlier to see why Stelson hadn't made the last finance team meeting, Stelson had tried to tell him the truth, but failed.

"I'm not feeling so well, Jim."

"Really?"

"Yeah. Got some kind of virus. Maybe something more, I don't know."

"Aaah, you'll pull through," Jim cheered him on.

A wave of anger had washed over Stelson as Jim dismissed the admission. He remembered all the people who had basically told him and his mother to be optimistic, look on the bright side of things even as his father entered the final stages of cancer. Their comments and churchy clichés could basically be summarized in three words: Buck up, buckaroo!

Still, Stelson played along, downplaying the breadth of his condition. "You're right. It's probably nothing. Send me the minutes."

Diverting Jim rather than reaching out for prayer wasn't helping anything, Stelson knew. Not to mention the fact that he was lying to LaShondra through omission. But what good would it do to get her worried? She'd just quit her job at his request. He had vowed to take care of her and the kids. Would she be able to trust him if he let her down now?

The only One Stelson didn't lie to was God. He told Him the truth: He was in pain. Running short on patience and tolerance. And scared.

⁊Chapter 18

"The...c...a...t, cat...is...r...e...d, red," Seth sounded out the words in his take-home printed book. "The cat is red."

"You did it, Seth! You can read!"

My baby's face lit up like he'd won a million dollars. "I did?"

"Yes! That's how you read, Seth. You just put the sounds of the letters together!" I jumped from the kitchen chair, snatching him up with me, swinging him around and around.

He pumped both fists in the air as we chanted, "Seth can read! Seth can read!"

Zoe beat on her high chair. "Aaaaach! Aaaach!" she tried to join us.

"Momma, can I call PawPaw and tell him?"

"You certainly may."

I set my son on the ground and dialed my father's number for him. With all due enthusiasm, Seth informed Daddy that he could read. I heard my father yelling through the phone, congratulating my son who, by that point, was nearly out of breath from excitement. "One day, I'm gonna read the big black book about the slaves, PawPaw, but I can't now because I don't know how to read big words yet."

I reached for the phone. "Gimme."

"We'll talk to you later, Daddy. Seth just wanted you to know, all right?"

I hung up before Daddy could deny that he was still subtly pushing his agenda into Seth's mind. When a four year old sings "We Shall Overcome" and "Swing Low Sweet Chariot" in the bathtub, somebody is on the march.

"Seth, don't sing those songs around Daddy, okay?" I said.

"Yes, ma'am."

I had to pick my battles with Daddy.

Seth couldn't wait for Stelson to get home. He practiced reading the book three times as we waited on the couch. When he heard the latch turn, Seth grabbed his book, hopped down, and swished his footed pajamas across the living room floor to greet his father. "Daddy! Daddy! Guess what?"

"Not now, Seth," my husband pushed Seth aside.

"But I can—"

"I said *not now*."

Seth's shoulders slumped. His face followed.

Stelson fussed at me, "What's he doing up anyway? He should be in bed by now."

"I gave him special permission to stay up late for you."

"Bad idea."

Stelson hung his jacket on the coat rack.

I could have wrung his neck.

Seth sniffed, calling my attention to his bruised feelings. I walked him on to bed. "It's alright, Seth. Daddy's not feeling well, remember?"

"But he's *never* feeling well," Seth moaned. "Maybe if I read to him, he'll get better."

Blinking back tears, I knelt beside Seth's bed with him for bedtime prayers. "And God, please help my Daddy to feel better so he can listen to me read. I know he will like it. In Jesus' name, Amen."

I was glad somebody felt like praying for my husband because it sure wasn't me. But before I could get back to our room and let him have it, he was already in bed. With his work clothes on.

I switched on the light.

"Turn it off," he said, his head beneath a pillow. "I can still see the light."

"You're gonna see the light *for real* if you can't treat us any better than this." *Sit up here and hurt my baby like this. Who do you think you are anyway, buster?*

"Shondra. Please. I'm tired. My head hurts. I can't."

"*You* can't? How about *I* can't? *Seth* can't."

Enraged, he hopped out of bed, stepped toward me, and switched off the light himself. "If you don't stop, I'm going to a hotel. I cannot argue with you tonight."

"How you gonna go to a hotel? It's not in the budget." I slid my neck to one side.

"You can be really evil when you want to, you know?" he said.

"Look who's talking!"

He put his hands on his ears. "Stop yelling."

I lowered my voice. "I'm not yelling."

"Could you just leave me alone? That's all I'm asking."

"Must be nice to come home from work and not have to take care of anybody else."

He walked back to the bed, pushed his feet into his shoes. "Look, I've got travel points and I'm more than willing to use them if you can't control yourself."

I'm gonna be honest: If I'd had my own job, my own money coming in, there's no way I would have tried to stop my husband from leaving that night. I probably would have told him to let the doorknob hit him where the good Lawd split him. But when he grabbed his wallet off the night stand, I had visions of me, Seth, and Zoe sitting out on the curb homeless.

"Whatever, Stelson. I'm not going to push you out of this house."

"Thank you." He collapsed on the bed. Kicked his shoes off again. "Good night."

Lord, I got to get myself back together because I can't live with this foolishness.

Chapter 19 ⋧

My shoe selection was still limited to flats, preferably flip-flops, thanks to my almost-healed toe. I'd tried to attend a few classes at the gym but the moves were too much for my foot. My best bet was the elliptical rider. My feet stayed planted in one spot, and I could roll my weight toward the instep to relieve the pressure every five minutes or so.

In only three sessions, I had worked myself up to forty-five minutes, burning almost 400 calories. The children's play center was a godsend. I could take a shower and get dressed after the workout knowing that Zoe was in good hands.

The water temperature in the gym shower was not conducive to an invigorating experience. I guess they didn't want us getting carried away with our break from the kids, which would explain why there was no bath tub. Seriously, if they'd put a tub in there, I would have brought my Ajax and my Pine Sol, cleaned it out, and spent an hour soaking in peace.

I lathered up my sponge twice, thankful that I wasn't rushed by the baby swing's timer. Zoe liked the college-age young lady in the "Barnyard" 2-hour daycare, which was a relief to me because my baby girl could be really picky with strangers. Seth, on the other hand, would have stayed with just about anyone when he was her age. He was so ready to get around, he'd made up his own awkward way of scooting around on his bottom before he figured out how to crawl. Never a dull moment since then. And Zoe was bound to take off any day. She was rocking and moving backwards already.

Wait a minute. Are my kids and my family all I think about now?

I tried to remember the last time I had thought about something that didn't involve laundry, food, or someone in either the Brown or Smith household.

No luck. My days and nights were filled with…serving.

I needed recess already. Stelson probably needed one, too. We hadn't had any "us" time since before Zoe was born.

That's it. We need a mini-vacation. A quick flight, a nice hotel with a view, good food, easy conversation and great sex.

Seth would be happy to bounce between my father and Jonathan for a few days. And according to Peaches, her mother would be more than happy to keep Zoe, so long as we didn't mind her spoiling Zoe rotten.

After getting dressed and signing my sweetness out of the Barnyard, I checked my calendar to make sure there was no note about weekend business for Stelson. Next, I called to review the balance of Stelson's frequent flyer miles. We had enough to book roundtrip flights, but I needed to check with him about hotel points.

I was so excited about our soon-to-be plans I went ahead and made arrangements with the sitters. Peaches' mother squealed, "Ooh yaaas! I can't wait to get that butterball over here!"

Of course, Daddy had to say something negative. "Make sure you watch the weather forecast. Might rain."

"A little rain never hurt anybody," I chirped.

"Yeah, you right. But a lot of rain will. Watched the news the other day and they said a whole house fell into a sinkhole…"

I barely listened as my father recapped the top ten horror stories he'd probably been watching for the past twenty-four hours on news TV. "Is there any good news on television?" I finally asked.

"Naw. Ain't nothin' good happening," he fussed. "People just crazy these days. They'll blow your head off over an iPhone and sit up in the courtroom with no remorse at all!"

"All right. I'll catch up with you later, Daddy."

On second thought, I called Jonathan to see if he would serve as the main sitter. Maybe Seth and his girlfriend's son could have a playdate. I was fairly certain that Daddy knew how to entertain Seth for a few hours twice a week, but once Daddy ran out of energy on a full weekend with Seth, I had no doubt my father would park his grandson in front of CNN for hours on end so he could get a good dose of reality.

Jonathan agreed to step in, which put me at ease and reignited my giddiness. I couldn't wait until Stelson got home to finalize the plans. Dropping by his office unannounced wasn't my usual M.O., but the last time I'd done it, he'd been more than grateful.

"Hi, Helen. Is Stelson in?"

"Yes, LaShondra. He's with clients now, but they should be finishing up soon. You and Zoe want to take a seat?"

"Sure. We'll wait."

Helen, of course, reached out toward my baby, but Zoe snuggled in tight, clutching my clothes. "She has to warm up to you," I said.

"Awww. She's so adorable. You two thought about entering her in pageants? She'd win hands-down."

"You know, I've never considered it." Not to mention I had my reservations about pageants anyway. All that makeup and fake eyelashes on little girls didn't seem like something I'd want to subject Zoe to unless she somehow found out about them on her own and asked to compete.

"My niece puts her kids in them. They've won a ton of scholarship money already, and they're not near as cute as Zoe, if you ask me," she laughed at herself.

"I'm sure they're beautiful," I took up for Helen's peeps.

Stelson's office door opened and three people dressed in professional attire—two men and one woman—shook his hand as they exited. "We look forward to working with you, Mr. Brown. We'll be in touch," the older gentleman said.

"Same here," my husband agreed with a smile.

He's in a great mood.

I stood. Stelson held the door open and I followed him into the office. I tiptoed to kiss his lips.

He gave Zoe a kiss, too.

"Babe, I was thinking. Let's get away this weekend. I'm overwhelmed. You're overworked. We need some time together."

The strained expression covered his face again. He returned to his computer. "No. I don't think so."

My heart dropped. "Why not?"

"Because I don't want to."

"And why not?"

He released the computer mouse. "I mean, you barged in here with all these plans…we didn't have a discussion. We haven't figured this into the budget. We have to plan differently now with one income."

He never would have been able to throw the money situation in my face if I'd had a job. I sank into one of the guest chairs and bounced Zoe on my knee. "You've got enough frequent flyer miles. And maybe enough points—"

"I said no. I'm not going."

"So if it's not money, then what is it?"

He exhaled at me as though I was some nutcase asking him for five dollars. "I'm not *up* to going. I don't *feel* like going. I've had a few headaches lately, in case you've forgotten."

"How *could* I forget?" slipped from my mouth.

He shook his head and attended to the computer screen again. "Is that all you wanted?"

"No. I want *you*. I need you. The *real* you."

My husband leaned back in his chair and ran his fingers through his hair, catching the bulk at the nape of his neck. "I can't, okay? I'm not trying to push you out, I don't mean to upset you. But I can't be there for you right now. It's taking every ounce of energy, every prayer in me to come to the office and work through these headaches. Capiche?"

"You don't have to be so mean to me," I scolded. "I just watched you put on a happy face for your clients. You can act civilized when you want to. Why are you giving *me* the worst of you?"

He took a deep breath. "I don't know."

"Well, you need to figure it out. Soon. I don't deserve to be your emotional and verbal punching bag." I grabbed my purse from the back of the chair and hoisted Zoe to my hip. "Are we going on a vacation this weekend or not?"

"Not."

"Fine. I'll cancel everything. We'll continue in our own private hell."

"Stop being so dramatic. This is not hell. At least not for you."

I seethed, "You don't know what's happening inside my head."

"I couldn't have said it better myself," he barked back.

Helen said good-bye to me as I breezed past her with Zoe flopping up and down beside me. I threw a quick "bye" over my shoulder and dashed to my car. I locked Zoe into her seat then sank into the driver's seat in just enough time to avoid a public meltdown.

My intimate weekend plans had come crashing down, not only on my head, but on my heart. How could he be so abrupt? So brash and sullen?

The more I thought about what had just happened in Stelson's office on top of my upside-down-world, my heart broke.

Zoe must have recognized my despair. She started crying. We would just have to be two crying Browns that day because I was in no position to comfort her. I wished I could take her somewhere and drop her off for a few hours while I licked my wounds.

Alas, the task of caring for her continued. She downed a bottle of baby food. I wiped her face, changed her diaper, laid her on her tummy in the playpen for a nap. Meanwhile, I crossed as much off my to-do list as possible with cooking and cleaning. In an hour she'd wake up. In two hours, we'd pick up Seth and my main job would be to keep them both busy until Stelson got home with his sorry attitude.

This was my life now.

❧Chapter 20

"Mmmmm….mmmmm."

The low moan woke me from my sleep. "Stelson?"

"What?"

I raised up to find my husband clutching his head. Even in the darkness, I could see that he was in unbelievable pain. "Your head again?"

"Feels like someone wearing track cleats is stomping on my head," he groaned.

"Let's go."

"Go where?"

"E-R. Now. This has been going on too long. It's ridiculous."

"Stop yelling."

"I'm not yelling. I'm *telling* you we're leaving. I'll get the kids together. You change clothes or put on a robe. I don't care."

Leaving the house at five-thirty in the morning threw our routine off, which made Zoe extra fussy.

Seth was immune to his sister's crying. He was knocked out in his car seat.

Normally, Stelson would have ignored her, too. Not that morning. "Make her stop. Please."

I fumbled with the CD changer, settling on the kids' favorite Dora song. "If you're happy and you know it, clap your hands!"

"Uh, no. That's too loud. Turn it off," Stelson ordered even as Zoe began to quiet down.

"Well, you can't have it both ways. Either Zoe cries or Dora sings," I explained the choices.

"I should have driven myself," he muttered under his breath.

Father, Stelson is your son. Please help me. And please help him with this headache.

We left the E-R with a clinical diagnosis of migraine headache, which baffled me completely. From what little I knew about migraines, they were triggered by stress. But what could be stressing my husband out? I knew he had a great deal of pressure as co-founding partner, but Brown-Cooper Engineering was a well-established, fairly elite engineering firm. By God's grace most of their business came from repeat customers and referrals with deep pockets who weren't struggling. People called my husband's company when they were looking to expand and had enough money to afford the best.

Was it the kids? Seth was a handful. Zoe still woke up in the middle of the night sometimes, but I was the one who handled her after-hours issues.

Was it me? *No. Couldn't be.* Well…maybe. Maybe it was the fact that I'd quit my job and now everything rested on Stelson's shoulders. Really, that was the only thing that had changed in the previous weeks. Perhaps on the surface, Stelson wanted to be the man. But subconsciously, he was panicked about bearing the load for a family of four. Anyone would be, right?

Once I got Stelson home and took Seth to school, I ran back to the pharmacy to fill the migraine relief prescription. Zoe played with the toys dangling over her carrier while I ran my theory past Peaches on the phone.

"No. That's not it. Stelson's used to paying bills. He had his own house before you two got married," she shot me down. "It's gotta be something else. Is he getting along with Mr. Cooper?"

"Yeah. As far as I know."

"How's his family in Louisiana?"

"They're good. I talked to his mom after Seth's lost-in-the-forest incident. Everybody's fine," I discounted that possibility.

"Maybe it's not stress-related," she said. I could hear computer keys tapping away in the background. "I'm at my natural remedy website. Let me see. Hmmm. Maybe it's some kind of hormonal imbalance," she suggested.

"Men don't have hormonal issues."

"Yes, they do!" she argued. "They probably have more hormonal problems than doctors actually diagnose. Okay. So here's a personal question—just trying to get to the bottom of this. How are things in the bedroom?"

"Fine," I said.

"Fine like *okay* or fine like it could go down at a moment's notice?" she probed.

"Wait a minute," I stopped her. "*What* could go down—*it* or *us?*"

Peaches huffed. "I'm gonna have to break this down for you. Let me read from the screen." She cleared her throat. "Is he able to achieve an erection and does it last throughout the duration of sexual activity?"

"Yes," I answered, feeling like we were sixteen years old reading a magazine we had no business owning.

"How's his attitude? Mood swings?"

"No, not until the headaches started."

"Aaaa-hah," she contemplated. "Has he eaten any seafood lately?"

"No," I ruled out, exhausted with this wild goose chase. "You know what, I haven't even prayed about it."

Peaches fussed, "Well, what are you calling me for if you haven't even talked to Daddy?"

"I haven't had a minute alone all morning, all right?"

"Mmm hmmm. You get in the closet, I'll do some searching online. Amen?"

"Amen, girl."

My prayer time did nothing more than confuse me. I was reading a book on God's goodness by Bishop Desmond Tutu and his daughter, Mpho, during my prayer time. They described horrific torture and injustices people had suffered in South Africa and worldwide. And yet, somehow, God's goodness prevails.

I agreed. But I didn't see what any of that had to do with Stelson's headaches.

For days, I journaled my questions: Is it really migraines? Are the kids and I stressing him out? Is he worrying too much? Should I go back to work after Thanksgiving? Christmas?

I was growing tired of asking questions without receiving answers. I would have given anything to call my Momma. Even if all she told me was to keep praying, it would have been better than feeling like I was in limbo without somebody backing me up in prayer. Usually, I could count on Stelson to cover me. But since he was the problem, it was just me and God. And God wasn't talkin'.

Stelson kept getting up and going to work every day. He showered, took medicine, and dove into bed when he got home.

I bathed the kids and took care of business as usual. Kept telling myself to carry on like he wasn't even home, like he was working late. And I probably could have waited out this episode of migraines were it not for the fact that I had to serve him dinner in our dark, silent bedroom.

Witnessing the anguish on his face sent me into lecture mode. "Honey, just last month you made me go to the doctor over a stubbed toe that turned out to be a broken toe, remember?"

"We already went to the doctor. It's a migraine."

"I don't think so, Stelson."

He griped, "Since when did you earn a medical degree?"

"Since when did you get so disrespectful?"

"Please. If you'd...stop saying things that don't make sense. Arguing makes my head throb harder."

"I don't have to say anything at all to you," I sassed. "I could bring your little plate in here and set it on the bed and leave."

"Maybe you should," he agreed.

"Fine. I will," I said, standing.

He squeezed his eyes shut. Pinched the top of his nose with two fingers. "I...it's...I'm getting pretty close to a ten on the pain scale."

"I've been past ten. In labor. But I didn't go left on you," I stated. "Stelson, I've never seen this side of you."

"Neither have I. I've never been this miserable for this long in my whole life. Just leave me alone before I say something else stupid."

Well, at least he recognized he was being stupid.

Didn't make much difference to my feelings, though. I staved off the tears long enough to get the kids down for the night.

I cleaned up the kitchen with warm tears streaking down my face. Deep down inside, I knew Stelson didn't mean to be so rude, but he *did* hurl those mean words at me. And somebody wise once said: You can't unspeak words.

In the ten years I had known him and the nine we'd been married, I had seen him angry or grouchy after a hard day's work. He wasn't perfect. Everyone's entitled to a bad day here and there. And, of course, we had argued. But he had never insulted me or my intelligence. Never told me to basically get out of his face.

I didn't have the heart to lie in bed that night. I fumbled around in our room by the light of the hallway, looking for pajamas. Once I found them, I changed clothes in the guest bathroom and came back to the living room to watch television on the couch.

I threw a blanket over my legs and settled into several episodes of *The Golden Girls*, laughing at the re-runs as though I hadn't seen them all before.

Blanche, Rose, Dorothy, and Sophia. Friends for life. I wondered if Peaches and I would both outlive our husbands and move in together. Be roommates again, like we were in college. I would probably be Dorothy. Peaches would be Blanche without the sleeping around. Peaches was a flirtin' something before she got married, so I'd have to watch out for her.

We'd be single again. Kids grown. Grandkids grown, too. We'd take a cruise once a year, visit warm places for the winter. *Yeah. That would be fun.*

During the third episode, when I should have been quite sleepy, I felt a nudge to head to the prayer closet. Momma used to say that when you're all alone and you can't sleep at night, God's calling you to pray.

Only, I didn't want to pray. My feelings were hurt and I didn't want to go into the prayer closet and look at scriptures telling me not to take offense. I was offended already. Too late.

Plus, I was dirt tired. *Can we talk tomorrow, Lord?*

My phone buzzed from about ten feet behind me. Darn near made me jump out of my skin. If God had started texting people, that was gonna be all she wrote for me.

I shuffled to the kitchen island and read the message. From Stelson. *Where are you?*

I responded: *Living room.*

Coming back?

Maybe.

Sorry.

Against my feelings, against my will, I joined him in bed.

↬Chapter 21

Thank God for the frozen meals. They saved me from choking my husband and neglecting my children. Between Stelson's ongoing bad-attitude headache and running behind Seth and Zoe, I figured I'd be next for a migraine.

My prayer time, though productive by comforting me and buffering me in His love, still hadn't yielded an answer to my husband's health challenge. He had run through his prescription medications in a week and another bottle of Excedrin Migraine while we waited on the insurance company's approval of an appointment with a neurologist.

Peaches had decided that Stelson was suffering from a vitamin deficiency, and WebMD had me thinking he had a brain tumor. I put the whole thing on the back burner and went into survival mode because if I thought about it too much, I'd get discouraged on top of angry.

Keeping up with Seth's homework and finalizing plans for his fifth birthday party gave me enough to do anyway. One would think that, seeing as I was a stay-at-home mom (which I'd learned was abbreviated SAHM), I would have planned an elaborate shindig with a clown, a bouncy-house, some Pinterest party ideas, and a whole buncha hot dogs.

No. I didn't feel like cleaning up after a slew of kids. Chuck E. Cheese to the rescue. I had invitations sent home with several of his children's church buddies, along with my father and Jonathan's marathon-girl's son.

The very last person I told about the party was the birthday boy himself because he would have bugged me to death if I'd told him too far in advance.

With the cake and Seth's birthday gift in tow, we arrived at the pizza party half an hour early so I could meet with the hostess and scout out the area.

As the guests arrived, Stelson remained in one spot with Zoe at the main table while Seth and I ran around with his friends playing games.

Jonathan and marathon-girl, whom he introduced as Krista, arrived a few minutes after our starting time of three o'clock. She was short with an athletic build and a cute teeny-weeny afro. "Nice to meet you. Where's your son?"

"He's spending the weekend with his father," she said. Her thin grin said it all. She and the ex were obviously not friends.

"Awww...I'm sorry I didn't get to meet him, too."

"Maybe next time," Krista said.

"Well, come on over. Let me introduce you."

In doing the rounds, I labeled her Jonathan's "friend". He didn't correct me, so I figured it was accurate despite the Facebook status.

"And this is my husband, Stelson."

Krista continued to flash all thirty-two. "Hello."

Stelson's smile was more a grimace than a greeting. "Hi." No handshake, no nod. Only a blank 'Hi.'

He shouldn't have come to the party.

Daddy joined Stelson at his booth, relieving him of Zoe for a while. I tag-teamed with Jonathan, who took my place in the game of Skee-ball with Seth. Returning to our table, I found Stelson with his arms folded on the table, his head down. "Babe, do you want to leave? I can get Jonathan to bring me home."

"No," he flared, "I don't need you telling me what to do."

Unfortunately, my father's keen ears picked up on the nasty response. "She just asked you a question, man." Though Daddy had no business butting into ours, he'd only said what I wanted to say.

"You're right," Stelson smarted off. "The question was directed toward *me,* with all due respect. And I answered it."

"I couldn't care less if you respect me or not. But look like you slapped a little *funk* on your answer to Shondra, if you ask me," my father continued.

I could tell the two moms from church at the adjacent booth were trying hard to keep from turning around to watch my family unravel.

"Well, since nobody asked you—"

"Really?" I intervened. "This is Seth's birthday party, for crying out loud."

Stelson exhaled heavily. "It's too loud in here. I'm going to the car."

"What?" We weren't even close to the stage because I had requested an area far enough away to make the music bearable for Stelson.

He scooted out of the booth and walked toward the exit doors.

Daddy muttered to himself, "He betta watch how he talks to my daughter. She ain't no negro slave."

"Would you stop with the negro slaves, Daddy?"

"I'm gonna speak my mind. I knew it was just a matter of time before the *real* him came out. White folks are sneaky like that."

"I will not let you disrespect my husband." I stood up for Stelson's position even though he wasn't exactly on my good side.

"Well, I'm not gonna let him disrespect my daughter, either. You can put up with it if you want to, though I know me and your Momma raised you better than that. She'd be 'shamed to hear how he talked to you today. Downright ashamed."

Me with my emotional self, I stomped off to the restroom and holed myself up in a stall to get composed, keep from crying like a big forty-two-year-old baby. *Who does this?* By that point in life, I should have been well-versed in strapping on a mask to get through difficult moments. Save the melt-downs for later.

But this was my baby's fifth birthday party. One of the first ones he'd actually be able to remember. And Stelson wouldn't be a part of that memory, all because of some stupid headache and an argument with my father—which everybody knows is futile from the get-go.

Pull yourself together, Shondra! Get your game face and your big girl bloomers on.

With this smidgen of self-therapy, I was able to plaster a smile on my face and graciously answer the questions about Stelson, including Seth's. "Where's Daddy?"

"Oh, he wasn't feeling well," I replied casually.

"Migraine again?" Seth asked, his face growing long. He'd heard the medical term dozens of times by that point.

I nodded. "You go ahead and eat your pizza."

Zoe became the perfect distraction. She didn't want to be passed around—or at least that's what I told anyone who asked. "She has her days, you know?" I clung to her throughout the party, hoping people wouldn't see which one of us was holding on more tightly than the other.

Stelson left me the task of putting the kids to bed that night. *What else is new?*

"Did you have a good time at your party, Seth?" I rubbed his hair.

"Yeah. I wish Daddy could have stayed."

"I know." I tugged gently on my son's ear. "But don't worry about him. He'll be fine soon."

"Mommy, is Daddy down?"

"Down like what?"

"Like when it was in Ecc…leese…mastes?"

"Ecclesiastes?"

"Yes. When we had home church."

Seth amazed me with the odd things he remembered sometimes. "Yeah, I guess he is down."

"Then somebody's supposed to help him up, right?"

Ding! My heart took the punch. "Yes. Somebody is."

Seth pointed at me. "Is it you?"

"Yeah. I guess it is."

"Okay. Thanks, Mommy."

"Mmm hmm."

Father, God, I don't know what's going on with my husband's head, and neither does the doctor who was supposedly a specialist. But You know what's wrong. Please heal my husband. Otherwise, I don't know how we're going to go on with all this arguing. I'm trying to remember that he is under duress. In pain. It's hard, though. Protect my heart, too, from bitterness.

Initially, I had wanted to go to the women's fellowship so that I could meet other women. Now, I was going to preserve my sanity. The fellowship was from nine until noon, but the "Mommy's Day Out" childcare went until three, which meant I had some hours to myself before Seth's school released, before Stelson got home.

He had said the headaches were decreasing in intensity, but I wasn't sure if he was just telling me that so I wouldn't worry or if he really meant it. Honestly, I didn't know what to think about the things that came out of my husband's mouth anymore. I was beginning to wonder if, maybe, Daddy had been really nice to Momma for a long time before he turned into a sourpuss. Maybe I had done what so many women do: married a man just like the one who'd raised me.

God forbid. Daddy was hardly talking to me after Seth's birthday party. Given all the tension in the Brown household, I was almost glad to be on non-speaking terms with my father. Less drama for me. We were both content with Jonathan as a go-between, transporting the meals from my kitchen to Daddy's.

I know the Lord says to honor our parents. He also instructed married people to cleave to one another. I wasn't sure how to do both when they were pulling me in different directions.

A break with a bunch of other SAHMs and retired women would do me fine. Followed by a massage would be even better.

After signing Zoe into childcare, I registered at the sign-in table. The young woman who was attending the table asked, "Are you a member here?"

"Yes."

"Is there any particular group you'd like to sit with?"

"Umm...no. I mean, what are the group types?"

She smiled graciously. "Well, there are moms with small children and older, more seasoned women, women who have certain things or interests in common," she listed.

Given the fact that I was often the oldest one in the bunch of pre-schooler moms, I wasn't trying to join a group where I would feel the pressure of inadvertently mentoring somebody ten years younger than me. No, I wasn't coming to this fellowship to give. I needed to be the baby in the group. "I'd like to sit with some older women, please."

The hostess led me to table four. And, just as I'd requested, everybody there had at least one swath of gray hair, which did my heart good. *Thank You, Father.*

The room was set up with roughly twelve round tables. Each table was covered with pastel-colored cloths and a centerpiece with silk flowers. This space doubled as a fellowship hall, so it had a homey-feeling, perfect for receptions and small dinners.

"I need thee, oh, I need thee," we sang at our tables. The first chorus activated my water-works. When I was a little girl, I used to hate when they sang those slow, long, drawn-out songs with the same ten words repeated over and over again. Songs like "Yes"—which only has one word, actually—and "I say yes to my Lord."

This song comforted me now. "I need you, Lord. I need you, Lord!" If He didn't help me, there *was* no help. "I neeeeeed you, Lord!"

Someone tapped my arm and passed me a tissue. "Have your way. Have your waaa-aay."

I could have sang that song for hours. And I did, actually, in my heart. The humility of petition rested on me all through the morning's Bible study. One by one, the women introduced themselves to me: Hattie, Beverly, Janice, Linda, and Doris. Linda had been at the picnic and remembered praying for Seth's saga. The rest of the women recalled the news report or the next day, when our congregation rejoiced together.

"Your son is a handsome one," Janice said, her smooth brown skin looking like it might have belonged to someone my age. Were it not for the wispy silver hair and the cat glasses, she might have fooled somebody.

"Thank you. He's a handful."

"Well, enjoy him now because he'll be a man before you know it," Hattie laughed.

I wished I had a quarter for every time somebody told me my children's childhood would flash by. Perhaps it would feel "fast" ten or twenty years down the line, but from my vantage point, there was no end in sight to the grind.

Miss Hattie, who was clearly the leader by virtue of her white binder, handled some administrative business. She collected donations for the fellowship coordinator's birthday gift, then sent a sympathy card for a bereaved family around the table for everyone to sign.

We discussed plans for a potluck. I took the easy route—drinks and plastic ware. If I couldn't freeze it, I wasn't trying to hear it right about then.

Our speaker, introduced as Sister Olivia Windham, was a tiny, short woman with long, black wavy hair braided into a ponytail that landed at her behind. I didn't recognize her from our church.

When she took the podium, I expected to hear a mousey voice. She looked like she was better suited for teaching nice, sweet topics like gardening and caring for kittens.

But when she opened her mouth, bay-bee, I knew it was on.

"The hour has come to hear the Word of God. I command the voice of the enemy to be silent in the name of Jesus. Cease from distraction. Spirit of the living God, manifest Yourself in our presence today. Teach us, guide us, lead us and comfort us, as Jesus promised You would. Your Word is established. You gave the prophecy in Ezekiel that You would put Your Spirit in us and cause us to walk in Your statutes and keep Your ways. Abba, Father, we agree with You. We agree. Let all God's people say…"

"Amen."

I sat completely engrossed in her presence. Arrested by this contrast of a little woman with a big message on intercessory prayer. As she read from the Word, I wrote the scripture references furiously. Simultaneously, the Lord wrote this lesson directly on my heart. Every time she admonished us to "intercede" the word bounced around inside me like a pinball machine. *Intercede. Intercede. Intercede.*

"Don't let the enemy come in and steal your children. Kill your family. Destroy your joy. According to John 10:10, that's all he comes to do. He's not here to hurt your feelings, make you sad and angry. That's just the tip of the iceberg. Honey, his goal is to *kill* you. Don't play with him. Fight him. Stand up to him. Defeat him. The victory belongs to God's people!"

She pumped me so full of the Word, I was ready to drop-kick the enemy. How dare he try to come in and destroy my family? Take my husband's health? Take my children's good memories of their father? *I don't think so!*

After the lesson, I hopped up on my feet and applauded to thank her for being a vessel for the message, as did most of the women gathered.

We were instructed to have a discussion among the people at our table, centered on questions which had already been distributed to the group facilitators. "Glory to God. Bless His name." Hattie took a second to settle down enough to read the first one aloud. "Okay. Mmmm mmm *mmm*. She sure can preach. Let's start with question number one. What is the enemy trying to steal from you?"

"My peace," from Beverly.

"My money," Janice added.

Since I was near the center, I spoke up. "My family's joy and my husband's health."

"You don't say?" Hattie probed. "Well, we sure can't have that happening. What's the matter with your husband?"

Well, I did want to be the baby in the group. And the baby does get all the attention. "Lately, he's been having terrible headaches. He's been extremely cranky. Mean. But I know it's because he's in pain."

"Mmm hmm. Wonder is he...does he have any, you know, *sin* in his life," Linda suspected. "You know, sometimes, we get sick because of our *own* fault."

What in the world?

A chorus of "mmm-hmmms" spread around the table. I looked to my left. My right. Heads nodding in agreement.

"Well, I mean. My husband is not perfect, but he's—"

"Step one is a good soul-cleaning. We can't expect God to step in and clean up when we've been sinning," Hattie added. "That's what I told my sister. Doctor told her she had cancer. I told her the first thing she needed to do was forgive her ex-husband, else she wasn't gonna ever get better. She never did. Not even on her death bed. So now, before I pray, I tell people to get right with God first 'cause ain't no need in us praying when somebody *want* to stay sick."

"Yep," Doris cosigned. Then added, "Healing starts at home first. And you got to build up your faith, too."

Did we all hear the same message?

"Most definitely," Beverly echoed. "Without faith, it's impossible to please the Lord. You can't expect a *thing* from God without faith and obedience!"

"And a clean heart," Janice piled it on.

Awkwardly, I questioned, "Umm…Jesus didn't tell people they had to be perfect before He healed them."

"But what did He tell them afterward? Go and sin no more!" Beverly said.

"Yes. *After*, and—"

"You just keep on living," Hattie interrupted me. "You'll see. People that ain't livin' right can't lay claim to the promises of God. Period. He will *not* be mocked. Every woman at this table done lost somebody who wouldn't turn it all over to God."

"Mmm hmmm."

I might as well have gone to a prayer meeting with my father, with all this negativity. Thank God I knew enough of the Word to recognize when I was sitting at a table full of people who had more faith in their experiences than the Word.

I had to shut them out. Completely.

When it came time for us to pray as a table, Hattie asked the Lord to "do Your will" in my husband's life. "Lord, we know You can heal him. But like the Hebrew boys said, even if you don't, we'll still praise you."

Note to self: Do not sit at table four again.

I was so angry and disappointed; I didn't even want to come back to the church again to get my baby. I checked Zoe out of the nursery and walked to the parking lot. As I was securing her in the car seat, someone's shadow shaded me from behind. "I'm sorry. I'll be out of your way in just a second."

"Oh, no rush."

Sister Windham's distinct, heavy voice caught my attention. Up close and in person, she had an even more inviting demeanor than when she'd been teaching.

"Oh my goodness, you blessed me so much today," I straightened to greet her.

"God bless you, sweetheart," she reached for a hug.

She barely reached my neckline, and yet the love in her embrace overwhelmed me. "I hope you don't mind, but could you pray for my husband?"

She stepped back. "Surely. What's going on?"

"He's got migraine headaches. They just came out of nowhere. I mean, my husband is healthy, he runs, he doesn't eat a bunch of junk. We've been to a couple of doctors but they don't really know what the problem is."

"Well, honey, let's get one thing straight. Fitness and health is two different things. Fitness is about your body in the natural realm. But prosperous *health* comes from life in Christ. Don't confuse the two."

She didn't have to worry about me confusing the *two*. I, for *one*, was confused enough. I was sure she'd said something profound, but it escaped me.

"It's just that, normally, he's a strong, godly man. Lately, he's…miserable," I shared.

Her eyes softened. "And so are you, I bet."

"Yes, ma'am."

"I know by the Spirit—you're a good wife. A good mother." She waved at Zoe.

"Do you think, maybe, my husband is…doing something wrong?"

"You don't have to do anything wrong to be the target of an attack. A lot of Christians forget—we do have an enemy in the land. But don't let that worry you. We've been given power over Him through Christ. You understand?"

"Yes, ma'am."

"What's your husband's name?"

"Stelson Brown. Thank you."

I backed away so she could pass.

"Where are you going?" she asked.

"I was getting into my car so you can get into yours," I laughed slightly.

"Well, you asked me to pray, didn't you?"

"Yes." I was thinking she'd write his name on a prayer list and get to him later.

"Let's touch and agree *now*." She offered her spindly hands. This woman brought my husband, his doctors, me, our children, our jobs, and the strife from my family—which I hadn't mentioned to her—before the Lord. She spoke healing and peace over us. And then she prayed for more patience for me. Matter of fact, she spent most of the time praying on me, which came as a surprise. *Why are we praying on me?*

"Fill her with more love, Lord. Let her be slow to anger, quick to forgive. Let her not look to the left or to the right, Abba Father. Gird her up in Your strength."

The comfort in her touch was pure love. Almost as good as if I was standing in agreement with Momma. In a way, I was—we were—because I knew Christ was in our midst.

"Amen and it is so."

"It is so."

I was hoping that she'd ask me for my phone number or some way to keep in touch with her. But the finality of her prayer, "it is so" put a period at the end of this situation, like when Jesus told the ten lepers to go show themselves clean, and they were healed as they went. It was a done deal from the moment He spoke it.

This lady had believed she'd received what she had prayed.

And so did I. For a while anyway.

Chapter 22 ∂

Stelson

Stelson had no business driving on an expressway and he knew it, which was why he took the back roads to work. He could stomach the ride at 40 miles per hour much better than 70 or 80.

When he arrived at work, he parked as close as possible to the elevators. Walking had become a chore. Though no one seemed to notice him leaning, he felt off-balance when he took more than five steps.

After the previous day's blow-up with Cooper and Helen, Stelson wondered if he should bother walking into the office at all today.

They had been right, however, about how he'd dropped the ball by not returning messages. But Stelson didn't appreciate his partner and his secretary teaming up on him, holding a meeting to get to the bottom of what Cooper had called "a miscommunication".

The most important people in his life were turning out to be his worst allies through this illness, especially LaShondra. Instead of being there for him, offering compassion, she was turning cold and pulling away.

Can't blame her, though. Especially since he hadn't told her the whole truth. For all she knew, he had a bad headache.

And God wasn't saying much. Though he still believed the Word, what he needed more than anything was a friend.

Stelson texted Cooper: *Not coming in today.*

Cooper replied: *Good idea. I'll handle things. Take a few days off.*

Couldn't have come at a better time. Stelson left the garage and wandered around the city for a while, thankful for the overcast skies hiding the sun's glaring rays. The only quiet place that came to mind was a library. He stopped at the local branch, brought in his laptop and found an unoccupied corner.

Wish I could sleep here.

For probably the tenth time in a week, he searched online for hints about his condition. Individually, his symptoms were clearly linked to specific diagnoses. But taken altogether, he could have just about anything.

God, You have to show me.

His phone vibrated. Jim Moore's name flashed across the screen. Stelson rejected the call, as he'd done to all other calls from church members recently. All they wanted to do was pray and tell him to find the bright side.

Praying was always in order, Stelson knew, but right now, he was too discombobulated, too disoriented to pray. Besides, the Lord knew he was sick. If He didn't intervene, it wouldn't be because Stelson hadn't told Him already.

In a desperate attempt to find his own cure, Stelson Binged "multiple symptoms" and "misdiagnosed" which led him to a site called "HoldMyHand." On a whim, he scrolled through the message board topics. *Don't want to tell my wife, No one understands, Just want to go to sleep and wake up when this disease is over, Still don't know what's wrong with me.*

He could have written any one of those posts.

Finally, he'd found people who were walking in his shoes.

Chapter 23 ৵

"Hi, LaShondra. I'm so sorry to call you in the middle of the day. I know you're busy and all," Helen apologized.

"Is everything okay?" I could count on one hand the number of times his secretary had called on my cell phone.

"Yes. Everything's fine. Sort of. I have Mr. Cooper on the line. He'd like to speak to you if you have time."

"Certainly."

Talking to Cooper was even rarer than talking to Helen. Aside from the company Christmas party, Stelson's business partner and I didn't communicate.

"LaShondra," he started, "thank you for taking my call."

"No problem. How can I help you?"

He paused. "We've noticed some changes in Stelson around the office as of late. I'm wondering if you can give us any insight. Is he well?"

How could I answer that question without damaging my husband's professional reputation? I dodged him. "What kinds of changes?"

"All I can say is that he's not himself," Cooper summarized.

I understood his vague verbiage to mean that he wasn't at liberty to discuss my husband's work performance with me. From my conversations with Peaches, I knew that there were laws against divulging information about co-workers, even in a partnership.

"Oh. I. Yes. Stelson has been under a tremendous amount of stress," I excused my husband's behavior. "As you may know, I've taken a leave of absence. With our two kids and taking care of my father...we've both been juggling a lot." I slathered it on, though none of those reasons seemed weighty enough to explain the abrupt decline in my husband's attitude.

"I see. Has he been to a doctor?"

"Yes."

"Uh huh," Cooper huffed. "Well, I've told him he should take a few days off."

No! I don't want him home! You keep him!

"If there's anything I can do to help him, please let me know," Cooper said.

"Thanks for calling."

The garage door squeaked open. When Stelson walked through the door, I looked up from the row of seasoned chicken and acted surprised to see him. "Hey, babe. To what do we owe the pleasure of seeing you this early?"

"Got finished. Came home."

Oh, he wants to lie to me now? "Really?"

He answered with a malicious glare.

Zoe beat on her high chair for her father's attention, but he walked right past her to our bedroom. My baby's bottom lip poked out. Her beautiful smile turned upside down as she processed what had just happened.

"It's okay, Zoe," I cooed, picking her up and rocking her until she seemed to forget. She was already sleepy, so nap time came easy.

Once Zoe was snoozing in her playpen, I hopped on the internet. There was no way my kids and I were going to suffer because my husband could not manage his pain. Granted, I'd never had a migraine, but I knew people who worked with headaches and lupus and shingles and in between cancer treatments. They got up and went to work every day and they didn't snap people's heads off. They learned how to cope. "I will not, not, not let the enemy steal my joy," I chanted.

The question came from inside: *Who is the enemy?*

My initial thought, which I know the Lord heard, was "Stelson".

I tried to change my answer to something spiritually correct.

His loving chastisement stilled my hands on the laptop keys. What exactly was I looking up on the internet anyhow? A way to stop my husband from being mean? Ten steps to ignoring your spouse? How to live a parallel life in the same house?

"I don't know, God." Giving sound to my confusion led me to the prayer closet like a puppy with his tail between his legs. I knew better than to go to Google before going to God. Why was I acting so brand new? How could I have forgotten so quickly that we were under spiritual attack?

Here I am, God. Let's whip this thing.

Wrapped up in His Word and His love, I learned the first rule of spiritual warfare real quick: The war is not against people.

Fresh from the prayer closet, I finished dousing the chicken, put it in the oven to cook, and then made Stelson a sandwich.

He was sitting up in bed reading his Bible. He had kicked his shoes off, but his clothes were still intact.

"I brought you something."

He took the plate of food. Set it on the bed. Without veering from the book, he said, "Thank you."

Since he hadn't said anything smart, I crawled in bed next to him and bundled myself against his right side. "Baby, I'm praying for you."

"I need it."

My flesh wanted to ruin the moment: to ask him if there was any way he could stop acting bully-ish and let him know how much he had hurt my feelings over the past weeks.

I glanced down and noticed that my husband was reading from the Psalms. Books of woe and lamenting written by David when he felt most neglected by God.

No, this wasn't the time to start fussing and demanding improvement. I sat there next to my husband and wept for him, for us, while holding on to his arm.

He rubbed my forearm. "It's going to be all right."

"I know. It's hard watching you go through this, though."

"I'm better this week than I was last week," he confessed.

"And you'll be better than this next week," I prophesied over my husband. "By His stripes, you were healed."

"Amen."

The words from my mouth to his ears became our truth the next week. Stelson reported less intense headaches and his attitude showed marked improvement. I should have been shouting for joy, but I wasn't.

I was still angry. Hurt. Stelson did render a two-second apology and thank me for nursing him during his bout with migraines. My feelings, however, were not satisfied. I knew Stelson wasn't perfect and we had both done things and said words we recanted later.

This was bigger than me, though. He'd been rude to our kids, my father and our friends. And he'd *lied* to me. I couldn't just dismiss all this behind migraine headaches. These were *character* issues lying dormant inside my husband before this sickness brought out the worst in him.

Maybe the ladies at table four were right after all. Maybe my husband *was* doing something wrong that I knew nothing about, which the Lord wanted to bring to light. Maybe his sudden changes were not as sudden as I thought they were. Had I been blinded by love? So busy working and taking care of the kids that I failed to see the signs? For all I knew, he could be having an affair and I'd be clueless. All those late nights at work. "Business" trips. *Hmph.*

I didn't put anything past him, and I certainly wasn't going to give him an opportunity to trample on my heart again in the future, headaches or not.

"Babe, can you take my shirts to the cleaners today?" Stelson asked as he repositioned his laptop case on his shoulder, preparing to leave.

"Got it," I sang to cover myself.

He pinched my waist and kissed me. "See you this evening. Seven-ish."

"Got it."

I must have spoken a little too sharply because he asked, "Are you okay?"

"Yeah, I'm fine," I nodded rapidly and smiled.

Stelson peered, like he wanted to ask another question, but he didn't. "I love you."

"Love you, too."

My prayer time was short, but not sweet at all because I was getting tired of God giving me all this information about *me*. What about Stelson? What about the way he'd acted? What about the fact that I didn't want to find myself stuck-out, without a job should my husband ever start trippin' again?

My Momma raised a Christian, but she didn't raise no fool.

As soon as Zoe's first naptime came, I was on the internet searching through my employer's website to see if there were open slots listed for principals or even in the curriculum office. I called Terrie Meunse, a fellow administrator with whom I'd taken several graduate level classes. We were study buddies and we'd both risen in the ranks with Plainview School District over the years. She worked at the central office now.

"Hey, Terrie, thanks for taking my call. How are you?"

"Not as good as you, obviously," she teased. "Wishing I was home, too!"

"Girl, I'm tryin' to get back in the mix after the semester, if I can. You know of anybody leaving?"

She hummed, "Mmmmm. I think Ms. Adams, over at Lakeview, may be pregnant. But she had a miscarriage with the first one. You know how that goes."

It seemed heartless to be discussing someone's infertility issues so trivially, seeing as Stelson and I had wandered through our own barren years when we first married. "I hope she makes it to term this time."

"Yeah. But other than Adams, I can't think of anyone. Who took your spot at the high school?"

"We hired a lady named Natalie Lockhart-Gomez."

"She's from the valley, right?"

"Yeah."

"I heard she was a pretty good administrator down there," Terrie said. "Thanks for the memo."

"But you're great, too!" Terrie quickly recovered. "Anyway, I'll keep an eye out for you and let you know if I see any vacancies coming up."

"Thanks. I appreciate it."

There. I had done it. I'd put the wheels in motion to get my life back on track. I felt better already knowing that if push ever came to shove in this marriage, my kids and I could survive.

Since I'd crafted an escape hatch for me and mine actually improved my attitude. Since I didn't envision myself depending on Stelson for my livelihood much longer, I figured I would not be as vulnerable to the possibility of him acting the fool.

Life went back to my new normal. Taking care of the kids, the household and Stelson. Praying in my silent space every morning. Trying to make sure Daddy didn't turn Seth into a Black Panther.

I still loved Stelson. He still loved me. But I had roped off a corner of my heart. Just in case.

Chapter 24 ❧

When the headaches came back a few months later, Stelson didn't tell me. He didn't *have* to. Walking past me and the kids without acknowledging us when he came in from work was all the clue I needed. Not to mention he'd started texting me rather than returning phone calls.

Ain't this somethin'?

I sent Terrie an email the week before Christmas break, reminding her to keep me in the loop. My in-laws usually joined us for Thanksgiving, but he had told his mother about the headaches and she'd decided it best not to come up this time around. Normally, I would have welcomed a nice, quiet Thanksgiving at home. The last thing I wanted this holiday, however, was some alone time with my five year old, my 9 month old, and my grouchy husband.

Attending church on Sundays gave me a slight reprieve; although we couldn't sit in our regular spots because Stelson needed to put distance between himself and the loud speakers at the front of the sanctuary.

The one thing I had to look forward to for Christmas was Peaches and her family coming home. Their flight arrived on the twenty-third so I'd had plenty of time to get fed up with the Brown household between Seth's school break and Stelson's decreased business hours due to the holiday.

On the way to Peaches' parents' house, I darn-near gave Stelson a lecture about how to behave. Told him if he couldn't act cordial, I didn't want him to come.

"You think I'm a heathen?" he defended himself.

"No. I just...don't want another argument."

"What do you think you're starting right now?" he questioned.

I sighed. I was tired of going in circles with this man. He knew he wasn't himself, and yet he expected everyone else to adjust their expectations about normal, everyday common courtesy due to his frequent headaches.

"All I'm saying is, if you are in too much pain and you don't think you'll be good company, you shouldn't go."

"If I stayed home with every headache, I'd never leave the house."

We certainly can't have that happening, buddy.

We had gone to another doctor who'd tested for allergies. Another one tested for pinched nerves. All to no avail. After the third specialist, we were referred to a psychiatrist to find out if Stelson's problem was psychosomatic.

He had been incensed. Insulted that doctors were insinuating the pain was all in his head, mind over matter.

After seeing all those physicians, I wasn't sure what I believed anymore. I knew Stelson was hurting physically. But with so many physical causes ruled out, perhaps the root was psychological. I didn't want to think that maybe my husband was having a nervous breakdown. And yet his attitude…

Christmas Eve was the first time I'd seen my best friend in almost three years. We held on to one another for dear life. Or at least I did. "Girl, girl, girl! I could kiss you!"

"Don't get carried away," she joked.

While Peaches and I continued to hug, our husbands shook hands. After properly greeting Peaches' parents, Seth took off running toward the sound of all the other children in the house and with all of Peaches' kids plus nieces and nephews, there were plenty.

Zoe squirmed to get out of Stelson's arms and lean over to Momma Miller's thick arms. She smothered our daughter with kisses and took her to the kitchen where Zoe was sure to be passed around from aunt to aunt. She'd gotten more social since learning to crawl.

Peaches' husband, Quinn, almost didn't make the trip. He had fractured his ankle in a 3-on-3 basketball tournament at their church and undergone emergency surgery the week before. For some reason, I almost hoped Quinn would be as cranky as Stelson. I guess, then, Peaches and I could have vented together.

However, Quinn showed no signs of ill temper. His bright smile portrayed a man as sweet and kind as my husband used to be. "Hey, LaShondra."

"Hey, Quinn. So good to see you again. I see you've been keeping my girl busy in Philadelphia." I raised an eyebrow. "I hardly ever get to speak to her."

"You, too?"

Peaches poked him in the side, but she might as well have been poking me. Watching their playful interaction reminded me of how Stelson and I were, once upon a time. We used to smile. Touch. Enjoy each other's company.

"We've got the game on back here," Quinn invited Stelson to join the menfolk.

"Sure thing." Stelson followed as Quinn hobbled along.

Peaches and I made a round through the house. The aroma of the women's cooking wafted through every square inch. Two televisions two rooms apart competed for center stage as the menfolk watched sports and the teenagers danced to gospel music videos. Peaches' smallest children weren't so small any more. She introduced me to them and I gushed over them, though they didn't recognize me.

I spoke to all her family members, including aunts, uncles, and cousins I hadn't seen since Peaches' wedding. Peaches' oldest son, Eric, who also happened to be my godson, was visiting his biological father. I'd have to wait until later to catch up with him, *if* he was so inclined. Seventeen-year-old boys aren't always fond of having their cheeks pinched.

Peaches and I ended up back in the front parlor. Finally, we were alone. "Girl, you look sooooo good," I complimented and squeezed her again. Her short, coily hair was the perfect accent to the sharp angles of her face. Her well-moisturized, deep cocoa skin reflected slivers of light from her gold and rhinestone earrings. The added touch of gloss made her lips go "pop" and my self-esteem go "poop". Thankfully, *one* of us was keeping herself together. For once, I felt like the unkempt one.

"Having babies back-to-back ain't no joke. They stole all my poor little calcium. I got three crowns. Can you tell?" She lifted her top lip with her fingers.

I inspected her teeth, on my toes, then dipping to observe from below. "They look real to me."

"Good," she exhaled. "I knew *you* would tell the truth."

"Well, the guys are watching a game. The kids are fine. Whatcha wanna do?"

I thought she'd never ask. "Get away from everybody, for real."

Peaches rubbed my arm as her face knotted in concern. "I hear you, Shondra. Let me say bye to Momma."

As a courtesy, I texted Stelson to let him know we were leaving the house.

Peaches grabbed her purse and we were off. "Where to?" she asked, starting the ignition in their rental SUV.

"Anywhere with adults. No sing-along songs, no baby-changing stations," I demanded.

She stared me down. "What? You wanna go to happy hour?"

"If I drank, I would *so* be there," I said.

She threw the car in reverse. "I gotcha. How about age twelve and over?"

"That'll work."

"Cool. I was planning to go to this place with Quinn, but since he's on crutches, he's out. You're in. But don't ask me any questions until we get there."

"I'm down for an adventure." Wherever she was taking me had to be better than where I'd been for the previous weeks, so I didn't ask any questions.

"How's your Daddy?" she asked.

"Same old. Still trying to make Seth appreciate his African descendants."

Peaches laughed. "What, exactly, is Daddy Smith doing?"

"Girl, teaching him negro hymns and spirituals. Buying him black action figures," I told her.

"Shoot, I can't find black action figures for my boys. Where's he getting them from?"

"Who knows? Probably some place he delivered to. I don't have a problem with Daddy introducing Seth to his black heritage. But we have to watch him so the message doesn't turn hateful and make Seth feel like he's fighting an uphill battle."

"Well, he will be," Peaches sided with Daddy.

"I get that, but does he need to start fighting it at five? I mean, dang, can he please have an innocent childhood first?"

She tilted her head. "I guess."

"When did you have the black talk with Eric?"

She bit her bottom lip. "Hmm. I guess shortly after he was diagnosed with dyslexia. I just laid everything on the table for him. You've got a reading disability, you're black—you're going to have it hard, dude. But you can make it. And that's exactly what he's done. He's graduating with honors, getting ready for college."

"Yeah. Eric's amazing. You done good, girl," I congratulated her.

She streamlined onto I-35 and then I-75, taking us into north Dallas. We talked about trivial things and laughed like sixteen year olds again. I wanted to tell her how angry I was with Stelson, but I didn't want to ruin her trip home. Ruin our time together. So I shoved all of my problems aside, hoping to savor every moment with my best friend.

When she parked outside of a place with bright, colorful lettering—JUMPUP!—on the outside of the building, I protested. "I said no kids tonight!"

"There are children present. But there will not be anyone under the age of twelve in our dodgeball game tonight."

"Dodgeball?"

"Yes. Dodgeball. On trampolines." She pumped her eyebrows up and down.

My word, what has she gotten me into?

The gym-like atmosphere, noisy and energetic, took ten years off my age from the start. Reminded me of my high school days, when life was carefree and I had an adventure ahead of me. Hopeful, joyous, giddy with anticipation.

There was a 12-and-older game already in progress, which gave me an opportunity to scope out our strategy before we entered the arena while Peaches signed us up.

These grown-ups were serious. Way too serious.

"You watchin'?" Peaches asked when she returned, her eyes as much glued to the action as mine.

"Yeah. Looks like you need to just keep bouncing at all times. Always a moving target," I surmised, studying the gray-haired gentleman who hadn't been hit the whole time. He was good. I hoped he wouldn't play again because I didn't want to hurt an old man.

The game's timer fizzled down to five minutes. "It's time," Peaches ordered.

We stuffed our shoes and purses into a cubby. She locked it and safety-pinned the key on her shirt. "Let's do this." We fist-bumped and gathered near the entrance of the giant trampolines, where a teenager explained the rules and safety precautions. No sitting. No climbing on the walls, no aiming at the head, etc. We also had to sign waivers releasing the facility from liability for any medical mishaps we might incur.

Six other people—including two noticeably attractive African-American men—joined our group. They were somewhat younger, dark-skinned, probably brothers, judging from their matching dimples. One of them looked up from his paperwork and smiled at me.

I smiled back with far more toothage than I'd consciously intended to display.

And then it was time for our game. The older man was still in there. On the other side. Looking like he wanted to smite us with a big, red ball.

Again, the employee reminded us of the rules. He gave four balls to each team of eight and pointed out a general "time out" area where we could recuperate when necessary.

The timer started, and the first thing I felt was rubber against my arm. *No he didn't!* That elderly man got me! One of the handsome brothers avenged me immediately, throwing his ball hard across the rows of trampolines. Our nemesis dodged, however.

"Dang! I missed him!" the brother hissed.

"Next time," I encouraged him.

I bounced over to Peaches. She caught one of the balls and managed to bop a librarian-looking lady square on her behind.

"Yes!" I screamed. A second later, my hip got hit.

"Keep bouncing," Peaches reminded me. "Moving target."

Honestly, I didn't care to hit anybody. I was just doing my best to stay mobile and dodge the balls coming at me. I pretty much used my teammates as shields and bounced like crazy, but it was fun jumping higher and higher with everything in me.

As children, Jonathan and I had begged our parents for either a trampoline or a pool. All we got was a swing set. It didn't even have a slide. Daddy told us if we weren't grateful for what we had, he'd take it down and give it to someone else.

My brother and I had joked that Daddy could never make good on the threat since the poles were cemented into the ground. That was Daddy for ya. All bark and no bite. I hoped Seth would soon learn to take what his grandfather said with a grain of salt while remaining respectful.

Bam! "Ow!" I hollered as the rubber bounced off my upper shoulder.

"Hey! No aiming at the head!" my self-appointed guardian hollered at the other side.

He bounced over to me. "You all right, my sister?"

"Yeah. I'm fine."

"I can see you're *fine*. But are you *okay*?" he flirted.

"You know that line is retired, right?" I said.

We both laughed. Then a ball hit him in the back. "Aw, man!" He turned around and fired at our opponents, nailing one on the hip.

I found myself admiring the view. His behind, to be exact. Stelson was pretty flat, as was just about every white person I knew. Not that I went around staring at people's tushes…I'm just saying.

"Hey!" Peaches called to me. "Pay attention! You're slacking!"

Our game ended with no clear winning side from what I could tell, and I had a pretty good viewpoint from behind the action. Peaches and I bounced out of our cage, followed by three more of our teammates who had only signed up for one round, I guessed.

The guy who'd been helping me, per se, saluted me and then left us alone.

And the weirdest thing happened: I was sad. Genuinely sad that he was leaving without so much as a good-bye. He didn't try to sit next to Peaches and me while we tied our shoes. Didn't try to ask for my number, though I would have turned him down. But still...he didn't try.

I suppose that made him a decent man, one who respected the wedding band on my finger.

I am married, I reminded myself.

Peaches and I found a booth at the food court and ordered the greasiest, best-tasting concession stand food. She got nachos, I had a corn dog with fries.

She blessed the food and went in on me. "Okay. We gotta talk. You were way too happy about that man—all up in his face, I'm just sayin'. What's up with you and Stelson?"

I dipped my corn dog in a pool of mustard and chewed slowly while weighing my words. It was nearly impossible for me to lie to Peaches. How could I be honest without throwing my husband under the bus? *Show me, Lord.*

"Spill it," she commanded.

I waited, though. Chewed my food carefully. I even pretended I was chewing when there was nothing in my mouth while Peaches sat staring at me with an unflinching expression.

"Okay. We've hit a rough patch."

"How rough?"

"Rough enough for me to be excited when another man pays attention to me, obviously," I volunteered myself for the impending cross-examination.

"What about intimacy?"

"Nilch. And why do you always have to ask about our sex life?" I asked.

She explained, "Because you can gauge what's going on in a marriage by what's going on in the bedroom. Huge parallels."

"I see."

"So what's the plan?"

"What plan?"

She slapped the table. "The plan for fixing the problem? Hello! You can't just let the enemy walk up in your house and snatch your family from you."

Without knowing, Peaches had reiterated what the speaker at the women's fellowship preached and what God Himself had whispered inside me. Why was it taking yet another person to help me see the light?

Speak, Lord. Put me in remembrance of Your Word.

"I don't know exactly what to do. I've prayed for him. I've tolerated him. The headaches went away, but now they're back and he's out of his mind again. I've been writing him "sick man" passes because I realize these are extenuating circumstances, but the stack of passes is almost gone. He's about to see a side of LaShondra Smith he's never seen, either."

"I doubt that. I've seen you go off around Stelson. It was not pretty," she smacked. "Does Six Flags ring a bell?"

"You did *not* go there." Yes, she did, and yes I did go all in on an employee. First of all, it was a hot day. We had no business outside trying to have a double date to begin with. When I finally got the Sprite I'd waited almost fifteen minutes in line to receive, it was flat. So I very politely placed the cup on the counter and said, "Could you get me another one? This one has no carbonation."

This—well, I don't want to call anybody out of their name—young lady took a sip of my drink from my very own straw, placed it back on the counter, slid it toward me and said, "Tastes fine to me."

I can't think of anybody who wouldn't have had a hissy fit, Peaches included. "What happened at Six Flags…she had it coming."

"How you figure she had a cold drink thrown in her face *coming?*"

"You don't take a drink out of somebody's straw and then expect them to drink after you," I laughed. "She was nasty."

Peaches dropped her head in laughter. "You're right. I would have done it if you hadn't. Gosh…we were so young and hot-headed back then."

"Speak for yourself. Six Flags was an isolated incident for me." I clutched my imaginary pearls.

Peaches rolled her eyes. "Please. Everyone has their breaking point.

Maybe Stelson is at his or pretty darn close. The last thing he needs is you walking away."

"I'm not crazy. I'm not going to leave him. We're in this for better or for worse, right?"

"You don't have to *leave* to leave. The same way you don't have to actually mess around to have an affair, like you did with old boy tonight," she accused.

"I did not have a mental affair with him!"

"Oh, guilty as charged! Smilin' in his face. Checking out his behind," she recalled correctly.

"I plead the fifth."

Peaches smacked her lips. "And I'll plead *the blood* for you."

"Thank you," was the only fitting response.

Against all common sense, we made a mad dash to the mall for last-minute Christmas gifts. I had finished shopping for the kids but still had Jonathan on my list, though I knew he never expected anything.

I asked Peaches if she thought I should get his girlfriend or her son something.

"Not until she gets a ring from Jonathan," Peaches replied.

"You know what? I'm gon' stop talkin' to you."

Chapter 25 ❧

Peaches and I re-enacted our Celie and Nettie patty-cake good-bye. "Me and you, us never part..."

Momma Miller cackled, same as always. She reluctantly returned Zoe to me. "This one here is a sweetheart. You can bring her over any time."

"Thank you."

"She got your Momma's nose, too," Peaches' mother noted. "Wouldn't be surprised if she grows up to be her spittin' image. Beautiful woman."

"I appreciate it," I struggled to reply. Holidays and birthdays without Momma were the hardest.

Stelson bundled up Seth as we headed out the door wishing everyone a Merry Christmas. He seemed pleasant enough. I'd learned to watch his jawline for a hint of his pain level. The headaches must have given him a reprieve.

However, I watched his jaw clench when we turned into the dusk sun for our ride home. He stopped the car while he searched the center console for the pair of shades which—*uh oh!*—I had removed from the car when I took it to be washed the previous Monday.

"Who moved my shades?"

"I did. I'm so sorry, honey. I meant to put them back—"

"This is freakin' ridiculous," he spouted off.

"Oooooooh!" Seth sang from the back seat. "Daddy, you said a bad word!"

Stelson qualified, "It's not *exactly* a—"

"Yes. It *is* a bad word," I stopped Stelson from flinging us on the path to an embarrassing parent-teacher conference with Miss Osiegbu.

Without warning, Stelson swerved the car to the right and put the car in park. "I can't drive facing the sun." He got out and opened the passenger's back door.

He unhooked Seth's seatbelt, shooed him over. "I'm gonna have to sit back here with you guys, and you'll have to scoot over."

"What about my car seat?" Seth nearly begged.

"Not this trip."

Seth's world came to a halt. He'd never ridden in *any* car without a special seat. "But Miss Osiegbu said we must always sit in a booster or we could get hurt in an accident. She says I have to wear it until I get eighty pounds, which is almost a hundred!"

Stelson ignored my son's reasonable plea. He hoisted Seth from his seat with one arm, threw the booster to the floor, and set Seth down in the middle. "Let's pretend you're a hundred pounds."

"But I don't *want* to get hurt," Seth's voice threatened to break with sorrow.

"You won't," Stelson assured him. He buckled himself as well as Seth in place while I got out of the car and assumed the driver's seat. Stelson laid his head against the headrest and covered his eyes with a pair of gloves.

I checked all my mirrors and eased onto the street again and continue down the Millers' street.

"Daddy, what if the police see me? Won't they give me a fricket?"

Seth's mispronunciation tickled me, but Stelson didn't see the humor. "Everything's going to be fine, okay? Just...shut it up."

I know he did not just tell my baby to shut up! We were close to having another Six Flags moment. Now it was my turn to pull over. "Stelson, get out of the car."

"For what?"

"Get. Out. Now. We need to talk."

"I'm so not moving until we get home," he said.

I eyed him through the rearview mirror. "I'm not moving another inch with you actin' a plum fool."

"Ooooooh!" from our son.

"Really, LaShondra? In front of Seth and Zoe?"

"I *asked* you to get out."

"Not exactly balmy outside. Freakin' forty-two degrees."

"Oooooh!"

I twisted my body to get a view of my ridin'-dirty Seth. "Honey, I don't know why your father insists on saying the word freakin' today. It *is* a bad word. And we're going to pray for him to stop this foolishness, okay?"

"Drive home!" Stelson yelled like somebody who obviously wasn't in enough pain to shut his own freakin' mouth! *Lord, forgive me.*

"I'm not driving anywhere!" I took my keys out of the ignition and swung open the driver's door. I opened the back driver's side door and seized Zoe. "Come on, Seth."

"Where are we going?"

"Back to Miss Peaches' and Momma Miller's house."

"Yeah! But what about Daddy?"

"He can drive himself home when the sun goes down." I helped Seth hop onto the concrete. My son, my daughter and I stood there watching my husband play idiot-man.

"What are you now? A real housewife of Dallas? You should audition. I'm sure they'd cast you," he said through gritted teeth. He exited the passenger's side and began walking around the vehicle.

Suddenly, he went down. Jerking, twitching, convulsing. Clenching his fists. His eyes fixed on one inconsequential point.

"Stelson!"

Having worked in public schools with thousands of kids, I knew immediately what was happening.

"Daddy!" Seth yelled as he ran to Stelson's side.

I thrust the baby back into her seat and pulled my cell phone from my pocket simultaneously.

"9-1-1 what is the location and nature of your emergency?"

"Corner of Jonah Drive and Bethel. My husband is having a seizure." I fed her information as I pushed my husband onto his side. A dark spot spread across the crotch of his pants as he lost control of his bladder.

"Daddy!" my son hollered louder.

"Seth, baby, run to Peaches' house—the one with all the cars in front—and tell her to come quickly. Can you do that for Daddy?"

He took off at breakneck speed toward the Miller house, feet pounding the pavement double-time. I positioned myself to keep an eye on Seth while I comforted Stelson and listened to the operator's instructions.

"Turn his head to the side to keep his airway open."

"I did."

"Good job. Does he have seizures often? Is he epileptic?"

"No. There's something else wrong with him but we don't have a diagnosis."

Animal noises escaped my husband's nose. *Eech. Eech. Eech.*

Rubbing his forehead, I coaxed, "You're going to be okay, baby. I'm here. You rest in the secret place of the Most High. You abide under the shadow of the Almighty." I couldn't remember the whole psalm, but I knew at the end there was a promise to those who fear Him. "God is here, too. You're okay."

I looked up and saw the entire Miller family heading toward us. I promise you, they resembled the cavalry.

Peaches forced me to drink a warm cup of hot chocolate. "Next best thing to coffee."

I sipped tenuously to satisfy her bossy-yet-nurturing nature. "Thank you."

Peaches, Quinn and one of her brothers, Monty, had followed Stelson and me in the ambulance. Stelson had regained some consciousness and control of his body in the ambulance. After ruling out drug use, the emergency room physician ordered some kind of specialized MRI, something we'd been trying to convince the doctors to do all along. Shame it took a seizure and an emergency room trip for them to get with the program.

Peaches, Quinn, Monty and I perched in a waiting room. The soft yellow paint and bright lights cast a soft shadow on everyone waiting patiently for news. I had to give it to the hospital, the chairs lining the perimeter of the room provided adequate cushioning, and we would know since we'd been sitting for an hour and a half.

"You all right?" Peaches asked for the fifth time since they took Stelson for the MRI.

"Yes," I answered, annoyed.

"I'm not. That was traumatic," she said.

Quinn intervened. "But you kept your cool, LaShondra, by God's grace."

He was sho' nuff right about the grace. Peaches sat back in her chair and resumed the game of Solitaire on her phone. Quinn studied the television. I wished for nothing more than a trip home so I could fall apart in my prayer closet. The image of my tall, strong, manly husband writhing on the ground while my son stood over him yelling, terrorized me beyond belief... *This is too much, Lord.*

I approached the nurse's station and asked how much longer it would be before we were able to see my husband.

"Last name?"

"Brown."

She studied her screen. "Oh, an M-R-I. We only have one in machine operation tonight. So it may be another half hour or so before he's ready."

"Thanks."

With some idea of the timeframe, Peaches ran me home so I could get supplies for Zoe and clothes for me in case I had to spend the night at the hospital.

"I'll be right back," I told Peaches.

"You sure?" she tilted her head, concerned.

"Yeah."

"If you're not back in five minutes, I'm coming in."

I released my purse at the door and rushed straight to the prayer room. A stream of pent-up emotion flowed out of my eyes as I prayed to my Father between heaving sobs. This was the big one. The ugly cry. The epic bubble-snot, head-jerking cry.

God, I don't even know what to say. Stelson had a seizure. You were there, weren't You? Why didn't You stop it? And my baby saw it. Father, this is crazy. I need You now. This very second.

As I prayed, I remembered reading Smokie Norful's testimony behind his first big hit, *I Need You Now.* Like Stelson, Norful's father was lying in a hospital bed. He had wires running everywhere from his body, and the singer had felt the same way I felt, which is why the song resonated with so many people. *Not a second or another minute.* From deep within me, I began to hum the tune.

And then a scripture came. *I will never forsake you.* And then a translation from somewhere popped up in my head. *For God Himself has said I will not in any way fail you.* Scripture after scripture, promise after promise flooded me as The Comforter personally lifted my head with His Words. All those scriptures Momma made me memorize, all those hours in consecration and study kicked in and took over.

"Thank you, Lord," I said aloud. Knowing that He was there for me, I could be there for Stelson.

Peaches rapped on the front door. "Shondra!"

I let her in. "Come on in," I said, wiping my eyes.

"Girl, I knew you were in here breaking down." Peaches snatched me into a hug and squeezed the rest of my tears onto her shoulder.

We were both slobbering messes by the time she let go. "We'd better get back."

"Yeah. Let me get what I came home for."

"I know kids. I'll get Zoe's and Seth's stuff." I pointed her to the kids' hallway and she headed to Zoe's room while I went to the master bedroom for my things.

I took a tote bag from my closet and filled it with another shirt, a pair of jeans and fresh undergarments. I grabbed my toothbrush and toothpaste, a comb and a brush.

I got Stelson's toothbrush, too. And that's when I heard Stelson's computer ding in his adjacent office. *He must have left it on.*

I moved the mouse, expecting to see some work-related file pop up on the screen. Instead, a discussion thread appeared. The title: *Sick and don't know why.* In the upper right, I saw my husband's screen name. *BrownBrother.* I sat in his leather chair. Scrolled down and read my husband's heart on a 15-inch screen.

I have no idea what's wrong with me. I've alienated my wife, my kids, my mother, my church family. My biggest fear is that I'll leave them like my father left me. He died when I was nine.

Beneath his confession, dozens of people responded, telling him that they were praying for him. That what he felt was normal. They'd been there and done that and he shouldn't feel guilty. He should tell his wife what he felt she needed to know, but feel free to come online and vent with them. They'd be right there for him.

The conversation took place over several days.

I clicked my husband's name and saw that he'd been a part of several discussions full of encouragement, venting, and amateur medical advice. The weight of his despair shocked me. *I didn't know.*

"Shondra?"

"Yeah, I'm coming. Just shutting down Stelson's computer."

I couldn't process what I'd just read at the moment. I closed the top without exiting the site. "Let's go."

Just as we rejoined Monty in the waiting room, a nurse dressed in tie-dyed scrubs stepped in. "Mrs. Brown?"

"Yes."

"Dr. Coyle would like to speak with you."

Peaches literally pushed me so my feet would move.

I followed the nurse beyond the white swinging double doors, to Stelson's bedside. He was upright, wearing a light blue hospital gown. The miniscule upturn of his lips nearly crushed my decidedly confident demeanor.

Words would have betrayed me. I pecked his forehead with my lips and concentrated on breathing normally.

"Mrs. Brown, your husband has asked that you be present as we discuss the findings. I think that's best, especially considering this whole episode may be foggy for him."

"I understand."

Dr. Coyle sat down on his stool and turned on both his laptop and a monitor at the foot of Stelson's hospital bed.

The days of doctors slapping X-rays and scanned results against luminescent panels must have passed without me knowing. *All this technology—he'd better have an answer.*

"I need to forewarn you. These findings are...concerning," he prefaced.

Stelson slipped his hand into mine and squeezed once. I reciprocated, taking it further by lacing our fingers together. Whatever the doctor said, we'd have to face it together. Period.

Chapter 26 ❧

"The scan revealed old lesions."

"Lesions?" I gasped.

"Yes, but they were old. Whatever you've got, you've had for a while or you're experiencing a relapse."

"I've never been this sick."

"I have a few questions for you, Mr. Brown." Dr. Coyle swiveled the laptop toward himself and pressed a few buttons. "In addition to the headaches, have you experienced numbness in your hands or feet?"

I was relieved to hear him ask questions that sounded foreign.

Until Stelson answered, "Yes."

What?!

The doctor continued, "Dizziness, off-balance?"

"Yes."

I choked Stelson's hand. He wriggled out of my grasp and rested the hand on top of the white linens.

"Fatigue?"

"Yes."

"Difficulty breathing?"

"No."

Thank God for one no! Dr. Coyle was going to have to put me on a stretcher in a minute. Why was my husband hiding all these symptoms from me?

"Blurred vision?"

"Yes."

The doctor took off his glasses and got busy clicking and scrolling away.

Stelson avoided my glare, keeping his eyes on the doctor alone.

"Well, there's good news and bad news. The good news is, now that we know you have lesions on your brain, we can narrow this down to a specific category. The bad news is, the types of syndromes and diseases we're likely dealing with can bring life-changing, life-long challenges."

Immediately, something inside me rejected this report. Not because I didn't want to believe it, but because the Witness inside said the doctor wasn't accurate. The same Witness, the Holy Spirit, had spoken when Stelson's headaches started. I knew then that we weren't dealing with migraines, just as I knew when the doctor was speaking that Stelson's problem, while serious, was not in line with the doctor's suggestion.

"What kinds of diseases?" Stelson asked.

I didn't want to hear the answer and from the way Dr. Coyle rolled his head to the left, he didn't want to say too much. "There are quite a few."

"Name one," Stelson pushed.

"Well...there's MS, cerebral infarction, systemic lupus, epilepsy...it's too early to tell. We're going to keep you here overnight as a precaution. I recommend you work closely with your regular doctor to chase this down."

"Will do," Stelson agreed.

Dr. Coyle reattached his glasses to his face and patted Stelson on the shoulder. "Are you having any discomfort now?"

"No."

"Great. I'll check in with you again tomorrow morning."

"Thank you."

Dr. Coyle left the room.

I threw my hands in the air. They landed on my hips. I took a deep breath and tried my best to address Stelson without raising his blood pressure. "What was that?"

He rocked his head left and right on the pillow. "The truth."

"Why didn't you tell me you had all these other symptoms?"

"If this guy's a doctor and he can't help me, why would I tell you?"

"Because I'm your wife. Because we're here for each other."

"Are we?" he questioned. "The sicker I get, the more we fight. Telling you would only make you worry more, which makes you more irritable."

I'm the irritable one? Thank God I caught the accusation before it escaped my mouth. Lord knows we didn't need another argument.

We did the only thing I knew to do: pray.

I texted Peaches and asked her and Quinn to visit with Stelson. We all prayed again, then I walked with Peaches and Quinn to the elevator. Monty pressed the 'down' button and the door chimed almost immediately. "I'll go pull the car around so Quinn won't have to hop around so much."

"Thanks for coming, Monty," I said.

"You got it. See you later, Shondra. I'll text you in a few. Y'all can meet me at the emergency entrance, Peaches."

Monty boarded the elevator.

"Momma says don't worry about the kids," Peaches said. "Focus on Stelson."

I reached in my purse, searching for my wallet. "Here, let me give you something in case we end up staying longer and Zoe runs out of milk."

"Girl, please. We got this. Plus, you know Momma's already whipped up mashed potatoes. Zoe will not go hungry."

"Please thank her for me tonight," I begged.

"Do you need anything before we go?" Peaches offered.

"No. You being here was more than enough. I'm a basket case right now. I feel like I'm just going through the motions," I confessed to them as much as myself. "Stelson has been so...not himself lately. And I've been fussing at him, thinking he needed to will himself to snap out of it. I didn't know he was battling something so insidious. I can't imagine how much pain he was in. *Lesions* on his brain. That's like...*lesions*."

"He was definitely in a lot of pain," Quinn seconded.

Confused, I asked, "What? How did you know?"

Quinn glanced at Peaches. She nodded. Obviously, they knew something I didn't.

"Tonight, while you two were gone, Stelson asked me if I had any leftover pain medication from my surgery. Said he'd even pay me for them."

God, he's serious!

"I was going to call you later and tell you, but then *this* happened," Peaches said.

"Quinn, I'm so sorry—"

"No need to apologize, Shondra. Stelson's my brother in Christ, but he has flesh. No telling what any of us might do under the wrong circumstances."

As an educator, I always had the greatest respect for doctors, partly because they stayed in school so long. And yet, there we were, surrounded by all this computerization and a doctor who'd studied and practiced long enough to handle critical patients in a major hospital, and we walked out of there Christmas day basically with a note telling us to go see *another* doctor.

This is ridiculous.

With Stelson pretty much resting in bed the rest of the day, Daddy and Jonathan came to our house so Seth could have some kind of semblance of a Christmas surrounded by family and friends.

I noticed something about my father while he was in our living room: He wasn't nearly as bold and abrasive when he wasn't in his own house. He spoke to Stelson cordially and minded his manners. Held his tongue quite well, actually. Perhaps this was something he'd learned to do back in the '60s, when he'd perfected his public persona for mixed company.

Whatever the reason, I was thankful. He and Jonathan assembled Seth's Big Wheel and took him outside to test it despite the cool temperatures.

Momma Miller must have coddled Zoe nonstop because she was clingier than usual, not wanting to be contained by her swing or the playpen. I searched my closet full of baby gifts and produced a harness that I hadn't ever used. I strapped her in it, slung her on my back, and she was full of peace and joy facing the world from five feet off the ground.

This new perspective, as well as me singing softly to her, kept her entertained while I finished our Christmas dinner.

Stelson sat up in bed and laughed when he saw Zoe's newfound orientation. "Must be nice."

"I guess so."

I set his lemonade and plate of food on the nightstand. Turkey, dressing, sweet potatoes and green beans, though not nearly as much as he would normally eat. "Need anything else?"

"You," he said tenderly, caressing my arm.

I froze. My heart had grown numb from its survival-mode default position on top of the calluses formed by weeks of abrasive comments.

He asked, "Can you come and sit with me for a while if you have time later?"

"Why?"

"Because I'm sorry. About everything. I know you deserve better, but I didn't have it to give. I still don't. And I'm afraid maybe I won't ever be able to love you and the kids with all of me again."

"Don't say that, Stelson." I left the room so he wouldn't see me crying.

If this wasn't temporary, I wasn't sure I could survive. A sick husband? Two kids? Hustling back to work so I could support all four of us in between what would probably be countless doctor visits? What if he had another seizure? What if he went to jail for buying pain meds on the streets?

If we were elderly, if we were both retired with no kids at home so we could focus on one another that would be different. No one imagines spending a good chunk of their lives as a caregiver for a spouse. At our age, we were supposed to be vibrant and mobile and hopeful. Not a wife serving her husband Christmas dinner in bed at six o'clock in the evening because he was too fatigued to join his family at the table.

You couldn't tell me this was the good, hopeful, prosperous plan of God for our lives.

Peaches and Quinn would only be in town through the twenty-eighth. I wanted to spend time with her, but I couldn't very well ditch my husband to go hang with my best friend. She did the next best thing by coming over to our house the day before they left.

She must have known I was completely spent. She kept the kids occupied while I took a bath. Helped me get them in bed, then helped me catch up on cleaning and laundry—something only the closest of friends would do. And then she ordered me to turn on my laptop. "We are going online and we are going to find out for sure what's wrong with Stelson," she declared.

"The doctors can't—"

She gave me the hand. "Don't get me wrong, I have the utmost respect for anybody who stayed in school long enough to rack up two hundred thousand dollars in student loans. But I'm telling you, our country's medical system was hijacked when the Rockefellers started funding certain medical schools."

I glanced toward the ceiling. "Umm…what difference does it make who the Rockefellers donated to?"

She clicked her cheek. "They only donated to medical schools they deemed *certified*," she held up finger-quotes. "And the only *certified* schools were the ones that would teach doctors to recommend pharmaceuticals using their supplies. Of course, the more patentable drugs prescribed, the more money comes in. Everybody in the loop gets paid big time."

"But doesn't the patent process and the FDA ensure that drugs—"

I couldn't even complete the sentence before Peaches gave me the *be-for-real* look and said, "Don't drink the red Kool-Aid. Rockefeller actually *created* the American Medical Association despite the fact that his personal doctor practiced homeopathic medicine. Rockefeller lived to a ripe old age of 97 while the rest of us are too blind to recognize that most of what we need for healing is already available in the raw. I mean, if you get hit by a bus, by all means go to the hospital. But a lot of what ails us is curable naturally."

"So you're telling me that there's stuff growing on trees that can heal just as well as what doctors can prescribe? I mean, I know I've filled plenty of prescriptions that actually helped me."

"First of all, if prescription drugs actually healed, the whole system would collapse. Really, any large-scale man-made system is going to have corruption. You're an educator. You know it's not right that every child in Texas has to pass a test in order to graduate, right?"

"Agreed."

"And you said yourself that, often, principals get hired and fired based on who they know rather than how well they can run a school, right?"

"Yes."

"Same thing with the field of medicine. Doesn't mean every doctor is greedy, but some are. Now, some drugs are fine. Antibiotics are not the devil so long as you don't overuse them and you know what caused the infection so you won't have to use them again. But you usually need a natural supplement to help your body absorb the drugs or to fight off side effects—don't even get me started on side effects. Really, most doctors are trained to alleviate symptoms. If they actually cured people, we wouldn't need them or drugs as much.

"Second, have you ever tried any natural solutions?"

"No," I admitted. "I mean, I've tried a few "old-wives' tales"-type remedies here and there."

"Did they work?"

Poking out my lips helped me think better. Momma had a few concoctions, but Grandmomma Smith was the do-it-yourself-healthcare queen. "Well, I do remember once, when I fell and skinned my knee racing down the street with my cousins, my grandmother mixed up something with what appeared to be oil, tea, and some other stuff she didn't let me see. She slathered it on my knee. That stuff worked so fast, even as a child I knew it was amazing."

"That's what I'm talkin' about. She probably used coconut oil, tea tree oil. Beeswax to make it stay in place. Way better than over-the-counter ointment."

"Why don't doctors prescribe natural remedies if they're so effective?"

"Because you can't patent what God made, and what can't be patented doesn't make much money."

This whole conversation reminded me of banter from Daddy's lips. He was the only one I knew who was completely skeptical of the government, despite the fact that he worked at the post office for over thirty years.

"Okay. We've tried everything else. Might as well go underground," I conceded, raising my laptop screen, pressing the power button and wondering why my best friend hadn't written a book yet. I was as impressed as I could be without actually seeing this whole natural thing work on a case more serious than a skinned knee.

Peaches navigated to a website that looked more like a place for a witch doctor than two Christian women seeking God's herbs. "This is spooky."

"You are so brainwashed. The system has taught you well that if it didn't come from man, it's evil. Quite the opposite is true. But don't worry, girl, Peaches is here to set the record straight."

"Look at that woman!" I pointed to the top of the screen, where a woman in clothes that looked like curtains smiled back at us. I guess she was our age, in her forties, probably living on an island with no electricity. "She's a hippie."

"She's not a hippie. She's sixty-three and runs two miles a day."

My mouth dropped. "Nuh uh! She is *not* sixty-three!"

"Yes, ma'am."

I exclaimed, "Okay, if she was black, I could see it. This is gonna sound wrong, but a white woman's skin looking that young at sixty-three is not normal."

"Well, white don't crack, either, if you stay away from foolishness," Peaches surmised. She selected the word "timeline" from the page menu. "This tool will help us start at the beginning. When did Stelson first begin to have symptoms?"

"Um…a few weeks after school started," I said.

"Not good enough. Pull out your calendar."

This girl was not playing with me. I pushed away from the table. "Be right back."

Stelson stirred as I rummaged through my purse looking for my phone. "Peaches still here?"

"Yes. We're online researching your symptoms. She thinks we need to look at natural remedies."

"I'm open to anything," he mumbled.

I walked to his bedside and kissed him.

"What was that for?"

"Not sure. Guess talking with Peaches has given me hope."

"Works for me."

Peaches and I dragged and clicked on the timeline. For a bohemian website, the tool was quite sophisticated. The teacher in me thought the gadget might come in handy for helping students keep outlines as they read.

She took our search to the next level. "Now, do you use a debit card or credit card for most of your purchases? Do you keep receipts?"

"Yeah. Why do they want to know all my business?"

"We're going to look through your purchases to see if you bought anything out-of-the ordinary or forgot to mention something on the calendar. Your checkbook is a map to your life."

"Are you serious?" I chided.

"As serious as your husband having a seizure. Come on. Open the checking account, chop-chop."

With Peaches nipping at my heels, I turned the laptop toward me and opened our checking account to search for unusual purchases. "Nothing we haven't already put on the timeline," I said. "What do they want next, my mother's maiden name?"

"No. But if you have your family menu for the weeks leading up to the onset of symptoms, I'll attach the file."

My goodness!

Once we'd plugged in all the information, Peaches submitted our case for analyzation. "Done. I gotta get back to Momma's. We should hear something in the next hour or so—depends on their holiday schedule."

"An hour?! Why can't it just spit out a diagnosis when you enter a few symptoms?"

"Because it's not run like a mainstream doctor's office. I pay a pretty penny for my subscription to this site. These timelines are actually reviewed by real people who are passionate about natural medicine. I'll text you as soon as I get the email."

She gathered her belongings and hugged me good-bye. "You coming to Momma's tomorrow?"

"I hate to see you go." What an understatement. Peaches had been a lifeline for me that week.

"Promise you and Stelson will bring the kids up soon?"

"As soon as he's better…"

"I'll change my sheets the minute I get back to Philly, then."

Her vote of confidence swept from her lips to my soul. She was so certain that my husband would be fine. I clung to her faith because mine was nearly depleted.

I slept as peacefully as possible with Stelson tossing and turning next to me as though he couldn't get comfortable.

Flat on my back, I stared at the ceiling wondering what God was thinking about this situation. What was the conversation in heaven? In the spirit realm? What were the angels telling the demons and vice versa?

For Seth's first birthday, Momma had given us a framed illustration of a little boy praying with his eyes closed. Right behind the boy were silhouettes of majestic, towering angels listening and watching intently. The cut-out matte showed Luke 4:10. "For it is written, He shall give his angels charge over thee, to keep thee".

Personally, I wasn't feeling very kept. I felt loose. Out there. *What's up with my angels? They on break?*

I nearly jumped when my phone vibrated on the nightstand. *You're funny, Lord.*

The screen showed one text message.

From Peaches: *EUREKA!!!!!*

Chapter 27 ❧

I fell trying to get out of bed and get to a place where I could freely talk to Peaches. "Ow! Shoot!"

"Shondra?" Stelson asked.

"I'm all right," I answered from the floor.

"What are you doing?"

"I just got a text from Peaches. She says she has the answer."

He switched on the light. "Call her."

I wasn't expecting him to jump on the trail so quickly. "I'm all over it." I snuggled up next to my husband and dialed Peaches.

The phone didn't complete one full ring. "Shondra, you are not going to believe this."

"Hold on, let me put you on speaker so Stelson can hear." I pressed the corresponding icon. "We're here."

She busted out, "Lyme disease."

Stelson and I waited silently, which I assumed meant he was as clueless about what she'd just said as me.

Peaches continued, "You remember when Seth got lost and Stelson was looking for him?"

I replied with, "Uh huh," although I wondered what Seth's disappearance had to do with Stelson's illness.

"Lyme disease is caused by the bite of an infected tick, carried by deer. North Texas is in the danger zone," she explained.

Stelson grabbed his phone from his nightstand. When the Google search engine page popped up on his screen, I knew he was already off to the races.

Stelson leaned in to ask, "What do we do now?"

"Take the test. But you don't want to take it at any old lab. There's a list of recommended labs whose equipment is sensitive enough to detect what we're looking for."

Isn't a lab a lab?

"They start you on a round of antibiotics. Now, this late in the game, I'd say you should probably take them in addition to the natural therapies since this thing already has a head start."

"What's the prognosis?" Stelson asked.

"It can be a very long recovery, but you can beat it, my white brother from another mother."

Peaches promised to send over the results and recommendations via email. We thanked her profusely for her time and for helping us in all matters bohemian.

"After this, you'll be one of us," she said. "Night y'all."

Lyme disease. Since Peaches first mentioned the name, I thought she'd meant "lime" disease, which sounded like fruit poisoning, if that's even possible. We Googled it and found a website with more information.

"Did you *see* a tick on your body?" I quizzed as we sat up in bed viewing the images together on my laptop. *This is gross.*

"No, but some people never see it." He pointed to someone's testimonial on screen and read out loud, "I…never… saw… a… tick."

The way he said it, like a new reader tackling a *Dick and Jane* book, cracked me up.

"What's so funny?" he said.

"You sound like Seth."

"Seth can read?"

"Yeah. He wanted to tell you."

"Why didn't he?"

"He tried." Rather than make my husband feel worse, I softened the truth. "You didn't feel like talking at the time."

Stelson covered his eyes with one hand. And he cried. We both cried, hoping the worst was behind us.

First thing in the morning, we tried to schedule an appointment with the lab, but Stelson's insurance said the request had to be written up by his doctor in order for them to cover it.

His doctor seemed quite annoyed that an online website had caught what he'd missed. Nonetheless, he conceded that Lyme disease was a definite possibility, given Stelson's day in the woods. The lesions, he surmised, might have been from a previous Lyme infection. This most recent exposure might have triggered a more potent reaction.

As was routine, he prescribed antibiotics immediately, even before the diagnosis was confirmed, because with this disease, every day counts.

When Stelson and I got the results from the lab a few weeks later, we clung to one another and thanked God for a definitive answer. He'd tested positive for Lyme disease.

◈Chapter 28

As Peaches had forewarned, the recovery process thus far had been slow, even with the antibiotics. Every few days, she'd ask me how he was doing. "He seems better."

"Nuh uh. You need to make a list of all his symptoms and chart how he's feeling every day. Scale of one to ten, ten being horrible. This will also help make sure no co-infections are starting and sneaking up on him."

I railed, "You're making this sound like a full-time job."

"LaShondra."

Her pause alarmed me. "What?"

"Taking care of Stelson *is* your new full-time job. I am soooo not trying to scare you. God did not give us the spirit of fear. I do want you to be aware, though. He's not totally out of the woods. There's a huge cloud of suspicion and political mystery around Lyme disease."

"Like what?"

"I'll send you the links. Call me after you've read the articles."

My computer dinged with her incoming message. Within a few clicks, I was dumbfounded. The titles of the first two articles alone caught my attention: *Lyme Disease Biowarfare. Diseased Ticks from Government Lab.*

If Peaches hadn't been so helpful already, I probably would have dismissed them. But she'd been right about everything else so far, and she had opened my eyes to the fact that I needed to open my eyes even more when it came to trusting my health to a man-made system.

I was almost late getting Seth from school. Couldn't tear my eyes away from the screen long enough to take a breath and process. Though no one in an official capacity had owned up to it, there was a theory floating around that Lyme disease was a man-made disease. An experiment in biowarfare gone wrong, which explained why something as complex as Lyme disease was officially "discovered" in 1975 despite the fact that ticks and deer have been around for centuries. The map of Lyme disease's progression across the United States also showed the heaviest concentration in areas nearest the lab, heading westward.

Online whistle-blowers alleged that Lyme disease, in particular, was engineered to progress slowly, in intervals, and mimic so many other diseases and affect people in so many different ways that enemies wouldn't know what hit them until it was too late. Depending on how the disease manifested, people could be diagnosed with rheumatoid arthritis, Multiple Sclerosis, Parkinson's disease, chronic fatigue, ADHD, fibromyalgia…

Undiagnosed, Lyme disease is a horrific condition. I couldn't finish watching some of the documentary videos.

"God, if this is true, it's terrible," I whispered to Him.

Peaches and I, of course, gabbed about it as I traveled to Seth's school.

"I cannot believe the government would let something like this happen," I said, "and then deny it."

"Girl, please," Peaches smacked.

"This is crazy. I don't think Stelson will believe it, though. He doesn't believe in speculation about conspiracies and big cover-ups. He's an engineer. Unless it's something spiritual, he defaults to facts. I'm not trying to make you feel bad, but the only reason he listened to you was because everyone else has been wrong."

"Well, maybe he can pray about the information. No matter what, he needs to know. The biowarfare researchers knew that doctors would prescribe antibiotics to fight the disease, so they infused components that could make the disease worse after antibiotics. From what I've read, this thing was engineered to confuse doctors, torture victims, and destroy lives. Stelson needs a major, systemwide detox to ward off co-infections."

"Got it. Bring on the owl powder and skunk extract."

Peaches laughed, "Quit."

"I'm serious. Whatever helps, we'll do it."

Stelson, as predicted, wasn't as receptive to the biowarfare theory, nor the alternative supplements despite the fact that God used a natural-medicine website to shine the light on his issue. "You sound like your father," he called from the bathroom as I lay in bed.

"You're right," I agreed because I didn't want to lose him to the politics.

Instead of focusing on the questionable origins of Lyme disease, I weighed in on Peaches' recommendation for detox. "Suppose the Plum Island theory isn't true. You must admit that after three weeks of antibiotics, your symptoms haven't completely disappeared. A detox would be good for your overall health. Can't hurt."

"Depends. I don't want to be tied to a toilet," he complained. "Got too much work to catch up on."

Stelson walked out of the bathroom wearing only a towel around his waist. Though he'd lost some muscle mass while ill, he was still a decent chunk of eye-candy. Took my mind completely off the subject. "You got any special surprises for me tonight?"

Our intimate time had resumed. Kinda. Nothing but the basics and only on weekends because he was pretty much pooped after work.

His complete healing couldn't get there fast enough for me. "If I pack your lunch every day, put your pills in little baggies and label them, would you do the detox then?"

He shrugged. "That's the only way it'll happen. I don't have time to read labels when I'm rushing between clients."

"Fine. Personal lunches it is."

Chapter 29 ॐ

Ebby, from the church's children's ministry, reached out to me by phone after we'd missed several Sundays. "Hey, lady. Just wanted to make sure my sweet Zoe and Seth are well. I see that you've checked the kids into the system here and there. I keep missing them, though. Is everything okay?"

"The kids are great," I eased her concerns. "I should have called to let you all know why our attendance has been spotty lately. My husband was diagnosed with Lyme disease."

She gasped, "Oh my. I've heard it's awful. Is he getting better?"

"Slowly. He's trying to stay away from things that trigger migraines. He has a hard time with loud noises and those flashing lights the praise dancers sometimes use."

"I see. Service can get pretty rowdy," she said.

"When we miss church, we have worship service at home whenever Stelson's up to being our pastor," I half-joked with her.

Ebby said in a lowered voice, "Quiet as it's kept, that's where church starts, really. At home. I wish more parents took time to teach their kids the Word on the couch and around the dinner table. Would make my job so much easier."

I couldn't rightfully say we'd been as diligent about teaching the Word as Ebby was giving me credit for. Her insight, however, gave me something else to add to our after-school schedule: scripture memorization. Now that Seth could read, it was *on*.

Another call came in later that afternoon, this one from the Tuesday women's hospitality team.

"Yes, Miss Willie Rose, everything's fine. Thank you for asking."

"Well, the last time you were here, you sat at table four. The table leader, Hattie, asked me for your phone number, but we're not at liberty to give out personal information between church members without permission."

Thank God!

"We're wondering if you might join us again this coming Tuesday. Sister Windham will be concluding her message on spiritual warfare and intercession."

She'd sold me already, except I didn't want to sit at table four again. "Umm...Miss Willie Rose, would it be possible for me to sit at a different table?"

"I-I suppose so. Do you mind me asking why you'd like to move?"

Answering her question directly would mean border-line gossip. "I'd rather not say."

"Hmph."

The way she *hmphed* me, I just knew my special request was going to get back to Hattie. "But on second thought, stop. Rewind. I don't want to cause any problems with the way things are arranged. I'll stick with my table for now."

"Are you sure?"

"Yes, ma'am." After all I'd been through with my husband, what could a table of women do to me?

"We'll see you Tuesday. And I don't know if you know this or not, but we extended Mom's Day Out to five o'clock."

"You don't say?" My soul cried out Hallelujah! I could have danced like David. "Be there with bells on. Bye."

Immediately, I began to dream up plans for my life between noon and five o'clock. Five whole glorious child-free, husband-free hours. *What will I do with myself? A massage? Shopping? Take a nap?*

The last option was the only one I wouldn't have to consult with Stelson about. Sleep was free. But I could do that any night. I dialed him at work. "Babe, you know how much you love me, right?"

"Yeeeeesssss," he slurred.

"And you know how hard these past few months have been for me, right?"

"Yeeeeesssss."

"I'd like to make a budget adjustment proposal. A massage and facial next week while Zoe is in the church nursery and Seth is at his piano lesson."

Without hesitation, he answered, "Go for it. You deserve it."

I hung up the phone before he could ask any questions. And then I went to my prayer closet and praised God. Not for the upcoming massage but because Stelson's reaction was…from my *old* Stelson.

My sweet, doting, even-tempered husband was back again.

Earlier, I'd *thought* about getting my David on. This revelation put the thought into action. I selected Amber Bullock's *Lord You've Been So Good* from my playlist and performed an impromptu praise dance for an audience of One.

From the two phone calls in one day, I gathered there must have been a church-wide thrust to contact members who had fallen off. We used to call such missions "roundups" at my old church.

Once, Momma tried to "roundup" Daddy. He only attended on special occasions, for Jonathan's or my sake. Easter and Christmas speeches or skits and choir solos.

"You ain't got to round me up to nothing," I remember Daddy fussing. "Jesus won't be rounding up half the folks *doin'* the roundup. Some of 'em will be looking for a rope to come their way and they'll be falling down a hot chute instead."

My father believed in God in a general sense. Like, he'd say "I swear before God…" and "I'll leave that to the Man upstairs." But he'd always harbored a severe dislike for church folk and preachers.

"Jonathan Smith, Sr." Momma reserved his whole name for her biggest points. She'd tapped her stirring spoon on the edge of her pot of greens and set the spoon on its holder. "It ain't your place or mine to judge who's goin' to heaven or hell. All you can do is try to walk upright before God. He'll do the judgin'. I wonder how you're going to answer Him when He asks you why, after all He blessed you with, you hardly ever turned around and gave Him any time."

Daddy had popped open a can of soda. Sat down at the table next to me while I peeled potatoes.

"Tell me something,"—I knew he was setting Momma up then—"when did they start the roundup?"

Momma thought for a second. "I believe First Lady announced it last week."

"And when do y'all start the fundraising for the pastor and his wife's anniversary?"

Momma narrowed her eyes at him. "You wrong, Jonathan. Pastor and his wife labor over us. They're good shepherds and they deserve to be rewarded."

"I ain't sayin' a man don't deserve honest pay for work well done. Mighty funny, though, how some shepherds don't go lookin' for the lost sheep 'til it's time for the fleecin'." He tilted his head back smoothly and gulped his soda.

Momma turned to the dishes in the sink.

I was too young to comprehend Daddy's implications, but I knew he'd said something Momma couldn't refute entirely.

All she could do was admonish, "You need to keep your mouth off the mand of God."

"He ain't a man-*d*. He's a ma-*nnn*, just like me. When church folk stop worshipin' the preacher and start doin' something worth my time, I'll be there."

As much as I despised my father's attitude about church, I gathered he must have been hurt by someone in the past. Momma tried her best to protect Jonathan and me from Daddy's cynicism without telling us outright that she thought he was foolish. "We gon' pray for your Daddy to see the light 'cause right now, the enemy's got him blind as a one-eyed bat."

I wanted to ask Momma what difference it made how many eyes a bat had if it was already blind, but I didn't want to be accused of talking smart, so I kept my mouth shut.

Even as a child, I knew my father wasn't right about a lot of things. I never doubted his love for me and, later, I grew to appreciate his glass-half-empty perspective because it helped me understand how to deal with people who had suffered rough childhoods and life-changing injustices. The fact that he'd been accused of a crime he didn't commit, then beaten silly by white police officers to the point that he was unable to take advantage of his college scholarship—his chance at a wonderful life—was something for which I had to cut Daddy slack.

Funny thing is, when I got into my secret place Tuesday morning before the women's meeting so I could get my mind right for table four, the Father asked me if I thought I was any better or worse than my father for not wanting to be around my assigned group?

My first thought was to try and reason with Him—tell Him exactly why I didn't want to be around them. Tell Him how disappointed I was that a group of women older than me had not encouraged me and lifted me up as I'd hoped. I was even getting ready to flip to the Psalms and quote David where he said, "I have more understanding than my elders..."

But I stopped. Didn't even go there. Slapped my palms against my forehead and said, "I repent. I receive the mind of Christ on this matter." I was too tired and getting too old to sit up and argue with God anymore. If His ways are good—and they are—why debate?

By the end of my quiet time with Him, I realized two things: First, I was the daughter of Jonathan Smith, Sr. For as much as I deplored his pessimism, there was a streak of it in me, too. Maybe I could blame Daddy for modeling negativity while I was a child, but I was forty-two years old now and Christ lived in me. No excuse.

Second, the Lord put me at table four for *His* purposes. If I thought I knew so much more than my sisters, it was my responsibility to share His truth, in love, with them no matter what age they were. *I* was discriminating based on age.

Table four received me as though Miss Willie Rose hadn't given a hint of my reluctance to rejoin the group. *Thank You, Lord.*

The order of service had switched. We had group talk time first. Naturally, they all wanted to know where I had been, how my husband was.

"He's improving every day. It was so hard taking care of him, but

God is faithful," I gave a generic answer.

"Well, you know what the Bible says," Janice added, "God won't put more on us than we can bear."

"Mmm hmmm," they all murmured and nodded.

I tell you, God didn't bit more let me get five minutes into the discussion and already I had to speak up against this misquote of the Word. "Well, you know, my sister," I tried to dash a little sweetness on the contradiction, "that scripture…" *How do I say 'ain't even in the Bible' without being disrespectful? Help me, Lord.*

"What about it? Been one of my favorite scriptures all my life," Beverly chimed in.

One of the fellowship facilitators casually interrupted our discussion. "How's it going at this table?"

Doris tipped up her hat. "Good. We were just discussing the verse about how God won't put more on us than we can bear."

"Oh," the facilitator laughed, putting a hand on her chest. "I know. People think that's a *real* scripture! We're gonna have to do some Bible drills one of these days."

The facilitator moseyed on to the next table.

"What she said," I shied away, thankful that the correction had come from someone nearer their age group.

Doris bucked her eyes. "Chile, I been quotin' that scripture all my life. You mean to tell me it ain't even in the Bible?"

"No, ma'am," I answered as innocently as possible. "God said he wouldn't put more *temptation* on us than we can bear. Not more *troubles* or *problems.* I mean, if we could bear everything that happens to us, we wouldn't need Him."

Hattie threw her coffee napkin on the table and gasped, "Shut your mouth!"

"Yes, ma'am."

"Well, what other scriptures you know of that we need to revisit?" Hattie asked, pulling her Bible closer.

I snatched my phone from my purse and tapped a browser open. "There's a website. I'll go to it now."

My tablemates waited in anticipation, still awestruck about the revelation. Of course, once the site loaded, I gave them more. "Here's one. The race is not given to the swift or the strong, but to the one who endureth until the end."

"You got to be kiddin' me! We used to sing that song in the church choir!" Linda slapped the table.

"The verse is actually a mixture of Ecclesiastes 9:11 and Matthew 24:13. When you really think about it, the verse *can't* be true. The race is given to those who believe on Christ as Savior—not those who put forth the most effort the longest, right?"

Hattie's posture stiffened. "I'mma tell Willie Rose about you. You need to teach us a class or two next semester."

My mind said "oh, no" but a bell rang loudly in my Spirit. *Me teach a Bible class?* I couldn't see it. I begged the Lord to just give me one new task at a time. Please.

We all donated to the pot for the farewell offering to Sister Windham. Once again, she delivered more words of wisdom than I could capture with a pen and paper. I wished I hadn't been so condescending with my seasoned sisters. By judging them, I'd missed out on the blessing of hearing Sister Windham teach.

After dismissal, I rushed to approach her. "I wanted to let you know how much the message blessed me. And to thank you for praying for my husband. He's better now."

"Fully recovered?"

Odd question. The Holy Spirit directed me to tell her the whole truth, not the cheery version I'd given to everyone who'd asked. "Seventy-five percent, if I had to put a number on it."

Her intense focus on me in a buzzing crowd of sixty or so women was unnerving. Made me feel extremely vulnerable. Had the Spirit not arrested me moments earlier, I might have sidestepped her probe with humor or a churchy cliché.

Not today.

"You know, the last time we talked in the parking lot, you asked me to pray and ask God to heal your husband."

I nodded as my eyes began to sting. My heart was jumping at the chance to receive whatever she had to say. The fact that I was there, the way the Lord used me at my table, it wasn't a coincidence. This day was important, and I knew it even before Sister Windham laid it on me.

"I wanted to say something to you then, but the Holy Spirit said you weren't ready, so I didn't. I prayed what you requested. And if you remember, I prayed for *you* more than your husband."

A tiny smile escaped. "Yes, ma'am, I did notice."

"Well, God has answered my prayer for you. You're ready. And what I see is that you and your husband have been fighting this attack on his health like y'all are at the bottom of a hill, his health is at the top, and the enemy's standing between where you are and where you need to be." She lowered one hand toward her knee, the other she raised high. "But y'all got it backwards. In Christ, you *already have* health. Your fight is to *protect* your health, not *get* it. You understand what I'm saying?

"You're at the *top* of the hill swinging the sword down, not up. The enemy is beneath you, never above. *You* tell *him* what to do, not the other way around. We been singin' Jesus, He will fix it after while, when all the time, He left the power with us. You hear?"

"Yes, ma'am. How, exactly, do I fight him?"

"I see you missed a lot of sessions," she semi-fussed. "Your sword is the Word. Every time you speak it from your lips, you strike a blow to the enemy."

"Yes, ma'am."

"Let me sum it up for you. You and your husband, speak to what's left of the mountain and tell it to be removed. Keep your thought-life in check, and don't let your mouth utter anything contrary to the Word of God. I don't care what the doctors say, what the TV say, what the internet say. You"—she poked my shoulder—"fear not and believe only. Find you some scriptures to stand on and don't be moved."

I wiped my face. "Thank you." Such inadequate words. "Thank you so much."

She gave me a big Grandmomma-hasn't-seen-you-in-a-while hug. "Bless Jesus."

Chapter 30 ❦

Stelson's groaning permeated the midnight silence. "Baby?"

He was upright, groping his knees. "All of a sudden, they just started throbbing. Maybe it's—"

"Don't even speculate. Get the scriptures," I declared before he could confess something we'd have to strike down later.

He hit the light and pulled the index cards out of the drawer. I leaned into him as we professed in unison, "My son, attend to my words; incline thine ear unto my sayings. Let them not depart from thine eyes; keep them in the midst of thine heart. For they are life unto those that find them, and health to all their flesh. Proverbs 4:22-23," we professed in unison.

"But he was wounded for our transgressions, he was bruised for our iniquities: the chastisement of our peace was upon him; and with his stripes we are healed. Isaiah 53:5."

Then, I placed both hands on his knees and spoke to them. "On the authority of the Word of God, we come against everything that's out of line with perfect health given to us through Christ. I command these knees to be healed and cease from throbbing in the name of Jesus."

Stelson rubbed my back as I continued praying for him. Normally, I would have just said a few words and given him an Aleve. But the Spirit pressed me to tarry over him. And that's exactly what I did. Led by Him, I spoke not only to his knees in a general sense, but to his cells. Mind you, I didn't remember anything about cells from my science classes.

But I knew He did.

My tears fell onto my husband's body as the cell-calling continued up and down his legs. "Sickness, be removed from his body. We cast you into the sea."

I prayed and commanded until Stelson's hand stopped moving and I heard him snoring again.

Music to my ears.

Poor Zoe. Her first birthday was in less than a week and I hadn't officially invited anyone to the simple gathering at the park. In truth, we had been blessed with unseasonably warm weather for late January—not that Texas weather follows any logic. A check of the 10-day forecast put us in the high 60s just in time for an outdoor party (with plenty of bug spray).

If the comparative lack of documentation in her baby book was any indication of how different things would be for her as a second child, I could see why so many people suffered from second-child complex.

Mommas be tired!

"Who's gonna show up besides Daddy, Jonathan's crew, Momma Miller and a few people from the church?" I asked Stelson as we waited in the doctor's office.

"Don't worry. No one remembers their first party."

"When she sees pictures of Seth's first birthday party, she's going to notice a difference. Remember? We had the bounce house, the cotton candy machine, face painting..."

Stelson winced as he read the latest issue of Time Magazine. "I remember it all too well. Two different flavors of cake, a Teenage Mutant Ninja Turtle, a piñata—"

"We did *not* have a piñata!"

He shrugged. "Might as well have."

Seth's first birthday party had been one of our biggest blow-ups. I believed in giving our kids things I never had. Stelson believed I was throwing the party to impress our new neighbors and the people at the church. There was some truth to his argument, but I was too hormonal to acknowledge his point. I went behind his back and planned a huge celebration. I thought Stelson was going to spit fire when he opened the door and saw that overgrown masked turtle.

I chuckled at the memory. "Okay. No turtle this time. But we will have a bubble-blowing machine."

"Works for me."

By this time, I already knew the number of stripes on the outdated wallpaper in the doctor's office. I had seen every segment of the continuously playing "educational" video twice. The testimonials read more like horror stories. One man was perfectly healthy until he woke up one morning and couldn't move his arms. Of course, the commentator ended his segment by saying that his doctor prescribed yada-yada.

Seriously, if I hadn't been immersed in the scriptures on health, coming to the doctor's office would have scared me silly.

Stelson and I had already prayed before we got out of the car. I'd drawn up the verses on my phone and we recited them together, though it was clear we both knew them by heart. For as much as I'd been slipping little index card reminders in his lunch, Stelson probably hid them in his heart before I did.

The nurse beckoned us to a patient room, where Stelson's doctor performed an examination and reviewed the most recent lab results. "So far so good. But there's always a chance of bizarre, random symptoms popping up later with Lyme disease."

"I understand," Stelson politely acknowledged without agreeing.

I winked at him.

We left the office holding hands. Actually, *swinging* hands like two nine year olds who had just shared a secret.

Daddy and Momma Miller had agreed to each watch a child while Stelson and I went to his late afternoon follow-up appointment. I had no doubt Momma Miller could handle them both, but I felt an obligation to divvy them up if at all possible. Now that Zoe was walking and getting into everything, I needed to save the double-up babysitting for special occasions.

"You want me to drop you off at home before I go get the kids?"

"No. I'm not going back in to the office today. I'll go with you," Stelson said.

First stop was Peaches' mother's house. Upon entrance, we knew she was at it again, baking cookies to send home with us. She kissed us both, squeezed Zoe, then gave her to Stelson while thrusting a plate of decorated sugar cookies in my hand.

"Zoe helped make these," she claimed.

"You teaching my baby to cook already?"

"Gotta start early," she joked. "She is such a joy, Shondra. And her golden brown color is really coming in. No offense, Stelson."

"Why would I be offended?" he asked with a hint of polite laughter.

"I'm just sayin'. *This* one ain't gon' look like you."

In the car, Stelson asked me what I thought Momma Miller meant by her comment.

"Nothing."

"Then why did she say it?"

"Stelson, people in her generation, in Daddy's generation…they had a different experience growing up. Can we leave it alone?"

Uneasiness etched in his forehead as he headed to my father's house next. "I wish we could all come to an understanding. Get on one accord."

"May not happen in our lifetimes. Can you live with that?"

"I suppose I'll have to."

To my surprise, he parked the car and slid the keys out of the ignition.

"You're getting out?"

"Yeah. I owe your father an apology."

"For what?"

He widened his eyes. "Does the name Chuck E. Cheese ring a bell?"

"Yeah." I popped my lips. "Pretty bad day."

Stelson faced me. "When your dad walked you down the aisle and gave you to me, he wasn't expecting to see his little girl be mistreated. Looking at Zoe—with her golden brown skin," he teased, "I don't know what I would do if someone disrespected her in my presence. I want to look your father in the eye and let him know I'm sorry I let him down. Man-to-man."

Now, if we had been talking about any other "man" except my Daddy, Stelson's sentiments might have actually been touching. Endearing. But this was Daddy and I knew my father had a hard, nearly impossible time forgiving people.

"You don't have to do this."

"Yes, I do."

"No, you don't," I tried. "My father isn't always a reasonable person. You might think you're going to talk to him about your behavior, but I guarantee you somehow, some kind of way, he will turn this into something else. Maybe you should write him a letter or—"

"I'm not a coward," my husband spat back at me. "I got this, babe." He unlocked the doors and exited.

I unlocked Zoe from her seat and kissed her gently. "Sweetie pie, your Daddy is going into a lion's den."

She grinned, showing off her little square white teeth.

"Yes, he is," I cooed.

Stelson knocked on the door.

I rushed up behind him. "Just tell him you're sorry and get it over with. No long, drawn out conversation. Check?"

"Check."

"Do not answer any questions. All questions lead to endless debate. Capiche?"

"Capiche."

Daddy answered the door. Saw Stelson. His face soured. "I'll get Seth."

"Great."

"Wait. Mr. Smith," Stelson said before Daddy could walk away. "I want to apologize for the way I talked to both you and LaShondra at Seth's party. It was rude and disrespectful, and I'm sorry."

Still partially veiled behind the screen, Daddy asked, "Heard you must have been real sick at the time."

"Yes, sir, I was…not that I'm making excuses for my behavior."

His eyes swept over my husband. "I accept your apology. You look like yourself again. Must have gotten over it."

"I did, by the grace of God."

"Uh huh. What'd you have, anyway?"

"Daddy, I told you he had Lyme disease. We don't want to hold you long."

"Shondra, can't you see I'm talkin' to the man?"

I rolled my eyes behind Zoe's back.

Daddy continued, "I told a friend of mine about it. He does a lot of studyin' and stuff on the internet. Told me Lyme disease is man-made, just like the government created AIDS and the West Nile virus. Printed off a bunch of papers and everything."

Stelson shifted. "Yes, LaShondra told me about the theories floating around, but you know, I don't really subscribe to these unfounded government, military conspiracy theories except, maybe, the one about who shot JFK."

I kicked my husband's foot.

"Say you don't believe in 'em, eh?" Daddy baited.

"No, sir."

"You ever heard of the Tuskegee Experiment?"

Stelson leaned his ear toward the door. "The what?"

Didn't I tell him not to entertain questions?

Daddy swung the door open. "Y'all come on inside."

"Are you serious?" I begged.

"I'm just gon' educate the man," my father insisted.

Stelson crossed the threshold.

I had no choice except to follow him. Otherwise, who knew what might happen? "Ooooh!" I fumed, stomping in the house. "Where is my son?"

"Back there by the washing room foldin' towels. You were right. Seth can sho 'nuff make a perfect crease. He can do sheets, too. And I told him he's off to a real good start. Needs to get used to doing things better than other people so they won't look down on him, look down on his race."

"I'm afraid we'll have to agree to disagree on Seth's need to represent the race," Stelson said.

"Maybe we will," Daddy said, "but let's at least understand what we're disagreeing about." He pulled out a kitchen chair for Stelson to sit. Then he scooted a chair close so that he and Stelson were almost knee-to-knee.

Disgust twisted my face. I stood over them both with Zoe dangling from my side. "You two are asking for trouble. Stelson, you *know* you don't need to get agitated. And Daddy, your pressure is not the lowest. Why can't y'all just let it go?"

"We're two perfectly sane men," Stelson set it up. "If we can't talk through our differences like civilized people, we're both terrible examples for our race and Seth is in deep trouble."

I shoved Zoe onto Stelson's lap. "She's young, impressionable, and very sensitive. Don't do anything to scare her. Either of you." I wagged my finger between my husband and father.

"Reach me those papers over there," Daddy ordered, pointing to a pile on top of the microwave.

My lips tightened as I fulfilled my father's request. I handed him the papers.

He slapped them on the table and pushed them toward Stelson. "*This* is the Tuskegee Experiment."

"I'm outta here." *God, I hope You got this.*

ᚶChapter 31
Stelson

Stelson leaned past Zoe's head to read the first paper. He read the headline and a few captions first: *The Tuskegee Syphilis Experiment. Government officials used black men as lab rats. Wanted to study their corpses.*

As a matter of habit, he noted the fine print at the top, which referenced the URL hosting the information: TheNewUndergroundRailroad.us. "No disrespect, Mr. Smith, but you printed from a no-name website. Anyone can post anything on the internet, whether it's true or not."

Stelson sat back in his chair.

Mr. Smith snatched the stack. "All righty, Mr. I-gotta-hear-it-from-somebody-I-know." He shuffled through the papers. "CNN good enough for you?"

Stelson raised one eyebrow as he bent and surveyed the article. *The Darkest Chapters of Medical Research.* He handed Zoe to his father-in-law and read the short report documenting the government's 40-year inhumane research on the deadly STD using hundreds of black, uneducated sharecroppers. The men were informed by the United States Public Health Service that they were being treated for "bad blood" when, in fact, they weren't being treated at all; researchers simply wanted to document the effects of Syphilis.

"You see the dates?" Mr. Smith interrupted.

"Yeah," Stelson said in awe, "forty years. 1932 to 1972."

"You were alive in '72, weren't you?"

"Yes, sir."

"Then you got to admit, it wasn't that long ago that the government was willing to risk people's lives for the sake of an experiment, right?"

Stelson nodded. "This is…terrible."

"Well, if you feel that way, then welcome to the club," Daddy announced with arms open wide.

"What club?"

"The Messed-Over-by-the-Man club. Just like the government experiments cost these men their lives, the government experiment got you payin' a price with this Lyme disease."

Daddy shoved the papers even closer to Stelson. "Read all these and tell me you still trust what they were doing on Plum Island."

Stelson leafed through the stack, skimming through the headlines. "If all this is true, we should be ashamed of ourselves as a country."

"*We?*" Mr. Smith pointed back and forth between the two of them. "As in me and you?"

"We as a *people*. As a *country*."

"This ain't the black man's country. This land don't belong to *all* the people. White people gonna always have the upper hand, and they gonna always use that hand to slap black people back to the bottom, 'cause y'all can't stand to see us get ahead."

"What about President Obama? Tons of white people voted him in office."

Mr. Smith crossed his arms. "You ever seen a man in the office of the President of the United States of America be so disrespected?"

"Yeah, Bush Junior. People made a calendar of the ignorant things he said. They've written books, posted a ton of YouTube videos online. The compilations are hilarious, actually."

"See the difference!" Mr. Smith jabbed a finger at Stelson. "When they don't like a white president, they make jokes. But when they don't like a black president, they get hateful. Write all kinds of rhetoric to discredit him, his intelligence, his character. Talk about his wife like a dog. You ever seen so many people criticize a first lady's appearance?"

Stelson frowned, obviously considering his father-in-law's viewpoint.

"You don't see no light-hearted humor about the black president and he's a hundred times smarter than Bush. 'W' used to say stuff so stupid, made me squint at the TV," Mr. Smith hissed.

The vision of Mr. Smith staring at the screen in disbelief during one of President George W. Bush's impromptu blunders sent a ripple of laughter through Stelson.

"I'm glad you think this is so funny now. Won't be funny when Seth gets sent to the office for doing the same thing the white kids get away with. Or when somebody say Zoe got a bad attitude 'cause she ain't makin' everybody laugh, which is all they expect us to do anyway— entertain and play sports. Can't come across like she's too intelligent or they'll say she's intimidating."

Stelson's smile slipped away, cognizant of the fact that he was in Mr. Smith's 'they' category. "What exactly do you recommend I do, Mr. Smith?"

"Tell 'em the truth. Tell them that, as far as the world goes, they're *black*. Let 'em know they got natural born enemies."

"But—" Stelson spotted a movement in his peripheral vision. He saw Seth standing at the door leading to the main hallway. He hoped his son hadn't heard much. "Hey, buddy."

"Hey, Dad. Hey, Zoe, Zoe, Zoe!"

She squirmed out of her grandfather's lap and tottered toward her brother, who swooped her up into his arms. She hung awkwardly as Seth leaned back to balance her weight. He kissed her three times, once on each cheek and then the chin. For as much as he must have been cutting off her circulation, Zoe didn't complain.

"Let's go, sissy." He struggled to carry her away.

"Seth, where are you taking her?" Stelson asked.

"Where I am. By the laundry room."

"Be careful with her."

"Yeah," Mr. Smith said, "and teach her how to fold clothes."

"Okay, PawPaw," Seth, nearly out of breath from lugging his baby sister, answered.

With the kids out of earshot, Stelson asked, "For a moment, let's forget about the fact that Seth and Zoe are both black and white, which you've never addressed at all."

He waited for a rebuttal from Mr. Smith, but there was none.

"Don't you think teaching kids—any kids, black, white, whatever—that their enemy can be spotted with their eyes is a huge disservice? What if the person who may be willing to help Zoe with something is white, and the person who wants to stab Seth in the back is black? Then what?"

Mr. Smith pounded a fist into his palm. "You're missing my point."

"You don't *have* a point—"

"How you gon' tell me I don't have a point?" Mr. Smith's voice escalated. "Just 'cause you don't agree, don't invalidate me."

Stelson raised his palms to chest level. "My bad. You *have* a point, but it's based on overgeneralizations and stereotype. Both equate to prejudice, which is quite ironic if you ask me."

Mr. Smith set an elbow on the table. Covered his mouth with his fist. "I'm not sure if the problem is that you *don't* get it or that you *won't* get it."

"Get what? You haven't told me anything except…" Stelson laid a hand on the article. "How awful white people have been to black people and how *my* kids need to embrace their blackness and be skeptical of all white people. You're teaching Seth to be suspicious of what he sees in the mirror."

"He may not always look white," Mr. Smith stated. "Sometimes it take a while."

"Let's say it never happens. What if Seth *always* looks white? What if he grows up and marries a white woman, then you've got bleach-blonde great-grandkids. Then what? You want them to come and tell you they're sorry about the Tuskegee Experiment?"

"We don't want no durn apology. We want respect!"

"In the ten years before I got ill, when have I ever disrespected you?"

Mr. Smith bit his middle knuckle.

"That's right. Never! I'm a good son-in-law. I'm good to your daughter, your grandchildren. I'll raise them in the fear of God, but never the fear of man."

"Then you raisin' 'em in ignorance and that shows *your* ignorance," Mr. Smith accused.

LaShondra stepped into the kitchen. "This conversation is

approaching destructive. I think we'd better leave now."

"I think you're right," Mr. Smith followed, "because I don't think me and Stelson ever gonna be able to see eye-to-eye."

Stelson didn't respond.

"Okay. Let's leave well enough alone," LaShondra wheedled. She stood beside Stelson and held his hand.

"But a grandparent's got a right to pass on the history," he mumbled.

"No, you don't," Stelson spoke up. "Not if it leaves Seth confused."

"Seth ain't the one confused. It's you two," he pointed at Stelson and LaShondra.

"Daddy, all we're asking is that you respect our rights as *parents* to raise up our children the way we believe is best. Can you leave the black history lessons to us?"

Mr. Smith threw an arm toward Stelson. "He don't even know black history!"

"I know we all need to stop living in the past and move forward," Stelson surmised.

To which LaShondra pivoted toward her father's side as she dropped Stelson's hand. "Wait a minute. Nobody's saying we need to forget the past. It happened. If we brush it under the rug, it'll happen again."

Stelson threw his hands in the air. "Then what is the solution? You two tell me the answer!"

"Own up to it!" Mr. Smith hurled over LaShondra's shoulder. "Be proactive!"

"How can you command me to do something *you're* not doing, and you're black?" Stelson laughed. "I mean, are you mentoring young men in this community? Are you going to council meetings? Voting in all the elections?"

Nostrils flaring, Mr. Smith stepped in front of LaShondra, which landed him directly in Stelson's face. "I ain't got to do nothin' but be black, pay taxes, and die."

Stelson backed up. "You're doing nothing to pay it forward, but you expect me to do something?"

"I paid it *backward*! Got the scar behind my ear to show for it, you hear me!"

LaShondra put a hand on either man's chest. "Enough."

"Whaaaaa!" Zoe's squeal reverberated through the house.

The adults froze.

"Whaaaaaa!"

In a millisecond, the argument died as they rushed to the laundry room.

ᴨChapter 32

"Seth!" I screamed at the sight of Zoe holding up her reddened arm. Stelson picked her up before I could.

"What happened?"

The smell of bleach scratched my nostrils.

"What did you do, Seth?" Daddy flared.

Seth looked at my father, my husband, and then me. His eyes filled with tears. "I'm sorry. I was trying to help Zoe."

"Help her how?" I noticed tiny bleached spots on his blue school pants and a green hand rag showing similar discolorations. "With bleach?"

"Yes. PawPaw said black people have bad lives. And I don't want Zoe to have a bad life. I used the bleach spray on her arm, and I rubbed it with a towel so she can be white."

In that millisecond, my gut ripped down the middle as I came to realize how heartbreaking it must have been for Seth to imagine his baby sister doomed for life because she was brown-skinned.

Stelson and I looked at each other, his eyes communicating the mutual pain undergirded by anger seeing as this was my father's doing. He growled, "I'm gonna go rinse her arm," and sped off toward the kitchen.

Seth raised his hands to his face.

"Don't!" I clutched his wrists to prevent him from getting bleach in his eyes.

My swift action must have scared him even more because Seth wailed in confusion. "I wasn't trying to hurt her!"

"We know you would never hurt Zoe."

"Are you mad at me?"

I didn't answer. Honestly, this was the kind of thing I would have gotten a whipping for when I was five. And yet, I couldn't find it in me to spank him. Made perfect five-year-old sense to use bleach to make things white, including his baby sister whose life was headed for disaster, according to his beloved grandfather.

Still in emergency-mode, I took Seth to the restroom and washed all the way up to his elbows with soap and warm water.

Once I'd dried him and was satisfied he was out of danger, we joined Stelson, Zoe, and Daddy in the kitchen. Stelson was at the sink with the bright overhead light turned on, examining her skin closely. "I don't see any breaks in the skin."

I dropped Seth's hand. He shot over to Daddy's chair and climbed to the safety of my father's lap.

I, too, inspected Zoe's arm at the sink as she panted through her last few whimpers. "Just irritation."

Stelson patted Zoe's arm with a paper towel. He twisted the faucet handle.

Absent the rushing water, the room fell silent.

Daddy looking at me and Stelson. Me and Stelson looking at him. Seth looking back and forth like he wasn't sure who was in trouble.

Stelson leaned against the counter. Crossed one ankle over the other. I stood beside him. "Mr. Smith, do you *see* what we've been trying to tell you now?"

Daddy rubbed his fingers across his lips roughly and gave the slightest nod.

My breath bottlenecked in my chest. I covered my mouth to avoid distracting Seth with my own overflow of emotions as little huffs of air escaped. *Breathe. Breathe.* I knew Daddy was wrong for trying to brainwash Seth, but he didn't mean harm. And I knew Stelson was right for vigilantly guarding our family from fear, but there was still the reality of life in the world even though we weren't *of* it. The bottom line, though, was my babies. Seth was too young to process the complexities, obviously. The timing was all off, and it was time for my father to set the record straight.

I prodded, "Then tell Seth, Daddy. Tell him about the wonderful life ahead for both your grandchildren."

My son looked into my father's face.

Daddy set his forehead on Seth's. Nose-to-nose. Daddy closed his eyes and exhaled as though he'd been holding his breath for fifty years.

Seth giggled. "PawPaw, your breath smells like peppermints."

"Good thing, huh?" Daddy managed a chuckle despite the hint of crackle in his voice.

Daddy sat back a bit. Cupped Seth's chin with his left hand. "Listen. You know your PawPaw is old, right?"

"Mmmm hmmm." Seth nodded as best as he could.

"Seth." Daddy cleared his throat. "A lot of bad things happened to black people, especially people my age and those gone on before. But the world is changing. It's not perfect, but it's better. I don't want you to worry about your sister being black. She's gonna be just fine. And so will you." He threw a glance toward us. "Your Momma and Daddy will look out for you."

Seth slapped his clumsy hands against Daddy's face. Pulled Daddy closer. "Jesus looks out for me, too, PawPaw. You want me to ask Him to look out for you so people won't do bad stuff to old black people anymore?"

Tears fell onto my shirt as Stelson massaged the back of my neck.

"Yeah. That would be nice," my father accepted the offer.

"Close your eyes," Seth commanded. "God, could you please help my PawPaw so no one will hurt him because he's black? And if a bad person comes, You kick 'em away, all right? Thank You. In Jesus' name. Amen."

"Amen," we repeated.

Seth didn't forget to pray for PawPaw again during our family bedtime prayer. After a talk with Seth about staying away from chemicals, we had family prayer and tucked the kids in bed. Stelson and I thanked God for intervening with my father. I felt better already about Seth spending so much time with Daddy.

Stelson gave me a recap of the conversation he and Daddy had before Seth tried to change Zoe's skin color. "Oh, I forgot. Your father inducted me into the M-O-B-T-M club."

"The *what*?"

"Messed over by the man."

I tugged the covers up to my chin. "I don't even want to know."

Stelson packed his laptop and power chord into his work attaché and set it by our bedroom door. "Gonna try to do a mile tomorrow morning," he said. "Keep your cell phone on vibrate."

Seeing him shove the laptop into place stirred up my desire to speak to him about the website forum. I hoped he wouldn't see it as an invasion of privacy. If he did, I'd just have to apologize. I didn't want anything else standing between us. "Babe, when you were at the hospital, I had to come home for a few things. I was looking for some information on your computer."

"You remembered the password, right?" he asked, climbing into bed.

I turned my body to face him. "Yeah. I did. And the computer opened to your last window. I saw the Hold My Hand website."

He turned on his side, facing me. Lying in bed talking was something we used to do for hours on end when we first married. Before the kids. Even more than the physical intimacy, I'd missed our long, drawn-out, heart-to-heart talks. I sensed we were "there" again, though. After all the issues that had come to test us—my job, the kids, my father, my attitude, a tick bite—none of them had overtaken us, by the grace of God.

Yes. We're "there" again.

"I read some of your posts in the discussion forum." Water trickled from my eye.

Stelson wiped my cheek gently with his thumb. "I know. I should have talked to you before I went to strangers."

"No, no, no," I said. "Well, yes. I'm sad that you wanted to hold their hands instead of mine. But I get it. Chronic illness isn't something that can be understood from the outside looking in. In some ways, I think you should apply that same philosophy to the black experience."

"I'm sure you're right." He continued caressing my face. Twirling my hair as his eyes stayed fixed on mine. "What else bothers you?"

"The fact that you think I'm so fragile you had to hide the truth from me," I confessed.

"What would you have done differently if I'd told you all my symptoms before I had a definite diagnosis?"

I twisted my lips to the side as I thought. *What would I have done?* "I don't know. Maybe gone online and looked up all the symptoms. Been more demanding with your doctors."

"Been more worried?" he suggested.

A few beats passed. "Yes."

"Worrying doesn't solve anything. And, in this case, neither would all those sponsored websites and doctors we visited have helped. You had just quit your job and started learning all the stay-at-home-mom routines. You were stressed already. Why would I add to your problems?"

"Because your problems are my problems, big daddy. Look, I know you're a man and all." I slapped his shoulder. "If you hadn't had the seizure, we'd still be back at square one."

"But I *did* have the seizure and it happened that Peaches was in town, able to come right over and help figure it out. His timing is perfect."

"I know. I don't like being left out of the loop, though."

"All we did was argue after I got sick. I didn't think you *wanted* to be in my loop."

I smiled. "My bad, my bad."

He tilted toward me and planted a kiss on my lips. "My bad, too. There's actually a name for my irritability. They call it Lyme rage. When I read it on the website, I realized I was wounding you and the kids because I wasn't in control of myself. I withdrew. It was the safest thing for everyone."

The words seemed sweeter from his lips than they had been on screen. We lay without words, just playing with each other's skin and hair. Gentle kisses here and there.

My phone buzzed. "Ignore it."

"I fully intend to," Stelson agreed.

But then it buzzed twice more within a minute. "I'd better take a look."

The message from Terri read: Umm...I'm pretty sure you can have your job back. Turn on any local news channel tonight. PHS the top story.

One from Jonathan: Was that your school?

One from the school district with a link to a public announcement document which I wasn't interested in viewing on my tiny cell phone.

"Honey, turn on the news. Something happened at my high school."

He hit the remote control and we both watched as the reporter narrated. "It all started with some very ambitious journalism students. After a stealthy, long-term investigation, they created and posted their YouTube video yesterday titled 'Grownups These Days' exposing an affair between the principal, Jerry Ringhauser, and his new assistant principal, Natalie Lockhart-Gomez. Both administrators are married to other people. The students shot several videos and pictures depicting these two, who are supposed to be setting an example for the student body, leaving hotel rooms, attending events together, kissing and holding hands."

Snippets of the video confirmed the students' allegations. "Oh my gosh. This has Michael Higgins' name written all over it. He was chomping at the bit to break open a scandal," I told Stelson.

The report continued, "When Mr. Gomez was informed about the video, he came to the campus around five this afternoon and opened fire in Mr. Ringhauser's office. Early reports say the principal was in the office and hid under the desk.

"As he left in handcuffs, Gomez pointed out that he had only meant to scare the principal."

Footage of the husband being escorted from my school building to a police car in handcuffs rolled. "If I'd wanted to kill them both, I could have."

The reporter's face popped back on the screen. "Now, there were no students present at the time of the shooting. But as you can see"—he walked toward the back wall and put a finger through one of the holes—" Mr. Ringhauser's office shares an adjacent wall with another office. One of the *warning* bullets penetrated the wall. Sources tell us that office used to be occupied by another principal. Thankfully for her, she's on a leave of absence."

The camera zoomed in to peek on the other side—*my* side!

"This is Ivan Raley reporting. Lisa, back to you."

Chills ran all over me. "Stelson, that empty office is *my* office. I could have been sitting there when that bullet tore through!"

"Wow," Stelson remarked. "Just wow."

We held on to each other for a long time, that night. Really, I should say Stelson held me because I was beside myself. First, that my office got shot up. And second, that my boss, whom I had such respect for, would do such a thing.

"Focus on the good part, LaShondra. No one was hurt."

When I was a member at Gethsemane, people used to stand up and testify that the Lord had kept them from dangers seen and unseen. I always envisioned God putting his hand down between a person and whatever harm was trying to attack them.

But given this incident, I had to bring God out of my box, 'cause evidently He could run to the future, then come back and tell me what to do *today* so I wouldn't be in the wrong place at the wrong time three months later.

All along, I'd been thinking the Lord wanted me to take the leave for other people's sake. Little did I know, obeying Him was as much for my good as the people I was serving.

"Yeah, baby, He's beyond good."

Chapter 33 ∽

Of course, Dr. Hunt called and asked if I might be interested in returning to the campus sooner rather than later. "No pressure," she said. "It's just a question."

"Let me get back to you."

I started to make a note to myself to pray about it the next morning, but I got an answer in my heart almost immediately: *Not yet.* I didn't waste another minute thinking about it. Called Dr. Hunt and told her I was out until further notice.

I had to make a stop at the natural food store. Somehow, I had managed to run out of raw almonds, which had become a favorite staple of Stelson's lunch bucket. He'd texted me earlier that day to ask if maybe they'd fallen out of his bag. Funny how a man who'd previously raised his nose to unprocessed almonds had grown accustomed to the crunchy, slightly sweet treats.

After the women's fellowship, I dashed into the market, poured a pound of almonds into one of the plastic sacks, and checked out so I could get to Stelson's office before the lunch hour ended.

True to his word, Stelson had asked Cooper to take on more of the out-of-town presentations so he could slow down *after* he caught up on the work he'd missed. I think Cooper was so happy to have the old Stelson back, he would have done just about anything to appease him.

Cooper wasn't the only one.

"Hi, Helen. Stelson's in, right?"

"Sure is. Where's the little one?"

"At Mom's Day Out. Gives me a break every week."

"Yes." Helen chuckled. "They can be a handful."

I knocked on Stelson's door.

"Come in."

Opening the door slowly, I thrust my arm through the space and dangled the bag of almonds.

"Yes!" he cried, clapping.

Joy at hearing my husband's squeal spread through me as I walked into his office, giggling like a school girl. "I hope you'll enjoy these."

"Thanks, babe. You didn't have to go the extra mile." He stood, leaned over the desk and kissed me.

"You're worth it."

He nabbed a handful from the bag and threw them into his mouth.

The pile of papers and two lit monitors on his desk attested to what must have been an enormous amount of work. "Chop-chop. I'll let you get back to business."

I sashayed away, knowing he was watching my backside.

"Shondra," he said as I held the doorknob.

"The almonds? Was that all?"

"Yep."

"Oh. I thought maybe you were trying to get lucky."

A deep laugh rumbled from my throat. "Mmmm. I don't believe in luck. I believe in makin' it happen." I slipped out the door knowing I'd put a little something on his mind; a reason to get home early.

Daddy had left me three long messages, all saying the same thing. He had some books he wanted to run by me, to make sure they were okay for Seth.

Thankfully, Jonathan had convinced my father via a 3-way-call that it was okay to let Seth be a kid and get grounded in his own identity before we threw on the other social layers.

"His identity is forming *now*," my father had argued.

Again, I realized he had a point. My studies in education confirmed that much of children's personalities were ingrained before they ever started school. "Daddy, we want you to take part in building Seth's self-esteem. We just don't want you to tear down other people in the process."

I supposed the books were the product of that conversation. When I got to Daddy's house, he took Zoe from me and sang to her, "PawPaw's got some books for you, PawPaw's got some books for you."

I put my father's prepared meals in the freezer and followed him to the den, where Seth was already on the floor, sitting next to two piles of colorful children's books. "Ooooh! PawPaw! Look at this man's face!"

My son held up a book with a picture of Dizzy Gillespie's puffed up cheeks.

"Yes, sirree. He was a great musician. Not just an entertainer, a *musician*. Big difference. Everybody loved him."

"He looks funny." Seth held a finger to his lips and tried to inflate his cheeks like Mr. Gillespie's.

Laughter gurgled from Zoe's mouth; she found Seth's face extremely funny. Her eyes closed to near slits, laughing at him. Seth took a deep breath and made the face again. Zoe snickered harder.

Daddy put her on the ground so she could explore Seth and the mysterious cheeks more.

Daddy and I stood side by side, looking down at the kids.

Lord, please don't let Seth pass out trying to keep this girl happy.

"You look just like him!" Daddy encouraged Seth. "Maybe you could take saxophone lessons after you finish with Mrs. Gambrell."

A quick glance at the titles and pictures showed books mostly by and about African-Americans, with big yellow and white stickers from Half-Price Books.

There were a few about post office stamps, which Daddy probably got for himself as much as Seth.

"You like the books?" Daddy asked.

"Yes. These are great. Thank you," I said, my eyes still on the children.

"Yeah. I had a coupon. I got a few white people books, too, you know. For balance."

"Balance is good." I nodded, knowing this was as close as I was going to get to an admission of error from my father.

He crossed his arms on his chest. "That Seth is smart, you know?"

"Yep."

"And Zoe's gonna be right behind him."

"She sure is," I said. "I'm glad you got the books, Daddy."

He cleared his throat. "Yeah. Me, too."

Epilogue ❧
Six months later

Father, thank You for Jesus. Thank You for victory in Him. Stelson has been symptom-free for two months. Daddy's behaving, for the most part, though I really need to make sure we're on the same page about what we consider cusswords in our household. He thinks we're raising Seth to be soft. I ask that You bring us to another understanding, as now Zoe thinks the world of her grandfather, too.

Why did You do that, Lord? Why did You make grandparents so special to grandkids and vice versa?

I know You know what You're doing, even if I don't get it. I really don't get why you've got me teaching a segment in the women's Bible study on not-so-real scriptures. Me, teaching people the Word of God? Who knew? I guess You did!

I'm going back to work next month. Thank You for the help system from such an unexpected source—well, unexpected to me, but not to You. Between Momma Miller and Miss Hattie, both of my kids will probably gain ten pounds.

I'm thankful for the opportunity to bless these ladies financially, too.

Father, in all of the things that have transpired over this last year, the good…the very best thing—next to learning to forgive my husband so the enemy can't strike from the inside—has been reconnecting with You.

My prayer, Lord, is that You keep me. Like David said in Psalm 119:10. Do not let me stray from Your commands. I want 1 Thessalonians 5:23-24 to be my testimony. You are faithful to do it.

And while You are at it, keep my husband, too. Keep our family under the shadow of Your wings, where no weapon formed against us will ever, EVER prosper.

In Jesus' name I pray. Amen.

Possible Discussion Questions

1. LaShondra and Stelson discuss "the black talk". LaShondra feels it's necessary to prepare Seth for the specific challenges he may face as an African-American. Stelson doesn't want to pour the fear of man into his children's hearts. Do you agree more with LaShondra or Stelson? Why?

2. Have you had a *black* talk, an *overweight* talk, a *girl* talk, a *disability* talk, or any such kind of discrimination talk with a child? Did one of your parents have this kind of talk with you? Is this a talk that needs to happen? If so, when?

3. LaShondra says she can't stay home with her kids because they will drive her crazy. Which do you think is easier—being a full-time mom or a full-time employee?

4. LaShondra didn't have time to take care of her broken toe. Though the injury was minor, it was a major issue for Stelson, who insisted that she go to the doctor. Do you ever skimp on taking care of yourself due to work or other obligations?

5. LaShondra admits to herself that she cannot successfully balance home and work, yet she makes the decision to keep trying. Can you relate to her struggle? Do you think it is possible to juggle commitments as a wife, mother, and career woman while nurturing your physical and spiritual health all in the same season? If so, how? If not, what area(s) tend to suffer?

6. Peaches mentioned that Stelson could just as easily leave his job. Do you think it's a godly arrangement for able-bodied men to be stay-at-home dads while wives work outside of the home?

7. LaShondra almost left Baby Zoe in the car. This was a major turning

point for her. Have you ever done (or almost done) something tragic that marked a turning point in your life?

8. Do you think the incident at the movie theater was racially motivated? What are your thoughts about what happened to this couple after shopping at a local Walmart (see link below)? http://www.huffingtonpost.com/2013/05/21/virginia-parents-walmart-biracial-daughters_n_3313143.html

9. In her first full week off from work, LaShondra reactivates her prayer life and discovers that she has resentment in her heart. How does your prayer life affect you?

10. LaShondra makes out a list of fears that kept her from fully surrendering to God. What would your list look like?

11. LaShondra has to consciously decide not to let herself slip into a cynical, anti-white mode while at the picnic with church members. She wonders if everyone is secretly fighting a battle. Do you think everyone is fighting a secret battle? Have you had to fight secret battles?

12. LaShondra's father reminded her of the Cheerios commercial portraying a biracial child with an African-American father and caucasian mother (https://www.youtube.com/watch?v=kYofm5d5Xdw). What was your reaction when you first saw the commercial?

13. As LaShondra discovered, Lyme disease is a hotly debated topic in the medical community. There are even allegations that the disease originated as a government experiment with biological warfare, since it was only "discovered" in the late 1970s despite the fact that deer and ticks have inhabited the continent for centuries. Are you suspicious of the relationship between doctors, insurance companies, pharmaceutical companies, and government? Why or why not?

14. Jonathan expressed his opinions about black women, particularly

those raised in the south by fathers just like his own. He says he likes a woman with "bite", but not if she bites him. Do you agree or disagree with Jonathan's perspective?

15. Peaches fussed at LaShondra because LaShondra called Peaches before calling on God. Whom do you call first for answers?

16. Stelson's attitude change was brought on by extreme physical pain. Do you think LaShondra should have been able to overlook his sharp comments under the circumstances? Are you quick to overlook people's ugly words when you know they are suffering physically, emotionally, or spiritually?

17. The older women at LaShondra's table tell her that in order to pray for Stelson's healing, Stelson may need to be clean from sin first. Do you agree or disagree? LaShondra had to "shut them out" in order to keep her faith in tact. Have you ever had to stop listening to someone's advice because you realized they were usually wrong?

18. LaShondra was surprised when Minister Windham prayed for Stelson on the spot. Do you usually pray for people immediately or later when they ask? Have there been times when you said you would pray for someone but didn't? How can we be more faithful to pray for others?

19. After Stelson's headaches begin to subside, LaShondra doesn't tell Stelson the truth about her lingering hurt feelings. Instead, she goes into self-preservation mode and tries to limit her vulnerability. Are there times when you need to cover yourself, or does doing so taint a relationship?

20. LaShondra feels better knowing that if push ever came to shove in her marriage, she and the kids would be okay because she would have her own income. Do you think it's important for a woman to keep herself in a position to support herself and her children financially without a man's help? If you are a SAHM, are you ever concerned about what would happen if your husband's income disappeared?

21. At the hospital, Quinn tells Shondra that while Stelson is a brother in Christ, he still has flesh and might do something unthinkable under the wrong circumstances. Do you believe in the adage "never say what you won't do"?

22. LaShondra never imagined that she might be a caregiver for Stelson at such an early age. Do you know someone who is a caregiver for a spouse or an aging parent? How has this role changed his/her life?

23. Throughout the book, LaShondra struggles to maintain her faith despite her close moments with God. How do you handle challenges to your faith? Is there someone who intercedes for you or speaks hope into your life?

24. LaShondra didn't speak up with the older women because she was disappointed that they weren't more mature believers. Later, the Lord teaches her that He can use her with any audience. How do you balance sharing your thoughts with elders who may have unbiblical beliefs?

25. Stelson was relieved to find people who were also dealing with illnesses. Do you find it helpful or detrimental to connect with others who are experiencing similar trials?

If you enjoyed *No Weapon Formed*,
You'll love this excerpt from the novel *Stepping Down*
by Michelle Stimpson

Chapter 1

Pastor Mark Wayne Carter, III cast his drooping eyes on the clock ticking away on the wall directly across from his desk. Last year his wife, Sharla, had lowered the clock so that it stared at him while he was sitting in his gold-studded leather executive chair.

"I know you're busy doing the Lord's work, but it *would* be nice to see you home before the sun goes down sometimes," she had nagged as she pounded a nail into the wall. She positioned the clock in its new location, then put both hands on her hips. "If you can see the clock, you might actually keep track of how much time you're spending here in your office."

Mark didn't like to fight with her about his devotion to New Vision Church. The church was his life's purpose, the reason he'd walked away from his short, but well-paying career as an insurance salesman. This church had given him a sense of accomplishment he'd never experienced in all his months as top-producer at StateWay Insurance.

More than anything, Mark hoped that New Vision Church would be the reason Jesus said, "Well done, my good and faithful servant," to him one day.

Late Saturday nights came with the territory, which was one reason he hired a very young man as his assistant and semi-mentee. At thirty-eight years old, Mark was no old goat, but he wasn't bright-eyed and bushy-tailed, either. He needed an assistant to knock on the door every hour or so and make sure Mark hadn't fallen asleep at the computer.

A recent graduate of Southern Bible School, Jonathan Lawrence had come with stellar references and an excellent transcript. Mark wasn't too crazy about seminary kids. Jonathan seemed eager, though, and he had been faithful to his previous mentor. Mark didn't mind showing a young minister the ropes, so long as he learned quickly and knew how to keep his mouth shut. Jonathan would do, unless he proved otherwise.

11:45. Mark did the math in his head. It would take him at least another half-hour to finish the outline. An hour to fill it out with scriptures and examples. Ten minutes to get home. In bed by 1:45, to be up again by six and back at the church for first service at 8:00.

If only the Jenkins' house dedication hadn't taken so long and the visit to Mother Morris in the hospital had gone as planned, he wouldn't be in this predicament. *Lord, I'll do better,* Mark prayed silently as he logged into SermonDepot.com to browse for a ready-made message. Briefly, he thought about the problems he'd encountered this week at the church.

He couldn't wrap his mind around anything in particular. In a church of almost 1500 in attendance weekly, the issues varied. Blessings, sin, healing, financial prosperity. Any of those topics would do.

Mark refined his search by checking the "60-minute" and "adult audience" boxes to decrease the number of results. "Lord, show me which one," he offered briefly, though he wondered if God would actually advise him about this shortcut. His eyes landed on a generic title: Seven Steps to Success, taken from the parable of the sower in Matthew 13.

Mark clicked on his "Used Sermons" folder to make sure he hadn't already preached this message. Six years ago, when he and Sharla founded New Vision, he wouldn't have dreamed of downloading a sermon from the internet. As he realized the growing number of lectures he'd copied from the web, it was hard to imagine how he'd gotten to that point.

He took a cleansing breath and reminded himself that he wasn't alone. There were, according to the site's banner, thousands of paying subscribers—other pastors and preachers, presumably—who utilized the sermons. *God's word is consistent and true. It doesn't change. No need to reinvent the wheel every Sunday,* Mark rationalized as he checked the "use" box and printed the accompanying four-page document.

His laser printer hummed softly as a display of lights signaled the connection between laptop and printer.

A soft rapping at the door gave Mark a second wind. He hoisted his smile into place and sat up straight in his chair. "Enter."

Jonathan poked his head in the office. "Pastor, you okay in here?"

"Yes," Mark said. "Leave if you need to."

Jonathan shook his head, "Oh no, sir. I'm in no hurry. I was thinking...you fell asleep in here last Saturday night, so..."

Mark could only laugh at himself. "Thank you, Jonathan. I'm good. I hit the gym this week. Got more energy." Mark swiveled his chair around and grabbed the papers from the printer. "About to wrap it up."

"Okay." Jonathan ducked out of the room.

Aside from sore muscles, the workout had given Mark a little more energy. Maybe, if he kept the exercise going and cut back on the fast food, he might actually feel like a thirty-eight-year-old is supposed to feel. At six foot two and two hundred-twenty pounds, he'd been able to maintain a healthy weight, thanks mostly to good genes. His father had given him that much, if nothing else.

Despite the appearance of health, though, Mark was well aware that his cholesterol and blood pressure levels were higher every year. Or in his case, two years—which is about how long it took for him to actually show up at one of the appointments Sharla made for him with their general practitioner. Mark much preferred to leave his health in the hands of the Lord.

Quickly, Mark threw his parallel Bible and the pages of the next day's sermon into the front compartment of his rolling attaché. The laptop and charger fit perfectly into the second section. He gathered the rest of the papers on his desk and the surrounding counters into one stack. He still needed to review the notes, but he could finish it at home. If he made it there before midnight, he might actually get to spend time with Sharla before she drifted off to sleep.

How long has it been?

Another tap on the door. "Enter." With his back turned to the door, Mark switched off his printer and locked the overhead cabinets containing confidential church information. He heard the door open slightly, then close. He pivoted, expecting to find Jonathan standing there.

But this was definitely not Jonathan. *All that's good and perfect comes from God.* And He knew what He was doing when He made *that* woman. A form-fitting red silk blouse defining her full rack. White linen skirt so tight it bunched up across her hips. Legs that must have run track in high school, maybe even college. And a pair of heels that added a good five inches to her height, accentuating her lower half even more.

It only took seconds for Mark to process her body. His eyes made it up to her face in enough time to hide his intrigue. Hopefully. Respectfully, he stood. "How can I help you?"

"Pastor, I really need to talk to you." She sat down in the chair across from him, blocking his view of the clock.

"Um...well, if you want to set up an appointment—"

"This will only take a minute," she pushed past Mark's safeguards. He sat.

"A long time ago, I made a big mistake. And now I need to fix it."

Her perfume wrapped around Mark's face. Sweet, but not overpowering. The whole scene reminded him of those cartoons where a bull's eye rotates around and around, hypnotizing an unsuspecting character.

She crossed one leg over the other, revealing a good six inches up the side of her thigh. Bare, taut skin. "I just don't know what to do. I was hoping you could help me."

Mark was no stranger to women's advances. Another thing he'd inherited from Mark Wayne Carter, II was good looks. Deep brown skin, a head full of short but wavy hair, and a sharp goatee could pull a woman from a mile away. But the one thing Mark could say he'd done right in his marriage was to remain faithful to his wife throughout their sixteen years together. He wasn't going to blow it on some misguided member who'd managed to outwit his new assistant.

Mark stood again. He'd played around with this fire long enough. "My sister, if you have accepted Christ as your savior, old things are passed away. It's late. I'm going to have to ask again that you to speak with Jonathan on your way out. He can put you in touch with the counseling ministry."

His abrupt end to their conversation obviously caught her off guard. "Um, b-but," she stammered for words. "But *you're* my pastor. Isn't this what you're *supposed* to do?"

Mark ripped the top sheet from the pad of sticky-notes on his desk. "The word of God is your counselor. Psalm one nineteen and twenty-four." He scribbled the reference on the note and handed it to the woman.

She snatched it from his hand, a scowl on her face. Mark noticed that one of her fake eyelashes slipped out of place. He had to hold in his laughter. "Meditate on His word. Have a good night, my sister."

Mark walked her to his office door, then past Jonathan and out to the door of the entire suite. "God bless you."

The woman didn't have a chance to respond before the weighted door shut behind her. With after-hours security on the church's campus, Mark was sure she'd make it back to her car safely.

Mark turned sharply to face Jonathan, who sat at his desk with a bewildered look on his face. "Sir, I-I, she said she was a frequent guest of yours."

Mark's eyes turned to slits as he tried to decide if Jonathan was deranged or just deceived. Since the boy was still in his 90-day probationary period, Mark would give him the benefit of the doubt. "With the exception of First Lady Carter, I don't allow women into my office alone, especially not women dressed like *her*, without one of the female ministers present. Do we understand each other?"

"Yes, Pastor. I'm sorry. It's just that my last supervisor had, you know, guests. I-it won't happen again."

"Jonathan, I don't know what kind of pastors or preachers you worked with before me, but I'm not *that* man."

Chapter 2

Mark was careful to watch the rear and side view mirrors as the garage lowered behind his eight-year-old Cadillac Escalade. Though his ride didn't turn heads anymore, he still made it a habit to survey his surroundings in case somebody wanted to try him. Maybe he'd slack up a bit once they moved out of their quaint 2500-square-foot home and into the mini-mansion behind security gates Sharla had her heart set on. Until then, he would remain on high alert.

A side effect of being raised in one of the roughest areas of Houston was a keen awareness of his environment. "If you get caught slippin', it's your own fault," his father had taught him during one of their rare free-world visits.

Mark had tried to teach his own son, Amani, how to look out for danger, but being raised in a fairly safe, middle-class world had distanced Amani from the lessons of living in survival mode. The boy had grown up in a world where kids left their bicycles on porches outside at night and people actually turned in lost wallets to the police.

Much to Mark's dismay, Amani hadn't been in a fight in all his thirteen years. Mark had been in at least ten brawls by the time he was Amani's age. He'd won some and lost some. Gave and took black eyes and busted lips with the best of 'em. No matter, he'd walked away each time knowing he could throw down when pushed to the brink.

This comfortable lifestyle Mark provided for his family had come at a cost.

Mark took his key from the ignition, clutched his bag from the passenger's seat and made his way around Sharla's bright red Benz toward the doorway of the laundry room.

The scent of fabric softener greeted him upon entrance. He wanted to be glad about the pleasant odor, but he couldn't. Sharla didn't do the laundry. She'd hired some older, foreign woman to do their cleaning and washing. The woman, whoever she was, did an excellent job. But Mark had to wonder exactly what Sharla did all day that warranted paying someone else to take care of the home he'd provided for them.

Sharla didn't work. She hadn't homeschooled Amani since he started junior high school. She'd delegated most of her previously held duties as First Lady to other women at the church, claiming that she needed to concentrate on home. Somehow, "concentrating on home" got translated to finding someone else to clean the house.

But Mark knew better than to question Sharla. The house was her jurisdiction. So long as she stayed within the family budget, he'd keep his mouth shut unless he wanted to handle the laundry himself.

"I'm home," he announced, not really expecting a response. Just seemed like something men on TV did.

He hung his keys on one of the hooks magnetically attached to the stainless steel refrigerator. He took off his tie and hung it on a bar chair, pried his shoes off and left them under the kitchen table.

Sharla would fuss. What else was new?

Mark traipsed through the family room and up the staircase to his home office to drop off the materials he'd comb through later. Down the hallway, he noticed the blue glow of the big screen television coming from under the door to the media room. He opened the door and found Amani stretched across the sectional sofa.

"'Mani, go to your bed," Mark ordered softly, shaking his son's shoulder.

Amani gave a loud snort, scratched his head a few times, stretched, and then obeyed his father's directive. "Night, Dad."

"Night, man."

As Amani brushed past, Mark noticed that they were nearly the same height. Another six months of this growth spurt and the youngest person would also be the tallest person in the house.

Mark grabbed the remote control and switched off the TV as his son trudged away to his own bedroom.

Back downstairs in his own space, Mark was surprised to find Sharla still up. She was seated in their bathroom, fooling with her hair.

Well, the hair that somebody put on her head. Granted, her style was always on point, but Mark couldn't remember the last time he'd seen his wife's *real* hair.

"Hey, babe," he said.

"Mmm," she moaned. To be fair, she did have several hairpins in her mouth. Apparently, the current style required her to position her mane a certain way before lying down on the satin pillowcases she dared not sleep without.

Mark stood in the bathroom's entry admiring his wife. He loved to see her like this—no makeup, hair swept off her face, a T-shirt and loose shorts. Her skin had always been a pool of caramel beckoning him to dive in when he studied her for more than a few minutes. Though she had gained some weight over the years, a part of him actually liked the fact that there was more of her to love.

Watching her breasts jiggle as she struggled to shove the hairpins in place reminded Mark that he was indeed a lucky man.

"What?" Sharla piped up.

"I'm just looking at you."

"Why?"

"Because you're beautiful."

She smacked her full lips. "Not beautiful enough for you to come home before midnight, though."

Why does she always have to ruin a good thing? Mark stuffed both hands into his pockets. As a matter of habit, he checked his phone's screen to see if there were any new texts or email messages.

Sharla rolled her eyes and carried on with the business of securing her hair. "That's what I thought."

He decided to backtrack. "Sorry I'm so late getting home."

"I'm not surprised," she quipped.

Mark leaned his weary body against the doorframe, trying to decide whether or not he had enough energy left to wiggle through his wife's brick-hard attitude and find out what was really bugging her tonight.

He gave himself the benefit of the doubt; maybe her problem had nothing to do with him. Anyone in her family could have put her in a bad mood. Amani might have said something crazy, something he'd been doing a lot more lately.

For the record, he'd give her a chance to vent. "What's really going on, babe?"

She shook her head. "If you don't know by now, I can't help you."

He racked the last bits of his brain. Nothing out of the ordinary. "I'm too tired for guessing games tonight."

"And I'm too tired to repeat myself."

She wrapped a black mesh thing-a-ma-jig around the base of her head. Somehow, it kept its place.

Mark figured there must have been some kind of Velcro strip holding it in place. Sharla was right up there with the best of them when it came to keeping herself up. As he understood it, this was something the women in her First Wives' Fellowship taught her she needed to do.

Mark remembered now. "The church?"

"Bingo. Mark, when are you going to start *delegating* more?"

"I do," he barely answered. "I delegate what I can. But some responsibilities at New Vision can't be pawned off on other people."

"How about the responsibility of being a husband to your wife and a father to your son here at eight hundred Evanshire Street?"

"What do you want me to do, Sharla? Ignore my calling?"

She pouted, "I know you have to do God's will. But I also know that I did not sign up to be a pastor's wife. I married a businessman, not a preacher."

With that, Mark dismissed himself and made his way back upstairs to the office. They'd had this conversation too many times in the past few months for him to count, and it never ended with compromise. Eventually Sharla would take a look around and see that she had it pretty good. Once she came back to herself, she'd offer to make him a red velvet cake—a most welcomed apology. He would have to wait out her current tidal wave of attitude issues.

In the meanwhile, all Mark could do was pray that the Lord would mature his wife in Christ to the point where she could appreciate what God was doing with New Vision. He'd keep praying for her until then, because it wouldn't be fair for him to have to choose between his God and his wife.

Mark set aside what had just happened with Sharla in order to finish reviewing his canned sermon. But the tension resurfaced as soon as he turned off the light in his office and headed back downstairs again.

Part of him hoped Sharla was sleep already. At least she wouldn't be awake to give him the cold shoulder. He always found it much easier to drift off with the comforting idea that Sharla didn't realize he was in bed than to think she was ignoring him.

Mark showered and climbed into their King-sized sleigh bed for what might as well be considered a nap. A captivating glow from the pool's lighting system streamed in through the window.

When he and Sharla spent their first night in the house, they had both been so spellbound by the blue radiance, they'd stayed up nearly half the night in the hot tub section drinking virgin strawberry daiquiris and enjoying sensual pleasures.

Memories of how much they used to enjoy spending time with one another kept Mark from sleep. *Really, how long has it been?*

He listened closely for Sharla's breathing pattern. Shallow and fast. She was still awake.

Slowly, he slipped his left hand across her waist. Rubbed his foot against her leg. Waited for some reciprocity.

Since she didn't show any sign of resistance, Mark nudged his chin against her neck. Kissed her ear the way he knew she liked it.

"Mark, if you want to make love, why don't you just say it?" Sharla blared.

"Because I'm trying to *show* it," he nibbled on her ear.

Sharla shot up straight in bed. "What I want you to *show* me is that you care about me and our son. You didn't even *ask* about the conference with Amani's counselor yesterday."

Finally, Mark had a clue about his wife's extended attitude. "Did you tell me about it?"

"Yes. I sent you a text, since I didn't see you Thursday *at all*."

Mark vaguely remembered seeing Sharla's text flash across his screen, but all it said was, "call me." He hadn't seen the message until after the YoungLife fundraiser at the community center. By then it was almost ten o'clock and he was on his way home. Sharla was sleep when he got back, so he guessed it must not have been important enough for her to wait up. Maybe she'd figured out whatever was on her mind earlier.

"Amani's grades are ridiculous. Four C's, a B, and only one A. And I had to sit there and let her tell me all this *without* you," she stabbed at him with words.

How the heck did we go from almost making love to discussing report cards? "I didn't even know, Sharla. I'm sorry. But can we talk about this *later?*"

"Like you're going to actually be awake and ready to talk when you finish doin' your business? Yeah, right," she gave a sarcastic laugh.

"How is it *my* business? This is *our* business," Mark corrected her.

"You can't just spend all day at the church, come home after midnight, spend another hour in your study, and then expect me to roll over and play lovey-dovey with you," she snarled, her delicate face marred with anger.

With his heart rate still slightly elevated, Mark tried again. "Look, I'll talk to 'Mani tomorrow. But right now, baby"—he ventured to kiss her shoulder again—"it's about me and you."

Sharla balled a handful of covers into her fist and yanked the mass over her head as she resumed her face-down, off-limits stance in bed.

It took every ounce of godliness in Mark to keep from entertaining the irony of refusing advances from a stranger only to come home and face rejection from his wife.

Stepping Down Available Now!

Other Books by Michelle Stimpson

Fiction

A Forgotten Love (Novella) Book One in the "A Few Good Men" Series

A Shoulda Woulda Christmas (Novella)

Boaz Brown

Divas of Damascus Road

Falling into Grace

I Met Him in the Ladies' Room (Novella)

I Met Him in the Ladies' Room Again (Novella)

Last Temptation (Starring "Peaches" from *Boaz Brown*)

Mama B: A Time to Speak (Book 1)

Mama B: A Time to Dance (Book 2)

Mama B: A Time to Love (Book 3)

Mama B: A Time to Mend (Book 4)

Someone to Watch Over Me

Stepping Down

The Good Stuff

Trouble In My Way (Young Adult)

What About Momma's House? (Novella with April Barker)

What About Love? (Novella with April Barker)

What About Tomorrow? (Novella with April Barker)

Non-Fiction

Did I Marry the Wrong Guy? And other silent ponderings of a fairly normal Christian wife

Uncommon Sense: 30 Truths to Radically Renew Your Mind in Christ

The 21-Day Publishing Plan

About the Author

Michelle Stimpson's works include the highly acclaimed *Boaz Brown*, *Divas of Damascus Road* (National Bestseller), and *Falling Into Grace,* which has been optioned for a movie of the week. She has published several short stories for high school students through her educational publishing company at WeGottaRead.com.

Michelle serves in women's ministry at her home church, Oak Cliff Bible Fellowship. She regularly speaks at special events and writing workshops sponsored by churches, schools, book clubs, and educational organizations.

The Stimpsons are proud parents of two young adults and one crazy dog.

Visit Michelle online:
www.MichelleStimpson.com
https://www.facebook.com/MichelleStimpsonWrites

Made in the USA
San Bernardino, CA
17 February 2016